His face went ashen with fury

Ailsa had never seen such anger mingled with despair, as Fergus took her roughly by the shoulder.

"What in heaven's name are you thinking about," he demanded, "going out in a boat that's been lying in a shed for six years without repair? You must be mad—out of your right mind! Didn't you know how dangerous it was?"

"I'm sorry. I should have realized—"

"You could have drowned!" He stood looking at her for a moment, his eyes deep wells of conflict as he seemed to conjure up a scene from the past.

Her heart aching for him, Ailsa knew he was reliving the dreadful accident of six years ago....

Jean S. MacLeod, the author of more than fifty romance novels, lives with her husband on an isolated peninsula in Scotland's Western Highlands. From her doorstep she has a breathtaking view of the Hebrides. ''In these surroundings,'' she says, ''it must surely be possible to go on writing for a very long time.'' Indeed, her ideas and words are as fresh and romantic as ever.

Books by Jean S. MacLeod

Legacy of Doubt

Jean S. MacLeod

Harlequin Books

TORONTO • NEW YORK • LONDON
AMSTERDAM • PARIS • SYDNEY • HAMBURG
STOCKHOLM • ATHENS • TOKYO • MILAN

Original hardcover edition published in 1989
by Mills & Boon Limited

ISBN 0-373-17054-8

Harlequin Romance first edition January 1990

CHAPTER ONE

LOOKING down on Loch Truan for the first time, she saw it in sunshine, the white-sanded road winding along the shore like a ribbon that had no end to it, now in sunlight with the moors above it, now in shade where the dark forest trees came down to the water's edge. There was no sign anywhere that her destination might be in sight, although she knew that there must be a village tucked away somewhere beside the loch.

Ailsa Sutherland Mallory had inherited a small estate in the Highlands of Scotland from her uncle, Gavin Sutherland, together with a small amount of money which he had hoped would bring her from Canada to the country of her mother's birth. Fiercely patriotic, he had always regretted the fact that his only sister had chosen to marry a Canadian, and before he died he had sought to put the matter straight by making his only niece his heiress, provided she came to Truan to see the estate for herself. Being the girl she was, Ailsa had decided to travel to Scotland to inspect her inheritance and decide what to do with it.

'Your uncle wouldn't have expected you to sell it,' her mother had said. 'He was a proud man, and although he hadn't owned Truan for very long, he had become greatly attached to it. I knew by the tone of his letters over the past few years that he wanted to preserve it as it had always been, a Highland estate with a long tradition behind it which shouldn't be lost.'

Ailsa thought it a pity that her uncle had only lived for six short years after he had bought it, and what she already knew about Truan had fired her imagination, bringing her all this way to see it for herself. Although it wasn't her only reason for leaving Canada, she thought as she looked down at the sparkling waters of the loch, it was the break she needed to put an unhappy love affair behind her and start again. Russell Forgreave had walked out on her six months ago, and even now she was conscious of shock and disillusionment and a heart so bruised that she believed she could never love again. The hurt had gone deep, deeper than anyone knew. It lay reflected in her deep blue eyes which now scanned the loch and the mountains beyond it, and the quick toss of her head as she willed herself to forget the past and look only towards the future.

A future at Truan? Well, perhaps, but Truan—and Scotland, for that matter—had still to prove themselves as far as she was concerned. They had to offer her compensation, in a way, for all that had gone before, yet when she looked at them again she could not see those stern mountains bending to her will.

On the brow of the next hill the car she had hired at Prestwick for her journey north came to a halt with an ungallant stutter as she pulled into the side of the road where the County Council had provided a layby for just such an emergency. It was also a passing-place on a road so narrow that two cars approaching each other could scarcely scrape past without one or the other being propelled into the ditch on either side, which, at the moment, was full of water.

Ruefully aware that her talents didn't extend to a knowledge of mechanical engineering, Ailsa got out from behind the steering wheel, pushing back the dark hair from her brow to lift the car's bonnet and inspect the engine. It looked perfectly all right to her, although she had to admit in all honesty that the internal combustion engine was a complete enigma to her.

'Now what do I do?' she said aloud, wondering if a short cooling-down period would do the trick. After all, the car had negotiated all those hills on the road behind her, which was really a considerable feat.

Leaving the bonnet up in the hope of speeding the cooling process, she looked about her, aware of the beauty and the deep stillness everywhere which seemed to lay a balm on her spirit. It had been like this in Canada not so long ago when every holiday had taken her with Russell into the mountains from the rush and bustle of Toronto's busy streets. She had valued those moments of quiet and deep communion with nature more than she had realised at the time, believing that Russell did too, although she had also known him to be fiercely ambitious. Trading in furs, he had gone often to the wilds, but had always returned with a sense of relief to the noise and clamour of the big city where he had been born.

Determinedly Ailsa forced her thoughts away from the past to confront the present, realising that she was hungry and that this was an ideal opportunity to eat the sandwiches she had purchased in Oban on her way through. Unwrapping them from their protective covering, she saw them as immensely satisfying after her long drive, two sturdy-looking 'morning rolls' filled with cheese and a mixed salad which would prevent her from arriving at Truan Lodge gasping for a meal which might not be immediately forthcoming. She had written to her uncle's housekeeper from Canada, acquainting Mrs Birch with the date of her arrival but not the time, as she had had no idea of how long it would take her to reach Loch Truan from the airport, but she had not received a reply, which was disconcerting, to say the least of it.

Ah, well, she thought, I'm here, and no doubt Mrs Birch has taken it for granted that I'll arrive some time during the afternoon to take up my inheritance!

The sound of running water directed her attention to the ditch at the side of the road where she found a mountain spring gushing into a hollow of pebbles below the moss. The water was clear and cool, shaded by the young heather, and she knew it would be safe to drink. Cupping her hands together, she felt the water fresh on her lips like a still-remembered kiss, and then she plunged her face into it deliberately, only drawing back when she was suddenly conscious of being watched. Above her on the moor a tall, kilted figure was standing in the heather with two dogs at his heels and a long crook in his hand. A shepherd, she thought, although there was no sign of his sheep.

As if at some prearranged signal he came towards her, the black and white collies bounding joyously ahead of him to greet her in a flurry of wagging tails and panting, scarlet tongues.

'They're young dogs,' the man said, reassuring her. 'They won't hurt you.'

His quiet, measured tone reminded of her mother, but when he spoke to the collies it was in a different language.

'Is that Gaelic?' she asked.

He nodded briefly as he jumped down on to the road beside her.

'Yes, I'm training them to the Gaelic,' he acknowledged. 'It saves confusion when they're running with the other dogs and it often helps in competition.'

'Sheep trials?'

'When there's time.'

His smile was slow and deliberate, letting her know that these would be working dogs.

'Of course,' she said, recognising the fact that he had not been out here on the moor solely for pleasure. 'Why do you have to have such a long crook?'

'Sheep can get into awkward places where even a man can't reach in the ordinary way, so the *cromag* is made long for that reason. The crook part of it is fashioned from ram's horn and carved locally.'

Ailsa gazed at the *cromag* which she had called a crook.

'It's a sort of staff,' she mused. 'I can imagine you using it for your own benefit as well as for the sheep, to help you out of awkward situations too.'

He smiled at her suggestion.

'That's true,' he said. 'I wouldn't be without it on the hill.'

'You're a shepherd,' she guessed.

'You could say that,' he acknowledged, the distant smile touching his lips again. 'It's probably my true occupation.'

'And this is your home.'

It was hardly a question as her eyes sought the shining waters of the loch beneath them and the grand, dark mountains which closed it in. Without a doubt this man belonged here: he had the craggy grandeur of those dark hills about him and a look of freedom only to be found in such places where eagles soared and the red deer stood alerted, silhouetted against the forest green. He had not replied to her suggestion, and she looked up at him, seeing him, perhaps, for the first time. Eyes as dark as the loch where the trees came down to cut off the sunlight, eyes with a hint of sorrow in their slate-grey depths, challenged her from his superior height.

'It will always be my home,' he said. 'I was born here.'

Faced by a reticence in him which she could not understand, Ailsa turned back to the stranded car.

'You seem to be in trouble,' he remarked. 'I saw you exploring under the bonnet a few minutes ago.'

'I haven't a clue about engines,' she was forced to admit. 'It just seemed to hesitate a lot coming up that last hill, as if it was exhausted.'

Again the thoughtful smile spread across his dark face, banishing the sorrow from his eyes.

'Let me have a look at it,' he said.

She stood beside the car while he worked, his dark head half hidden under the bonnet, long fingers probing carefully for the fault.

'I don't suppose there's a garage around for miles,' she commented after a lengthy pause. 'There can't be many cars hereabouts.'

He said, his face still hidden, 'It might surprise you to know just how many there are, but apart from the sheep we're all fairly good mechanics around here. We more or less have to be, with the distance between garages quite often twenty miles or more.' Suddenly the engine spluttered into life. 'That ought to do the trick,' he said. 'It was nothing serious.'

He allowed the engine to run while Ailsa gathered up the remains of her alfresco meal. The collies had curled up at her feet, regarding what was left of the morning rolls with a suggestion in their alert dark eyes.

'Can I give them a sandwich?' she asked as their master straightened to his full commanding height again. 'They look hungry.'

'Collies always do, and one sandwich wouldn't go far between them.'

'And you?' she asked, conscious of an odd reluctance to let him go.

He shook his head.

'I'm going home to make my dinner,' he said.

It sounded rather bleak, living alone and catering for himself, but no doubt he was used to it.

'How far is Truan?' she asked. 'I ought to be near enough now, according to the map.'

'Four miles,' he told her. 'Are you making for the hotel?'

'No.' She stole a look at him, seeing the clear grey eyes in his suntanned face with the faint look of disappointment in them and the determination of the handsome mouth above the square-cut jaw. A man with a mind of his own and a deep purpose in life, she thought, but what was he doing here herding sheep with the look of something more about him that could even spell cruelty in a way? 'I'm going to Truan Lodge.'

Her confession electrified him, and immediately all the friendly banter dropped from his voice as his eyes hardened.

'As a visitor?' he asked.

'In one way—yes,' she admitted, 'but not altogether.'

His eyes were still steady on hers.

'What do you mean by that?' he asked.

'I've come to inspect my inheritance,' she told him.

His whole expression changed.

'You'll be the girl from Toronto, in that case,' he said coldly. 'What are you going to do with Truan?'

Of course, as a local, he would be interested, but she could not accuse this man of mere curiosity.

'How can I say before I've seen it?' she returned. 'My uncle died there six months ago, and I think he must have loved it very much, because he never came back to Canada after he bought it.'

'Six years ago.' The man was evidently well acquainted with Truan's history.

'You knew my uncle?' Ailsa asked eagerly.

'Quite well.'

'Then,' she suggested, 'perhaps you could direct me to Truan?' She indicated the car. 'You must know the way.'

He refused to help her.

'That would be impossible.' The quiet Highland voice was suddenly harsh. 'I'm taking the dogs over the hill, but you'll find your way to Truan easily enough. There's only one road—straight ahead.'

The brusqueness of his dismissal cut sharply across her first favourable impression of him, but what was the use of being angry if they were never likely to meet again?

'I'm sorry,' she said, 'but thanks for your help with the car. I would never have managed on my own.'

She watched him go, a tall, commanding figure with the two dogs at his heels, taking the steep hillside as easily and naturally as he would have done the road.

The hired car behaved perfectly for the rest of the journey into the village. Truan, nestling in a hollow at the head of the loch, was typical of many of the small villages she had passed on her way north, with its collection of one-storeyed whitewashed cottages following the line of the shore and its tiny stone-built church raised on a convenient knoll above it and half hidden by ancient yews steeped in hallowed peace. There was only one shop opposite the ubiquitous small hotel, and that seemed to be also the post office, since it boasted a faded red pillarbox in an adjoining wall. An incongruous-looking new telephone kiosk stood back a little way from the road as if it was ashamed of its blatant modernity in such a picturesque setting, and a ginger cat regarded her disdainfully from the windowsill of the store.

Going in, Ailsa half expected an overhead bell to announce her presence, and was agreeably surprised to see how updated the little shop really was. A girl in a blue overall smiled at her from behind the counter.

'It's a nice day,' she said in the soft Highland accent Ailsa was now beginning to expect and which reminded her sharply of the man on the moor. 'Can I help you, perhaps?'

'I'm looking for Truan Lodge,' Ailsa explained. 'I thought you could direct me.'

'Of course.' Without quite knowing why, Ailsa was conscious of some restraint in the quiet voice, the same reserve which she had discovered on the moor road. 'It really isn't far. Just straight through the village and a bit up the glen road. You'll see it easily in between the trees.' There was a pause in which the girl seemed to be considering her carefully and then she said without preliminary: 'You'll be the new owner, maybe? I hear you are expected.'

'Oh—yes, I am,' Ailsa acknowledged. 'I've motored up from Prestwick, and I wouldn't have believed that Scotland could be so beautiful, although my uncle's letters and my mother's memories were always full of its praise. I suppose I'm seeing it on a perfect day,' she said happily. 'I've had sunshine all the way.'

'The west coast is always best in the spring,' the girl told her. 'Mr Sutherland used to say it laid a healing hand on him and made him content. He would walk down here every day for his paper and sometimes a bar of chocolate and a wee dram at the hotel before he went back. He'll be missed at Truan,' was her final comment before she came round the end of the counter to point out the way to the Lodge.

'We'll probably be seeing a lot of each other,' Ailsa suggested on the doorstep. 'You are the postmistress, I suppose.'

'I'm her assistant,' she was told almost primly. 'When she's not in I look after the shop. My name's Moira Cameron. Miss Brisby is my aunt.'

The postmistress was evidently 'not in' at the moment and Moira was importantly in charge.

'If there's anything we can do for you,' she offered, 'a magazine or anything you would like delivered, we'll be happy to see to it. The papers come down from Fort William on the bus.'

'I'll remember that,' promised Ailsa, getting back into the car. 'Thank you for your help.'

And those few kind words about my uncle, she thought as she drove away.

Truan Lodge stood a little way up the glen road looking down over the sunlit water of the loch to the mountains on its far side where the westering sun was already far down the sky. It was much as she had expected from her uncle's description, a big, rambling house at the end of a tree-flanked drive with a wing on either side of the older, original dwelling and long windows overlooking a raised terrace where stone-balustered steps led down to an unkempt lawn. Over-grown rhododendrons and azaleas flamed at their unrestrained best, making a brilliant splash of colour against the darker hue of the trees, and a little deer pranced skittishly into the undergrowth at her unexpected approach. She put the car into second gear as she neared the house, turning on to the terrace before the stout front door. When she shut off the engine she could almost feel the silence.

No one came to greet the sound of her arrival. The heavy door remained closed, as if at the advent of a stranger, and the silence seemed to deepen as she waited. A cold feeling of dismay swept across her heart. Where was everybody, when they knew quite well that she was coming? Moira Cameron, the postmistress's assistant, had even said that she was 'expected', but surely this was no way to make her feel welcome?

The house itself seemed slightly forbidding, even though the sun still lingered on its grey stone façade and a thin column of blue smoke strayed from one of its tall chimneys into the still, clear air. Turning, Ailsa looked down towards the loch where half a dozen small craft lay idly in a tiny bay in the shelter of a dark headland. It was like a painted scene from a beautiful canvas with no life on it—only silence.

Squaring her shoulders, she walked along the length of the terrace, to encounter her uncle's housekeeper for the first time. Martha Birch had come round the end of the house from some back or side entrance, and she was in no hurry to make her feel at home.

'We don't open the front unless it's necessary,' she announced without preliminary. 'It's best to keep the door bolted these days, and we get a lot of wind and rain sweeping up the loch.'

A pale, thin woman in her late forties, she had done nothing for her appearance by dragging her lovely auburn hair close to her head and pinning it in a tight knot at the nape of her neck. Her sharp gimlet eyes were almost suspicious in their scrutiny as Ailsa moved forward to shake her by the hand.

'It's been a long drive, Mrs Birch, but I'm surely glad to be here at last. I've heard so much about Truan from my uncle, and it hasn't disappointed me. This is a lovely place. You must be happy to live here.'

Martha Birch turned to lead the way round the gable end of the house.

'Happiness is where you find it,' she remarked disconcertingly. 'I have lived at Truan for a great part of my life, serving the old laird.'

'And then my uncle,' Ailsa added, following her to the side door. 'He said it was a great relief to him to have someone in the house who knew the ropes.'

The merest hint of a smile relieved the stern lines of the older woman's face.

'It's good to know when you are appreciated,' she acknowledged. 'Mr Sutherland was a very generous man.'

Who could never have replaced the old laird in Mrs Birch's estimation; never, no matter how long he had lived at Truan, Ailsa decided.

'Is there someone who can carry in my luggage,' she asked on the worn doorstep, 'or shall I bring the car round?'

'Hamish will see to it,' the housekeeper told her. 'He comes in daily to attend to the garden and does odd jobs around the house, chopping wood and seeing to the fires. We have no other servants.'

Perhaps that was why half the house seemed to be closed, Ailsa thought, but even a quarter of this great rambling pile would serve her very well until she decided what to do with the rest of it.

Martha Birch led the way through a small entrance lobby to an inner hall where three doors lay open and a short, narrow staircase led to an upper floor.

'You'll be needing some tea,' she remarked. 'We take our dinner at half-past six, and seven o'clock when the days lengthen.'

There were established rules, Ailsa realised, and therefore, not to be questioned.

'That will suit me quite well, Mrs Birch,' she agreed.

'Of course, if you have other ideas——'

'No, not at all. I'm quite happy to fit in with your usual arrangements, although I suppose we could bend the rules a bit if we had company,' Ailsa suggested hopefully.

The housekeeper shot her a quick, unapproving glance.

'Mr Sutherland didn't entertain,' she said. 'He had the odd person in for a bite in the middle of the day, usually when there was a shoot, but he was a great reader and liked the evenings to himself.'

Ailsa had never imagined her uncle as a near-hermit, but she didn't argue the point as Mrs Birch ushered her into a cosy morning-room where a bright fire burned on the stone hearth and a round occasional table had been set with a white lace cloth, a cup, saucer and plate, and a large silver sugar bowl suitably polished for the occasion.

'I'll go and infuse the tea,' the housekeeper announced.

Ailsa took off her tweed jacket, laying it on a chair as she crossed to the long window which overlooked the untidy side garden where more rhododendrons and azaleas flourished without control. It would be impossible for one man to cope with all this lush growth, but the neglected garden held a certain charm which intrigued her. Tamed, it would have seemed out of place in that wild setting of shadowed hills and glistening loch, and it was a fitting setting for the old grey stone house which must have stood there for around three hundred years. Part of it, anyway. That's what we envy in the New World, she mused: all this reaching back into the past to an ancestry covering hundreds of years and the knowledge that we had belonged there for generations. Yet Truan had changed hands six years ago when Gavin Sutherland had bought the estate. Her uncle had become the new laird, she supposed, or had they never recognised him as that here in this lonely glen? The people of Truan, if they were like Martha Birch, would be loath to change their ways or their loyalty to the old order of things here in this remote place where her uncle had chosen to live. And he had never married. He had made her his heir because he had no children of his own.

She was still gazing out over the garden when the housekeeper came back into the room followed by a younger version of herself carrying a silver milk jug and a hot-water pot.

'This is Flora, my daughter,' she introduced them.

The relationship was obvious except for the fact that Flora had dancing brown eyes and wore her auburn hair curling round her face, letting it fall in a bronze cascade to her waist at the back. It was hair that seemed to fill the room with light, glowing against the drab wall-coverings and the shabby velvet furniture which spoke clearly of another age.

'Pleased to meet you,' said Flora, offering a shy smile. 'Did you have a good journey?'

'Excellent.' Ailsa realised that she would be expected to take her tea alone as Mrs Birch put a plate of scones and a jar of honey on the table beside the solitary plate. 'I'd like you to join me,' she said impulsively. 'Then we can talk.'

Surprisingly Mrs Birch accepted her invitation.

'Flora will bring the extra cups,' she said.

When Flora returned she stood back, allowing Ailsa to pour the tea. It was all very conventional, but no doubt they would relax in time.

'Do you live here?' Ailsa asked when Flora smiled at her.

'For the present,' her mother answered for her. 'Mr Sutherland was very fond of her. He sent her to college in Glasgow and he was always pleased to have her here for the holidays. Of course,' she added tentatively, 'if you wish to make other arrangements——'

'No,' Ailsa said, 'not at all. Flora must stay for as long as she likes and I'll be pleased to have her around. Someone of my own age.'

Flora's eyes glowed and her mother looked mollified.

'She won't get in your way,' she promised. 'That is— if you mean to stay here.' Mrs Birch put down her tea-cup, drained quickly of the tea. 'You may change your mind about Truan once you've been here for a while.'

The suggestion was wholly unacceptable to Ailsa in that moment, because she was already half in love with Truan.

'I don't think that will happen, Mrs Birch,' she answered firmly. 'I guess I've come to stay.'

The housekeeper rose to her feet.

'We shall see,' she said. 'These are early days yet.'

As Flora began to gather the used cups and saucers together she moved towards the door.

'Hamish will have taken your luggage up,' she said. 'You will be wanting to see your room.'

Ailsa caught up her jacket on the way to the door, managing to smile encouragingly in Flora's direction as she passed.

'See you at dinner,' she said, 'and we'll talk!'

Mrs Birch led the way up the narrow back staircase, turning at the top along a corridor which led to several bedrooms on the first floor. At the very end of the corridor she opened the door into a comfortable-looking room with a single bed in it, covered in a flowered cotton counterpane which identically matched the curtains on either side of the window overlooking the back terrace and an overgrown lawn tennis court, which Ailsa immediately decided to restore to its former glory, even if she had to cut the grass herself.

'It's just what I need,' she said, looking down on the court. 'It will be good exercise for me in the summer. Does Flora play?'

Martha Birch hesitated.

'She did at one time,' she admitted grudgingly. 'Now she is all for her books, because she knows she must study to pass her exams and make something of herself for the future.'

'But she has to have time off to play too,' Ailsa objected. 'What age is she?'

Martha Birch looked taken aback.

'Twenty-two,' she admitted almost reluctantly. 'A young woman, you might say, able to look after herself. If you wish her to go,' she offered again, 'I can leave with her once you are settled in.'

The harshness of her tone took Ailsa completely by surprise.

'That's not what you really want, Mrs Birch,' she guessed. 'You wouldn't leave Truan if you had a choice, and I'm not giving you one. I want you to stay here, and Flora too. I need your help and experience, because I wouldn't know how to manage Truan on my own.'

'It has been my home for twenty years.' There was a hint of nostalgia in the hard voice which a moment ago had sounded so resentful. 'I came as housekeeper to the old laird when he was first widowed and I helped to bring up his two boys.'

'What happened to them?' Ailsa found herself asking as she opened her first suitcase which Hamish had deposited inside the door.

'One is dead—the rightful heir to the estate. The other is still here, without any inheritance but the Keep.'

Uneasily Ailsa turned away, feeling as if she had been accused.

'He must find it difficult—the younger son,' she suggested, 'being so close to Truan now that it belongs to—someone else.'

'Ay, that he must—and does,' Martha Birch admitted, 'but he will not say so in so many words. He will not let anyone see his hurt. He is too proud for that, I'm thinking.'

When she had gone Ailsa unpacked both her suitcases, hanging skirts and dresses in the massive oak wardrobe which seemed to dwarf the room and laying her underwear and shirts carefully in the deep drawers of the dressing table beside the window. It was a temptation to look out across the garden again towards the hills, now in shadow as the sun went down, and an added temptation to explore the remainder of the house, which she finally decided against in case Mrs Birch had planned an escorted tour for the following morning under her strict supervision. Instead she went down the back stairs and walked round to the terrace to the car she had hired, remembering the man who had helped her on the moor road. Whatever he had done to the engine, it had performed perfectly ever since, and she wondered if she had thanked him enough.

Hamish ambled up to help her put the car away.

'You are to keep it in the stables,' he announced. 'There's plenty of room. What kind of car is it?' he asked with what she now considered to be native curiosity. 'It looks fairly new.'

'It's a Ford Cortina, and it isn't really mine,' she explained. 'I hired it at Prestwick for the journey up here, but——' she hesitated, 'I've half a mind to see if I can hang on to it permanently. I don't know if they would sell, but I've got sort of—attached to it now. Anyway, I've hired it for a month.'

'You'll have to remember to keep it filled up with petrol when you go to Oban or Fort William,' he advised. 'We don't have many garages in these parts and they often run short.'

'So I believe.' Ailsa was thinking back to her encounter on the moor. 'I don't expect to be using it very often,' she added. 'Not till I've finally settled in.'

Hamish gave her a long, calculating look.

'Maybe you won't be settling,' he said. 'Maybe you'll be like all the rest of the young people and be off to Glasgow half the time, or maybe you'll go back to Canada.'

She drew a deep breath.

'I won't do that, Hamish,' she said. 'Not till I've given Truan a fair trial.'

He went off, whistling under his breath, leaving her to find her own way to the stables, which she guessed would be at the back of the house.

The sun had set and streaks of gold and red lay across the sky above the mountain peaks, casting a bronze reflection on the water of the loch and etching deep shadows between the trees. The whole world seemed to be waiting for the coming of the night as the light faded, and the magic she had first experienced in her native Canada as she had stood waiting for the sun to go down over the Algonquin wilderness was the same magic she felt now. The still Arctic air might have been the same air she was breathing now, with just a chill of cold in it, and the forests she had known since childhood stood back as silently in the Algonquin as they did here, darkening the bays and inlets around the quiet loch.

When she had found a space in one of the stables to house the Cortina for the night she walked slowly back to the side door, where sounds of activity were coming from the kitchen across the hall. Mrs Birch and Flora were preparing the evening meal.

She did not join them, feeling instinctively that an offer of help would be resented. The kitchen would be Martha Birch's personal domain where she would reign supreme.

To her surprise, she found herself dining alone. A place had been set for her at one end of the long refectory table in the large, oak-panelled dining-room in the main part of the house, the wall sconces throwing a soft yellow glow on to its polished surface and picking out the moiré pattern of the faded paper which covered the upper part of the walls. It was an impressive room with its huge inglenook where half a tree trunk could easily burn in the open grate, and the shutters were already closed across the window alcoves and flanked by long velvet curtains faded to the colour of old roses.

'You shouldn't have put yourself to so much trouble,' Ailsa remarked as the housekeeper came in with a soup tureen on a tray. 'I can easily take my meals in the small sitting-room nearer the kitchen with you and Flora.'

Mrs Birch considered her request for a full minute while she served the soup.

'That would not be appropriate,' she said.

'But it would be practical,' Ailsa pointed out.

'The dinner has always been served in here.' Mrs Birch stiffened perceptibly. 'I see no need to change our ways. Your uncle ate his evening meal here and never complained. He liked to be alone.'

'I wish I knew more about him,' said Ailsa, leaving the matter of convenience alone now that Mrs Birch had expressed her strong views on the subject. 'He wrote to my mother occasionally, but you can never convey everything in a letter. All we were able to gather was that he was blissfully content here, with absolutely no regrets.'

'He took great pleasure in Flora.' Mrs Birch put the tureen back on the tray, preparing to leave. 'He knew how much she loved Truan.'

'That's only natural if it has always been her home,' Ailsa agreed.

The housekeeper paused beside the door.

'I brought her to Truan as a babe in arms. Truan was my salvation, you might say.'

'You were widowed?'

There was the faintest hesitation before Martha Birch replied.

'I was without a man—yes,' she acknowledged. 'He was killed in an accident before Flora was born.'

'I'm sorry.'

'You have no need to be. I have never asked for sympathy,' Mrs Birch declared. 'Not from anyone.'

Once again Ailsa was conscious of resentment, if not exactly directed towards her, then at least to the circumstances in which her late uncle's housekeeper now found herself and her child.

'I hope Flora and I are going to be friends,' she said spontaneously. 'There's not too much difference in our ages and we probably have a lot in common.'

Mrs Birch left the room without answering.

Well, I did try, Ailsa thought, but I guess I'll make the grade easier with Flora herself.

'Will you join me for coffee?' she asked when the housekeeper came to remove the dessert plates. 'You and Flora?'

'Flora is at her books. She has a lot of studying to do before her exams and I have the house to shut up for the night,' Mrs Birch said. 'You will not be going out again?'

Ailsa knew what the answer to that question would be.

'I'd like a walk by the loch,' she said, 'before I go to bed. It's a lovely night, and I can come in by the side door and lock up for you.' It was no more than eight o'clock, with the sky above the loch bright and clear, not really dark yet in this northern clime where the light seemed to be suspended above the mountain rims and the stars shimmered like small lanterns in the deeper blue. 'I feel refreshed after so good a meal, Mrs Birch, and I'm sure a walk would do me good.'

'You must please yourself,' the housekeeper told her, 'but I'll wait up for you. You'll no doubt be back before ten o'clock.'

Feeling guilty, Ailsa went up to her room by the narrow back staircase to find her coat. It might be cold at this time of night, although the sun had been warm on her face as she had sat eating her alfresco meal by the roadside spring up there on the moor. As she remembered the man who had come to her rescue, her lips curved in an appreciative smile as she thought that her first contact in the glen had not been a critical one, although he had seemed less disposed to be friendly once she had told him who she was. 'The girl from Toronto!' The phrase amused her. It was as if she had come from the far side of the moon.

Walking along the deserted shore road, she was aware of a magic which her uncle must have felt when he had first decided to buy Truan. Behind her the Lodge stood grey in the shadows, the starlight touching its slated roof, tall trees standing guard on either side, and she thought suddenly that it was too big a place for one person, although her uncle had been content in his isolation. Surely it had been built all these years ago to accommodate a family, and then those closed rooms on the first floor would have been full of children already asleep, and the unshuttered windows of the dining-room would have been pools of light in the darkness as their parents entertained? That was how the Lodge should be now if fate hadn't taken a hand to deprive Truan of its 'rightful heir'. But the second son was still here, she mused. What had he done about Truan after his brother died?

The uneasiness she had felt when she had discussed the brothers with her uncle's housekeeper returned, although she was in no way responsible for the younger son's deprivation. He had evidently sold Truan Lodge when he had inherited it for a reason of his own, but apparently there had been compensation in the shape of the Keep, wherever that was. No doubt, she decided, she would come across it very soon.

A figure appeared on the road ahead of her, coming up from the loch, and it was still light enough for her to recognise her companion of the moor, although he walked alone now without the dogs. He was carrying a pair of oars on his shoulder, one hand steadying them as he walked, and his feet were thrust into practical-looking gumboots.

'Been for a sail?' Ailsa asked companionably as they drew level.

'I've been on the loch,' he acknowledged, 'seeing to the fish-traps.'

She waited for an explanation.

'We're breeding trout,' he explained. 'It's a new venture which looks as if it might succeed, but at present it's more than time-consuming. We have a shed down there by the loch and half a dozen traps out on the water.'

'We?' she enquired.

'Tom Kelvin and I are in partnership. This is his night off.' He turned to move away. 'You'll be meeting him, I dare say, once you are settled in at the Lodge. He's quite a character. Came up from Glasgow for a holiday two years ago and decided to stay "because he liked the place". He has a B.Sc. in Engineering.'

'So—what made him want to breed fish?' she asked, falling into step beside him. 'It doesn't work out.'

The ghost of a smile touched his lips.

'You'd have to know Tom to discover why,' he told her, 'but it wasn't just a whim. He really does believe that he's found his Shangri-La.'

'Do you?' She paused to look at him. 'Do you think that you have all you will ever need here with your sheep and the fish?'

'It's where I belong,' he said without answering her question. 'I can't imagine myself being anywhere else.'

'I wish I could be so sure of my future,' she said after a pause. 'It must be tremendously satisfying to look forward with conviction and believe that you've done the right thing.'

'I can't imagine you racked with doubt.' He looked down at her in the starlight. 'Not when you have so much going for you.'

'You mean Truan, of course. That wasn't quite what I meant,' she confessed. 'I was thinking about coming so far from home to make a new start without being absolutely sure. Tonight I've felt vulnerable, very much alone in that big house up there with half of it closed and the main rooms far too big for me. I've only seen part of the Lodge so far, the part which was once the nursery wing, I believe, but of course, there's hardly been time for a tour of inspection.'

'You must have met Mrs Birch,' he suggested.

'And Flora! I'm sure we're going to be friends.'

'So—Flora is at home. I thought she was still in Glasgow.' He halted before the turn in to the drive, his back to the darkened Lodge. 'You will manage your way up to the house,' he said almost distantly. 'I'll be saying goodnight.'

Ailsa wanted to detain him for a few minutes longer, glad of his company on her first evening in the glen.

'I'd like to come and see the fish,' she said impulsively. 'It's something quite new to me.'

They were standing close in the starlight with the Lodge behind them and the dark mountains facing them across the loch.

'I'm sure Tom would be pleased to show you round,' he agreed. 'You'll have to come prepared with gumboots and something for your head.'

'Don't tell me I have to wade into the sea.'

He laughed.

'You'll have to wade through some disinfectant,' he told her, 'and there's always a certain amount of spray from the waterfall. Small trout start their lives in tanks of fresh water under cover, but we pass the falls on our way into the sheds. It can be wet.'

'I'll look forward to it.' She felt an odd lifting of the heart. 'Do I have to make an appointment—with Tom?'

'Come any day,' he said briefly. 'Tom or one of the boys is sure to be there.'

Reluctantly she turned towards the gates, closing them behind her before she went on up the drive and listening for his footsteps as he walked away. He could have seen her up to the house, she thought. He could easily have done that.

Mrs Birch was waiting in the small sitting-room with the door open.

'Have you enjoyed your walk?' she asked, bolting the outside door.

'Very much.' Ailsa took off her coat. 'I met someone I knew.'

Martha Birch turned to look at her, dark eyebrows raised.

'I met him on the moor this afternoon on my way here and he helped me to re-start the car when it broke down at the top of the hill. He's a shepherd of some sort.'

'It would be Donny MacKenzie,' Mrs Birch guessed. 'A wee fat man with a growth of beard.'

Ailsa laughed outright.

'No, he wasn't "a wee fat man" at all, Mrs Birch!' she said. 'He was every inch your Highland gentleman— or so he seemed. Maybe I was wrong to call him a shepherd,' she reflected. 'He was quite amused by that, but he had two dogs with him, both young collies he said he was training on the hill.'

Martha Birch walked towards the staircase in total silence. Evidently she did not want to hazard another guess about the true identity of the man on the moor.

'I'll follow you up,' said Ailsa. 'I'm really tired now after my walk.'

Slowly she mounted the narrow stairs in the house-keeper's wake, wishing her a brief goodnight on the landing where she had waited outside her own bedroom door. It was just after nine o'clock and a faint light still filtered through the windows facing the loch. With her hand on the door knob of her own room, Ailsa hesitated. The house was very quiet, hushed as if in sleep, but ahead of her was yet another window and she went towards it expectantly because she knew that it would afford her a view of the loch. Before she reached it, however, she realised that she had not come to the end of the corridor but to another door, stouter and heavier than the rest, which would probably be locked. She gazed from the window across the shimmering loch and back again to the firmly closed door, wondering what lay behind it in this rambling old house which seemed to be only partly her own.

The door opened easily enough, but she found herself in almost total darkness, groping her way along a wall which seemed to be some kind of gallery overlooking the main hallway of the house inside the front door. The door which Mrs Birch had told her was no longer used.

As her eyes became accustomed to the semi-darkness she finally made out a curving staircase climbing to the gallery where she stood and the vast area of the main hall far below. At the top of the magnificent stairway she stood quite still, aware of a feeling of trespass for which she could not account, an odd rejection of her presence there which sent a chill along her spine and a desire to run away into her sensitive heart.

Beneath her on the staircase wall she made out the heavy frames of several portraits hanging like dark custodians of this ancient house, the ancestors of the man to whom it had once belonged. They too must resent her, she thought, until she was able to laugh at the absurdity of the idea. Time I was in bed, she decided, till I can open the front door tomorrow to a breath of fresh air!

CHAPTER TWO

IN THE morning Ailsa knew that she had overslept when she was wakened by the sound of her door being opened and Flora's voice telling her that it was nine o'clock.

'It seemed a shame to waken you at seven,' she said, putting down the breakfast tray she carried on the table next to the bed. 'You must have been very tired from yesterday. It was a long drive.'

Ailsa sat up, blinking as Flora drew back the curtains from her window to let in a flood of light.

'I'm wasting all this wonderful sunshine,' she declared. 'You should have called me, but I promise you it won't happen again. Your mother must think me a laggard, sleeping my head off like this!'

'She gets up at six,' Flora admitted. 'Always has. It becomes a sort of habit after a while, I think, and you can't sleep afterwards. Seven o'clock is good enough for me, and eight when I'm in Glasgow.'

Ailsa was considering the lavishly set tray.

'I won't want my breakfast in bed after this,' she said carefully. 'I don't expect to be waited on, Flora, and your mother must have enough to do.'

'I help when I can, ' Flora assured her. 'She makes me study most of the time, and I don't really mind that, because it's so interesting.'

'What do you want to do—after college?' Ailsa asked, tapping the top of one of the boiled eggs on her tray.

'Teach, I suppose.'

'Aren't you sure?'

'More or less.' Flora stood with her back to the window. "I once thought I'd like to work with children—be a nanny or a nurse in a children's hospital, but I gave the idea up some time ago.'

When your mother put her foot down and decreed otherwise, thought Ailsa.

'You'll make a good teacher,' she said, 'and after all, that is to do with children. Flora,' she added, 'do you think your mother would mind if I opened up the main section of the house? It wouldn't cause a lot more work, and we could get someone in from the village to help. It seems a shame to keep it all shut up like that and the big door closed.'

Flora hesitated.

'It used to be open all summer,' she said at last. 'People coming in and out and things lying about all over the place—like a real home,' she added quietly. 'You know what I mean.'

'It could be like that again—the door open and the sun streaming in to that lovely hall.'

Flora looked at her enquiringly.

'I went through the door at the end of the corridor last night,' Ailsa explained, 'to the head of the staircase. It was all quite—ghostly with the furniture covered up down there and the family portraits on the walls. I suppose they *are* family,' she submitted.

'Everything is just how the MacNairs left it,' Flora agreed. 'Mr Sutherland—your uncle—bought the house as it stood, furniture and everything save for a few personal things of the young laird's which he took away with him when he left.' For a moment she stood wrapped in thought, her eyes on the scene beyond the window. 'It was a great wrench for him, as you can well imagine, because of the two of them Master Fergus loved Truan the most.'

'Your mother said he was still here, in the glen,' Ailsa observed. 'I think I would have gone away altogether to put the past right behind me, to forget completely in the end.'

'Fergus will never forget Truan,' Flora declared. 'He lives in a rented cottage in the glen now, but he can't be happy there, I'm thinking, always aware of Truan and what might have been.'

'I feel as if I've defrauded him in some way.' Ailsa bit into a piece of buttered toast. 'Being here when he should be at Truan instead of me, bringing up a family to fill this great house and producing an heir.'

'You are not to blame,' Flora told her reasonably enough. 'Nobody is, except——' She left the sentence unfinished as she crossed to the door. 'I'll come up for your tray later on.'

'I'll bring it down with me when I come,' promised Ailsa. 'You mustn't wait on me, Flora. You have other things to do.'

The other girl threw her an appreciative glance.

'Like studying most of the time,' she agreed. 'But I'll go with you through the glen one of these days and show you the view from Truan Beag. I'm thinking it's the most beautiful view in the world.'

When she had enjoyed a second cup of coffee standing in front of her bedroom window Ailsa dressed quickly and carried the tray and its contents down the narrow back stairs. She had cast a hurried glance at the heavy door at the end of the upstairs corridor, but there was no sense in exploring with a heavy tray in her hands, and no doubt it would be best to consult Mrs Birch in advance before she opened up more of the house.

The kitchen was deserted, and after she had washed her breakfast dishes she went outside. The garden was also deserted. It was as if Flora and her mother had disappeared into thin air.

Deciding to go for a walk at least to the end of the drive where she had parted company with her acquaintance of the moor the evening before, Ailsa returned to her bedroom to put on a stouter pair of shoes. The air had been mild enough outside, suggesting a perfect spring day, and she decided to go without a coat.

Closing the bedroom door behind her, she paused in the corridor, finally giving way to the same impulse which had taken her through the heavy door at its far end the night before. When she opened it, everything was just the same except for the fact that the hall beneath her was now flooded in morning light. It came from the two

arched windows high above the main door, slanting down
on the tessellated floor where the rugs had been rolled
carefully against the wall and it seemed as if the old house
was coming back to life. The massive main door was
still firmly closed, the furniture still draped in its dust
sheets, but there was a sense of freedom engendered by
that yellow, penetrating light which swept away the
feeling of dejection she had experienced only a few hours
ago.

She gazed down from the top of the staircase, one
hand tentatively on the fine brass handrail, before she
finally decided to go down.

The thick red pile of the carpet was soft under her
feet, but her eyes were immediately drawn to the portraits
on the wall above her. 'Everything is just how the
MacNairs left it', Flora had said, so these were surely
the MacNairs of long ago, the elegantly attired women
and handsome men, some of them in uniform, who had
called Truan their home for so long.

Slowly she walked beneath them, aware of a famili-
arity she could not put a name to and a strange,
mounting excitement running in her veins. They were all
here, all these MacNairs who had worked and perhaps
sacrificed to keep Truan as it was.

Looking up at them, she was met by a row of eyes,
some of them hard and demanding, others vaguely sad
as if half aware of Truan in its present state of near-
dereliction which they would abhor.

At the very bottom of the staircase a large portrait
hung a little way apart with the light full on the painted
face. Like so many of the others, it was the kilted figure
of a man pictured against a background of moorland
with two dogs lying at his feet and a *cromag* in his hand.
He was leaning slightly forward over the shepherd's
crook, and Ailsa's heart seemed to miss a beat as she
found herself looking into the accusing eyes of the man
on the moor.

For a moment she stood back, stunned by the sudden
revelation and once more aware of a deepening sense of
guilt, until she looked again and knew that this was a
different man. The eyes were harder, the mouth harshly
cynical as the lips curved in a half-smile—an older man

with the knowledge of the world behind him and a vague
indifference to the present. The fact remained, however,
that she had discovered the identity of the man on the
moor. This must be his immediate ancestor or, even more
likely, the older brother he had lost six years ago before
her uncle had bought the house. There was no way of
telling how old the portrait was, of course, because the
Highland garb had changed very little over the years,
but the tartan was certainly of the same weave in all the
portraits. She looked more closely to discover a signature and a date, finding them concealed among the
tufts of painted heather at the man's feet. The artist's
name didn't seem to matter, but the date was there.
Nineteen-seventy-eight. The portrait had been painted
eleven years ago and was obviously a portrait of the last
MacNair in the direct line of succession.

'That is Ewan MacNair.'

Mrs Birch was standing above her halfway down the
curving stairway, a steadying hand gripping the narrow
rail she had polished so often in the past. Her eyes were
on the portrait, hard and accusing, as if she blamed Ewan
MacNair for dying so carelessly before his proper
function could be fulfilled.

'And the young laird?' Ailsa found herself asking,
although she already knew the answer.

'He is living in a cottage in the glen,' the housekeeper
told her, coming slowly down the remaining stairs. 'This
is his elder brother, the rightful heir.'

Ailsa drew in a deep breath.

'I think I've met him,' she said. 'The young laird.
They're so alike I thought this was his portrait at first.'

'There was no time for painting pictures once Ewan
died,' Mrs Birch announced harshly. 'No time at all.
The money was needed for other things.' Suddenly she
turned from her contemplation of the portrait. 'When
did you meet Fergus?' she demanded.

'As a matter of fact, I've met him twice without
knowing who he was,' Ailsa admitted. 'It's the man I
was telling you about last night, who fixed my car, the
one who had two dogs.'

Martha Birch frowned at her. 'It would be Fergus,'
she said.

'It must have been.' Ailsa was still gazing at the portrait. 'He was carrying that carved shepherd's hook—the *cromag*—and the two collies look the same.'

'They are younger dogs and I suppose Fergus would be training them to the hill. They're pups of Nell, who was Mr Ewan's dog.' Mrs Birch looked sharply at her new mistress. 'You said you have met Fergus twice?'

'Last night, when I went out for a walk,' Ailsa explained. 'He was coming up from the loch.'

'It's a wonder he spoke.'

Ailsa turned quickly.

'Why do you say that? There was no one else around, and after all, we had met on the moor earlier,' she pointed out.

'He'd have little time for idle conversation,' Mrs Birch declared. 'He works every day God sends, and sometimes I wonder if it's not too much. It's as if he was trying to compensate for something, as if he had something to repay. You'll not get anywhere with him,' she added bluntly, 'if that was your idea. He doesn't take kindly to—strangers.'

'Mrs Birch,' Ailsa protested, exasperated, 'I wasn't trying to impress Fergus MacNair, if that's what you mean. I wasn't even trying to make a friend of him. I guess we were only being civil, and I didn't know who he was.'

'He would know who you were, though,' Martha Birch pointed out. 'It must have cut him to the heart, standing there talking to you at his own front gates.'

'I'm sorry if he felt that way,' Ailsa returned, 'but what can I really do about it? I'm willing to be friends, but if he can't accept that there's no other way I can—compensate for what he has lost.'

'Nobody will ever be able to do that,' the housekeeper declared stoutly, her lips thinning as she looked about her. 'And now Flora tells me that you are thinking about opening up this part of the house, so you will need help. Hamish can see to the door and I'll put the rugs in place. The stairs will make far more work, but that won't have to matter.'

'We can get extra help,' Ailsa suggested. 'Someone from the village, perhaps.'

'I'll have to see.' Mrs Birch stood aside to allow her to ascend the staircase. 'Flora can lend a hand in the meantime.'

'Flora has her exams coming up,' Ailsa pointed out, pausing on the first stair. 'She shouldn't be doing domestic work.'

'Just as you say, Miss Mallory.' The housekeeper's tone had been faintly derisory. 'I'm sure Flora will be pleased.'

Ailsa went slowly up the stairs, aware of all those watching eyes looking down at her from the wall but more fully aware of the hostile attitude of the woman who followed her to the floor above. No doubt Mrs Birch could be excused for her loyalty to the old order of things, for her allegiance to 'the rightful heir' and her undoubted concern for 'the young laird', but she felt that the older woman's dislike went even deeper than that. The housekeeper's distant manner was almost personal, as if she would never forgive her for inheriting what should have belonged to someone else.

A smile broke suddenly at the corners of Ailsa's mouth. Was everyone given a by-name here in this silent glen? 'The young laird', 'the rightful heir' and—'the girl from Toronto'! Was that what she would always be, the stranger from a distant land who had taken possession against everyone's will?

'I'm going out, Mrs Birch,' she announced at the head of the stairs. 'Unless you have something else you would like me to do.'

'You are your own mistress,' Martha Birch assured her. 'You will be back for something to eat at one o'clock.'

It was more of a command than a suggestion, and Ailsa's smile deepened.

'I have a reliable watch,' she said, 'and I don't intend to go far. I may call by the post office and get some stamps on my way back.'

'You'll get all the news down there too,' Martha Birch sniffed. 'Kate Brisby attends to everybody's business but her own.'

Ailsa laughed.

'I'll risk going in for the stamps!' she declared.

At the end of the drive she looked to left and right, wondering which way to choose and wishing that Flora had been able to come with her. They were almost of an age and she felt that they could become friends.

Finally she chose the loch, walking along the narrow road which skirted the shore until she left the trees behind and came upon a view which took her breath away. Loch Truan had opened out into a broad bay where the water was still and calm with a vista of more water on its far side and the all-pervading mountains rising against the skyline to the north and west, but what had riveted her attention so dramatically that she stood quite still on the narrow road to look and look again was the sight of a ruined tower rising in stark beauty on a rocky island just off the shore, an ancient castle obviously built there to repel the invader all those years ago when danger had come mostly from the sea. Her vivid imagination pictured the Viking hordes in their high-prowed boats sweeping in across the bay from the distant Hebrides and the castle waiting there on its rocky vantage point to drive them away.

Then she saw that the island was not an island at all. Stark and forbidding, it was linked to the mainland by a narrow causeway over which sheep grazed leisurely on their way to the tower.

Where sheep could go she could undoubtedly follow, she decided, picking her way between the rocks with a flutter of excitement in her heart. This was really exploring in the true sense of the word. She would come here often.

Swept on by her enthusiasm, she jumped from stone to stone, reaching the grassland around the keep to find herself surrounded by sheep. They were different sheep, darker in the fleece, with strong, curling horns which made them look formidable, but they continued to graze quite placidly as she made her way towards the tower itself.

It stood alone, its stout curtain-wall excluding all comers, its central elevation ruined in places where time and the elements had wrought havoc on what had once been an impregnable bastion of defence. Intrigued, Ailsa circled it, coming to the expected doorway high in the land-facing side where a broken stone stairway led up to the door. The door itself was made of wood and was protected by an iron grille which looked as if it had just been hoisted into position. The tower, then, was being repaired.

Suddenly she knew that it was being brought back to life by Fergus MacNair, the young laird who had inherited it apart from the Lodge. The absolute conviction stunned her for a moment, although she had reason enough for her conviction. Martha Birch's words were very clear in her mind in that moment as she looked at Fergus MacNair's stark inheritance.

'The one is dead—the rightful heir to the estate,' the housekeeper had said. 'The other is still here, without any inheritance but the Keep.'

'The young laird', as Martha persisted in calling him, had taken on a tremendous task. Ailsa looked up at the forbidding curtain-wall above which the battlemented tower stood almost in ruins, wondering how long it would take even a determined man to restore his ancient inheritance to some semblance of its former glory. Years, perhaps, she decided, and a great deal of money into the bargain.

Slowly she walked round the encircling wall which rose in places steeply from the sea, leaving little more than a narrow pathway for her to clamber over the jutting rocks till she came to an unexpected little plateau facing west where the grass was lushly green and the view heart-stopping in its absolute magnificence. Nowhere else, she thought, would the grandeur of hill and loch appear so entrancing, with Fergus MacNair's ancient Keep behind her and blue water and dark mountains straight ahead.

Sitting down on a mound of grass and heather with a clump of bluebells blowing in the wind at her feet, she let time slip away from her as she listened to the bleating of the sheep and the slap of water, like an intimate whisper, moving against the rocks, and in that moment she thought she understood why a man like Fergus MacNair must want to live there.

She stayed there for an hour, sitting with her back to the wall and her face to the sun, before she retraced her steps to the other side of the Keep, realising with a gasp of dismay that the tide had come in and now she was really on an island. The water had covered the causeway, leaving her high and dry under the castle wall.

Gazing down at the seaweed which festooned some of the rocks, she wondered why she hadn't realised that the causeway would be covered at high tide twice in a day, and coming to the rueful conclusion that she had been far too eager to reach the Keep—far too curious about it—to consider such details as an incoming tide and the long wait she was going to have before she could return to the lochside road and make the journey back to Truan Lodge in time for a midday meal. Mrs Birch would be furious, but surely she wouldn't consider sending out a search party to look for her till late afternoon. By that time, she assured herself, she could walk back across the causeway and be at the Lodge in time for the main cooked meal of the day. She would be hungry, of course, but that would be entirely her own fault, after all. Strange, she thought, how you don't think too much about hunger when there's plenty to eat close at hand!

Should she try to wade ashore or even to swim? Perhaps not, since it was only eleven o'clock and she now had plenty of time to just stand and stare. She could apologise to Martha Birch, explaining her predicament, and that would suffice.

Intrigued by the work that had been started behind the thick curtain-wall, she paused in front of the yett-guarded entrance, but even when she had climbed to the topmost crumbling stone step the solid door beyond it stood as a barrier to curiosity, shutting her out.

With all the time in the world to spare she returned to the far side of the Keep to sit on the grassy ledge under the sea-gate from which the ancient occupants of the tower had repelled invaders long ago with courage and determination until they finally departed, beaten and discouraged, to set sail for their own homeland.

An hour fled past before she returned to the causeway to find a boat approaching and a man rowing strongly against the tide. It was her acquaintance of the moor, the hill shepherd who had helped her in an emergency once before. It was also Fergus MacNair, owner of the

ancient Keep behind her which was his only true
inheritance.

She waited with an odd sort of alarm stirring in her
heart for him to reach the island, aware that this was an
angry man who had taken her invasion of his solitary
domain as an intrusion and was determined to terminate
it immediately.

'What are you doing here?' he demanded as soon as
he had grounded the dinghy on the pebbles at her feet.

'Exploring, I suppose.' Ailsa offered a smile. 'I walked
across the causeway without realising that the tide would
come in and leave me stranded.'

'You are not welcome,' he said bluntly. 'I'll take you
back.'

'Thank you.' She glanced at her wristwatch. 'It isn't
terribly urgent—getting back, I mean—so if you have
anything else to do I don't mind waiting.' She glanced
beyond him to the pile of boxes and rope in the stern
of the dinghy. 'You were coming to work?'

'Yes,' he acknowledged, 'but that can wait.'

'Oh, so can I,' she assured him. 'Please go ahead with
what you came to do and I'll sit on the shore till you're
ready to go back. I've been over on the other side of
your island, dreaming dreams.' She glanced up at the
curtain-wall. 'This is such a romantic place! What are
you doing behind that forbidding barrier of stone when
you have to guard it with so strong a door?'

He turned back to the dinghy, some of the initial anger
gone from his face.

'I'm reconstructing it a bit at a time, trying to get it
back to what it was,' he explained. 'The yett is essential.
It was wrought by a local blacksmith to a copy of the
original found among my mother's possessions at the
Lodge.'

Ailsa took a step towards him.

'Now that I know who you are I want to say "thank
you" again,' she said, holding out her hand, 'but perhaps
I should also say I'm sorry about trespassing like this,'
she added. 'I had no idea it was private property and
when I came across I didn't realise it was an island. Like
the usual sightseer, I was fascinated by all this.' She

looked back at the Keep. 'I didn't mean to behave like the proverbial tripper, I can assure you.'

'No,' he said, 'you're not a tripper, are you? You're here to stay, at the Lodge, at least.'

'That was my idea.' She looked at him, completely perplexed by his change of manner. 'Mr MacNair,' she said, 'whatever I have done, it wasn't from any desire to—hurt anyone. I came to Truan because my uncle willed the estate to me and—and because I was ready to leave Canada at the time. If I decide to stay here—to make Truan my home in the end—I want to be absolutely sure of my decision. I'm on my own now. My mother remarried in Toronto about a year ago, and I can't expect her to uproot herself and join me in Scotland, no matter how badly I feel about being alone. I'm old enough to fix my own life the way I want it, and at present I can't think of a better way than taking up my inheritance and doing what I can for Truan. If that sounds a little pompous,' she added quickly, 'I'm sorry, but it's the way I feel for the moment, anyway.'

He had heard her out without interruption, standing in the shallow water beside the boat.

'I hope you understand,' she ventured, waiting for his reaction with a sense of urgency she had no right to feel on such a short acquaintance.

'You sound as if you are making a convenience of Truan,' he said without turning. 'That is no good to the estate, I can assure you.'

'Believe me, I'm not.' Ailsa felt that she had to get through to him if only to prove that her intentions were genuine. 'I could love this place with all its wildness and beauty. You see, in some ways it's like Canada, where I was born. Although you may think so, I'm not a city girl. I've lived in Toronto and worked there for the past three years, but we were near enough to the Algonquin to be up there camping as soon as the snow cleared in May. All this'—she turned to look again at the pine-clad hillside across the bay—'reminds me of Canada, of Little Joe Lake and Arrowhon Pines and hoping to come across a moose or a wolf, or even a straying bear, when we were very young.'

'You make it all sound idyllic,' he remarked, 'but life isn't just one big holiday camp up here. When you really have to fight the elements for a living I think you have to be born to it.'

'That's true, and I suppose I've never had to fight very hard, but I do mean to try with Truan. This morning I opened up the main hall to let in some light, and it made a lot of difference.'

When he did not respond she looked back to the Keep.

'Are you building inside the wall,' she asked, 'or is there already a house there?'

He bent to pick up one of the boxes from the dinghy.

'It was a home at one time, but ever since I can remember and even long before that it was no more than a shell. It belonged to my mother's family—the MacKinnons of Nant—and she left it to me in her will, since the Truan inheritance was my brother's by right of succession. You will hear all this, I have no doubt, once you start moving about the glen.'

'But now I have it first-hand.' Ailsa smiled at him. 'How long do you think it will take to finish the tower? I'd love to see it completed.'

He seemed surprised by her enthusiasm and somewhat disconcerted by her obvious friendliness, but the look of hardness was still in his eyes.

'I doubt if either of us will see it finished,' he answered. 'It's the sort of thing that can take a lifetime when it must be tackled a bit at a time. With plenty of money to spend on it, of course, and outside labour, it could be done in a matter of months. The basic structure is undamaged and the foundations go down into the rock where the dungeon is still as it was hundreds of years ago.'

'A dungeon!' Ailsa exclaimed. 'You make me more eager to explore than ever!'

He bent to the dinghy without answering and she felt a hot wave of embarrassment rushing to her cheeks, knowing that she had been intruding again.

'Let me carry some of that up for you,' she offered as he slung a heavy sack over his shoulder. 'I'm quite able to help.'

He hesitated.

'You'll find some of the boxes heavy,' he warned. 'They're slates.'

'Not to worry!' she assured him. 'I'm used to lugging stuff around—that was half the fun of the Algonquin in the spring.'

As he handed her the first box their fingers touched, drawing her eyes instantly to his to meet the barrier of resentment he had erected between them for a very good reason of his own. He would never forget that she was the new owner of Truan which had been his cherished family home for so many happy years.

When they reached the foot of the steps leading to the ruined Keep he stacked their burdens in an untidy pile.

'I'll leave everything here,' he decided. 'The steps are a bit of a hazard in their present state.'

Ailsa glanced up at the forbidding door.

'Why was it built so high?' she asked, knowing immediately that she had made a mistake.

'To repel the invader,' he said. 'No matter which way they came—by land or by sea—they had to fight their way to the top.'

'And if they ever did get in they were immediately clapped into the dungeon!' she suggested.

'These were cruel times,' he admitted, 'needing ruthless measures. Every Highland castle had its dungeon and most of them have survived to tell the tale. This one is very narrow and very deep and full of mystery, to say nothing of the real horror of being actually confined in it.' He smiled suddenly. 'When we were young we used to play there, letting down a torch to show the way until my father decided to put the Keep out of bounds because it had become dangerous.'

'You must have been disappointed,' she remarked.

'Very! We spent whole days there.' His face darkened. 'It was a wonderful place for a boy to grow up.'

'Yes, I can see that.' They stood in silence for a moment but with the bond of understanding between them, looking back to an adventurous childhood. 'When the Keep is habitable, will you come and live in it?' she asked.

'I use it now,' he said. 'Often at weekends when I can camp inside and do some work.'

Hence the tiles and ropes and the wood which still waited to be unloaded from the dinghy!

'There'll be enough room now to get you back to the mainland,' he decided, moving the wood to one side.

'I'll help you unload. Then you can leave the wood on the shore.'

'Quite safely now that the tide has come in,' he answered, 'but it's after twelve o'clock, and Mrs Birch is a stickler for punctuality.'

'I've gathered that.' Ailsa met his eyes again. 'Was she always so—aggressive?'

'Not always, although she did rule us with a rod of iron where meals were concerned,' he conceded. 'After my mother died she was in full control most of the time because my father's work took him to Edinburgh and in some ways he lost interest in the estate once he was alone.' He stood for a moment in contemplative silence. 'Perhaps if Mrs Birch knows you want to stay it will make a difference,' he added without much conviction.

'I hope it will.' She helped him to lift the planks of wood out of the boat. 'I don't much like tussles.'

'Flora will be a help,' he assured her.

'Flora won't be here all the time,' she pointed out. 'I understand she'll be going back to Glasgow to sit her exams, and then—I don't think she really knows what she wants to do.'

'She wants to get married and have children and settle down in the glen where she was brought up.' He seemed to know a great deal about Flora's desires, but after all, they had been youthful companions at least during those long summer months when Loch Truan would be the ideal place to be. 'Flora is the sort of person who should stay here,' he added briefly. 'She is much needed in the glen.'

'Because so many young people go away?'

'The right young people. There are a few incomers, of course, like Tom Kelvin, who come here because it is all they want from life, but they are few and far between.'

'I'm looking forward to meeting Tom,' she confessed, 'and seeing the fish farm.'

'Any time,' he agreed, stacking the wood. 'Tom will be pleased to show you around.'

When all the wood was on the shore he stood aside to make way for her to get into the dinghy, forced to offer her a helping hand, and once again their fingers touched, but it was Ailsa who drew hers away first.

'Is it a question of "Who pays the ferryman"?' she demanded, stung by his silence as they approached the shore. 'Do I get out and promise faithfully not to return?'

'That is up to you,' he said, although she imagined him concealing a smile, 'but you should be warned that you will not always find the Keep occupied. Now that the spring is here I have other work to do, mainly on the hill.'

'How many sheep have you got?' she asked.

'At present I run about two hundred, most of them in lamb.'

'I like the idea of that,' she mused, 'but I guess it's pretty hard work too. Do you have any help?'

'Now and then, when the weather's really bad.' He helped her ashore, standing up in the dinghy to steady it as she got out. 'If you walk very fast you won't be late.'

'It's not the first time I've had to run home,' she said, regretting the final word instantly as she saw the smile in his eyes falter and all the darkness come flooding back into his face.

This time, however, she did not apologise, because as far as she was concerned Truan was her home too. Perhaps it could be argued that it wasn't hers by absolute right, but there was very little she could do about it.

Standing quite still on the pebbled beach, she watched him push the dinghy out with an oar, his powerful body etched against the grey stone of the tower behind him, his dark head bowed to his task as if he had already dismissed all thought of her from his mind.

When she finally reached the Lodge Flora was waiting for her.

'Did you think you were going to be late?' she smiled, noticing her breathlessness. 'You look all flushed and put out. Don't worry about Mother,' she advised. 'She's still busy in the kitchen.'

'It wasn't your mother I was thinking about,' Ailsa confessed.

'Who, then?'

'Fergus MacNair. He's just given me a very definite brush-off for going across to the Keep.'

'Och, he wouldn't mean that!' Flora declared. 'It's just that he isn't a lady's man in the usual sense of the word.'

'And what does that mean?' Ailsa demanded, already smiling. 'Is he the one-woman type or just a mysogynist.'

Flora hesitated.

'He was at one time,' she admitted.

'Which?'

'A one-woman man, but we haven't time to talk about it now, I'm thinking. Would you like to use my bike?'

Ailsa laughed.

'That's a change of subject, if ever I heard one!' she declared. 'I thought you used your bicycle all the time when you were on holiday.'

'Not *all* the time, and it would save you petrol on your car when I'm not here,' Flora pointed out. 'Why did you go to the Keep?'

Flora had a habit of going off at a tangent once she had thought a statement through.

'It's a hard thing to miss if you walk round the shore,' Ailsa pointed out. 'And terribly intriguing. I had no idea we had an ancient castle in the vicinity.'

'I like to think it's much more than a castle,' Flora answered. 'The ancient keeps are often older and, in a way, far more romantic, than a well-preserved castle which has been inhabited since it was first built. The keeps are still standing there defying the elements after hundreds of years, defying time itself.'

'Is that why Fergus MacNair wants to restore his?'

'Perhaps.' Flora gave her a long, penetrating look. 'Did he invite you in?'

'My goodness, no! I might as well have asked for a look inside the Pearly Gates!'

'That might be because he hasn't finished what he means to do,' Flora suggested diffidently.

'He said it could take a lifetime.'

'Which means he's going to stay here,' said Flora. 'I was worried about that.'

They had reached the open door of the kitchen where Martha Birch was working.

'Ailsa has been to the Keep,' Flora informed her. 'It's a lovely walk on the right day.'

Her mother turned to look at them, her face hard with disapproval.

'What took you there?' she asked bluntly.

'Curiosity, I suppose,' Ailsa admitted. 'I was stranded out there because I didn't realise that it was an island at high tide.'

'You wouldn't be welcome,' Martha told her. 'Fergus likes the Keep to himself.'

'I got that impression,' Ailsa had to admit, 'although he said I was perfectly welcome to go to the fish farm whenever I liked.'

'That's a different thing.' Martha considered her daughter. 'Were you there too?' she asked.

Flora's cheeks were suddenly pinker than usual.

'No,' she admitted. 'I went for a run up the glen on my bike and I met Tom Kelvin on the way back.'

'I see.' Her mother cut into a home-baked loaf with unnecessary vigour. 'You might have spent your time more profitably by studying your books.'

'Oh, Mother, I can't be studying all day long,' protested Flora, 'and Ailsa has just told me that Fergus is going on with building the Keep, which means that he's made up his mind to stay in the glen!'

Martha looked up from her task, eyeing them both with equal dissatisfaction.

'He'll tell me about it in his own time,' she said. 'I don't need to hear it from a stranger.'

There was more than venom in her deep voice and Ailsa had been aware of an added resentment at the mention of Tom Kelvin's name. Consumed by admiration for the MacNairs, she no doubt resented the fact of Tom, the intruder, walking clandestinely in the glen with her daughter whom she had sought to 'better' by accepting Colin MacNair's generous offer of a college education for her clever offspring. Her ambition might even have gone further than that to the ultimate union of Flora and 'the young laird' himself.

That was a thought! Flora and Fergus. It would be all of every desire Martha Birch could have cherished, and certainly Fergus had been pleased to hear that Flora was back in the glen, even if it was only for a short break in her academic career. 'Flora is the sort of person who should stay here,' he had said. 'She wants to get married and have children and live in the glen where she was brought up.' Was that what he wanted too?

The following day was Sunday and Mrs Birch summoned them early to breakfast.

'You'll be expected at the kirk,' she told Ailsa.

'I'd like to go,' Ailsa agreed. 'Have we plenty of time?'

'We have to be in our pew by ten o'clock,' she was informed.

The walk to the church took them through the village up to the mound on the hillside above the loch where the tiny kirk stood quietly close to the mountains with a stout wall running round it and a holly tree at its gate. An ancient tree, gnarled and bent before the onslaught of a prevailing wind, it seemed a fitting emblem of all the striving and patience which had prevailed at Loch Truan for so many years.

Walking up the gravelled pathway to the stout oak door, Ailsa was aware of the interest she evoked, but Mrs Birch marched purposefully ahead, looking neither to left nor right and obviously determined not to enter into any conversation until the service was over and she had dutifully approached her Lord.

Ailsa followed with Flora by her side.

'It's only a tiny church,' said Flora, 'and sometimes it's full to overflowing on special occasions like a wedding or a funeral. Then people have to stand outside and Donny MacKenzie plays his bagpipes away up there on the hill.'

Ailsa looked up towards the hills, imagining the scene on either occasion when all the village and the surrounding crofters came to pay their respects here in this tiny stone-built kirk which had stood on its rocky knoll for over five hundred years and was still the emotional centre of the village at its foot. MacNairs would have

been married here, and christened and finally buried in
the walled-off enclosure near to the hills. In that moment
she understood how Fergus MacNair must feel now, the
last of an ancient line who had no other inheritance than
the Keep.

Sudden guilt flooded over her as she followed Mrs
Birch into the church and slowly down the central aisle
until the housekeeper paused before a raised box-like pew
opposite the pulpit.

'"The laird's loft"!' Flora whispered. 'In you go!'

Ailsa hesitated, but the church was almost full and
Martha Birch was waiting. Flora followed her along the
pew to its farthest end while her mother settled herself
in the middle, straight-backed and aloof, although Ailsa
got the impression that she was well aware of how many
of the villagers had turned out on this auspicious occasion to take a good hard look at the new owner of the
Lodge.

Dutifully she bent her head, wondering what to pray
for when she still felt this overwhelming sense of guilt.

When she looked up again a tall, kilted figure was
standing at the entrance to the pew. It was Fergus
MacNair, and her heart seemed to miss a beat as she
looked at him. Gone was the suede jerkin and open-
necked shirt in which he had roved the hills that first
day of their meeting, and now he wore a lighter coloured
tartan and the conventional jacket that went with it. In
his hand he carried a light blue Balmoral which he set
down on the ledge in front of him as he took his place
in the pew. His rightful place, Ailsa thought as Mrs Birch
acknowledged him with a careful smile.

'Fergus hasn't been in the church for weeks,' whis-
pered Flora, 'but he always sits here when he does come.
Your uncle said it was where he should be, and I think
Fergus agreed.'

'It must be—difficult for him,' Ailsa said as Mrs Birch
looked in their direction, 'but maybe we'd better stop
whispering!'

During the service she was acutely conscious of the
man at the other end of the pew, but Fergus looked
straight ahead without even a hint of acknowledgement
in his eyes. Finally, to the strains of the organ, he rose,

nodded briefly to them without smiling, and strode up the aisle to the open door.

Evidently that was that!

Ailsa made her way slowly along the aisle in Mrs Birch's wake while Flora got caught up in the crowd as she chattered to this one and that, most of them anxious to meet 'the girl from Toronto' who had usurped their favourite's place in the glen.

Feeling curiously isolated, Ailsa stood aside, waiting for Flora to catch up with her.

'You've certainly done the right thing,' a voice said at her elbow. 'Coming to church on your very first Sunday in the glen.'

She turned to find Fergus MacNair at her side.

'I wanted to or I wouldn't have come.' She looked at him with a plea for understanding in her eyes. 'All the same, Mrs Birch made it difficult for me to refuse.'

'I know the feeling.' A fleeting smile touched his lips. 'We never got away with it when we pleaded that we had other things to do.' He settled the Balmoral on his head, its ribbons fluttering in the fresh breeze from the loch. 'You're the object of everybody's curiosity, by the way. Do you wish to be introduced?'

She didn't know what to say in the face of such a magnanimous gesture because she had been quite sure that he would stride off, leaving someone else to effect the introductions which the village people evidently expected. Almost instinctively she looked behind her for Martha Birch who was shaking hands with the minister.

'I—are you quite sure?' she asked. 'I thought you might find it—difficult.'

'Why should I?' His eyes were steady on hers, half smiling at her confusion. 'It would be the conventional thing to do.'

'I can't imagine you being a slave to custom,' she said, 'but I would like to meet one or two people, since it's such a nice morning and the sun is coming out.'

'Who do you already know?' he asked.

'Oh—Moira Cameron from the post office. There she is over there in the tweed suit, talking to the man with the beard. Then there's Hamish and Duncan Carmichael who came to the Lodge with some groceries.'

'Come and meet "the man with the beard",' he invited.

Moira Cameron stood back as they approached, obviously amazed to see the young laird escorting the girl who had taken his place in the glen. Not so her companion, however. The man with the beard was taller even than Fergus, with a mass of curling hair much in need of a barber's attention and thick eyebrows beneath which sparkled two wicked blue eyes as he surveyed her with avid curiosity.

'This is Tom Kelvin,' Fergus introduced them. 'If you really want to know about breeding trout, he's your man!'

Ailsa found her hand imprisoned in a big, engulfing paw.

'So,' Tom Kelvin said, 'this is the girl from Toronto!'

Ailsa laughed.

'I wonder how that got about,' she said. 'It seems to be something of a label now.'

'You'll never live it down, no matter how hard you try,' Tom assured her, looking hard. 'You're not what I expected.'

'That's going to need some explaining,' she told him. 'What *did* you expect?'

The briefest of glances passed between the two men before Tom replied.

'Oh, the usual thing. A city girl who would never settle down in a month of Sundays!'

'I see.' Ailsa drew in a deep breath. 'Well, if you want an answer to that I can give it to you straight away. I'm not a city girl and I'm not easily defeated. I mean to stay in Glen Truan, at least until I'm convinced that I've made a mistake by coming here at all.'

'Nobly said!' applauded Tom. 'I can see you mean it.'

'Every word!' Ailsa was acutely aware of the silent man by her side. 'I'm not going to try to revolutionise the glen, but perhaps I can fit in since I'm half a Scot, anyway. My mother was a Sutherland from Caithness, and although she married an American and went to live in Canada, she never forgot her native land.'

'I think you'll do very well,' said Tom, turning to the postmistress's niece. 'You've already met Moira, I understand.'

'Yes, she directed me to the Lodge when I first arrived.' Ailsa turned to shake hands. 'I met your aunt when I bought some stamps the other day.'

'She was telling me,' Moira acknowledged. 'I'm glad you're going to like the glen, Miss Mallory,' she added. 'Have you been about much?'

'Only as far as——' Ailsa hesitated, looking at Fergus. 'I found my way to the Keep,' she added carefully, 'and got stranded by the tide.'

'You didn't mention that,' Tom accused, looking quickly in his friend's direction. 'When was this?'

'It wasn't important,' Fergus assured him. 'I went over with some material and managed to put matters right.' He looked down at Ailsa with a deliberation she had seen before. 'Was the situation saved as far as Mrs Birch was concerned?' he asked.

'About being late?' She smiled at him. 'Yes, I was in plenty of time and I'm thankful for your help. I had visions of having to stay captive on your island until the tide turned, but I was able to walk away with dignity.'

Looking behind him, she could see Martha Birch approaching, a deliberate smile lighting her dour countenance, and Fergus turned immediately to shake the housekeeper by the hand.

'How are you, Mrs Birch?' he said. 'It's some time since we had a word.'

'Far too long,' Martha agreed. 'I'm very well—considering,' she added. 'How are you?'

'Getting by.' He gave her hand an affectionate squeeze. 'You'll enjoy having Flora with you for a day or two before she goes back to college,' he suggested.

'That I will.' Martha Birch looked as if she wanted to say more, but decided against it, unwilling to cause him even the slightest embarrassment. 'You'll be seeing her before she goes back to Glasgow, no doubt.'

'I thought she might bring Miss Mallory down to Cuilfail one morning,' Fergus suggested.

'To the fish farm? I can't imagine Miss Mallory being interested.'

There was a tightness in Mrs Birch's voice which suggested antagonism, prompting Ailsa to exclaim, 'But I'll be more than interested!' She turned to Tom Kelvin. 'When can we come?'

'Tomorrow would be OK,' Tom told her. 'We're never very busy on a Monday.'

Flora, who had been listening eagerly, asked quickly, 'Morning or afternoon?'

'Either,' Tom assured her. 'We'll be looking forward to your visit.'

He had included Fergus in his welcome, although Fergus himself looked disinterested. Not hostile, Ailsa decided, just uncaring one way or the other. Mrs Birch moved towards the gate.

'We must go,' she intimated. 'I've left the dinner in the oven.'

Tom looked down at Flora.

'Don't forget to come,' he said.

'As if I would!' She gave him a fond smile as her mother moved away. 'See you tomorrow,' she promised.

'Do you think Fergus really wanted us to go to the fish farm?' Ailsa asked, falling into step beside her as Mrs Birch hurried on ahead, mindful of the joint of beef she had placed in the oven before they had left for the church. 'He didn't sound quite so—welcoming as Tom.'

'Oh, that's the difference between these two,' Flora told her. 'Tom is the complete outgoing type while Fergus always thinks twice. Of course we'll be welcome! I thought you said Fergus had invited you.'

'He said I could go any time,' Ailsa remembered, 'but he also made a point of the fact that Tom would show me around.'

'That would be because of the sheep,' Flora assured her. 'Fergus often has to go on the hill in an emergency. What did you think of Tom Kelvin?'

'Exactly what you've just said! He would call a spade a spade no matter what happened,' Ailsa decided, 'and never hold a grudge.'

Flora nodded.

'That's Tom,' she agreed. 'I knew you would like him. Mother still thinks of him as a foreigner, of course, an incomer the glen could well do without, and she doesn't expect him to stay. She says he'll wander off one day as mysteriously as he arrived, but I don't think so. Tom has found what he wanted here. He hasn't much money, but that doesn't count with him because he has freedom and peace of mind. He also has a boat which he sometimes puts in the water,' she added wickedly, 'although I wouldn't like to sail in it, because it leaks like a sieve!'

'Which means it could be dangerous.'

'I suppose it could if you took the risk,' Flora reflected, 'but nobody would. Tom just likes painting it and knocking in a few nails in his spare time.'

'Does Fergus sail?' Ailsa asked innocently enough.

'Not any more.' Flora's brow was creased in a frown. 'At one time he was never off the loch—we were all keen sailors before we broke up and went our separate ways— and now Fergus has other things to do. He hasn't sailed since Ewan died.'

'His brother?'

'Yes.' Flora quickened her pace to overtake her mother. 'We don't really talk about it much.'

It was a warning, in a way, not to discuss the past which had apparently brought tragedy to the Lodge and an uncertain future to the young laird.

'We'll take the car tomorrow,' Ailsa suggested, 'unless you specially want to ride that creaking old machine you call a bike!'

'We can walk,' Flora told her. 'It isn't all that far to Cuilfail.'

The idea of an invigorating walk to the fish farm delighted Ailsa.

'I'm really looking forward to this,' she admitted as they set out early the following morning with a light breeze fanning their cheeks and the promise of sunshine above the low-lying clouds. 'I suppose you'll call that a Scotch mist up there, hiding the hills.'

'It'll drift away quite soon,' Flora assured her. 'I'm looking forward to this visit too,' she added. 'I haven't been to the fish farm for nearly a year, and everything changes so rapidly. Hamish was telling me yesterday that they have five more traps down there on the loch and several new tanks for the fish. You will use my bike, won't you, once I've gone back to Glasgow?' she added, going off at her usual tangent. 'It isn't nearly as decrepit as it looks.'

'I'll be grateful,' Ailsa assured her. 'It will be much better than a car for getting about the glen.'

'Except when it rains. That's what people don't like about the West Coast,' Flora pondered. 'They think it rains here all the time, which it doesn't. This morning is going to be just perfect, so you won't be disappointed.'

'I know I won't,' answered Ailsa, wondering if it was the promise of good weather or a new experience or just the fact that she would be meeting Fergus MacNair again that lightened her step and put a new meaning into their journey to Cuilfail.

'Cuilfail?' she asked. 'What does it mean?'

'The sheltered corner,' Flora translated promptly. 'You'll love it!'

They had taken a narrow path by the lochside where alders and birch made a light screen between them and the water and quite soon they had reached a small, hidden bay where a waterfall plunged down from the surrounding hills. Framed by oak and mountain ash in amazing flower, the descending water splashed into a deep pool by the roadside, reflecting trees and sky in a dark mirror on the ground.

'Here we are!' Flora announced, leading the way. 'It looks as if we're going to surprise everybody.'

The sound of the falling water was loud in Ailsa's ears, shutting out all other sound as she looked about her.

'There's nobody here,' she remarked.

'Bound to be,' Flora declared. 'They know we're coming.'

When they had negotiated the pool and the waterfall they could see the huts more plainly, three in a row, all neat and well-maintained with a barrier fence between them and the road, and somehow it made Ailsa think of the lonely Keep on the far shore of the loch, although this time she was Fergus MacNair's invited guest.

It was Tom who finally came towards them.

'You'll have to put these on to walk through the disinfectant,' he explained, holding out two pairs of green Wellington boots. 'Maybe they won't fit very well, but they'll serve their purpose for the time being. We have to be careful about disease,' he explained, turning to Ailsa. 'It could wreak havoc in next to no time when the fish are so young.'

Flora was struggling into a pair of the boots.

'Tom, they're miles too big!' she complained.

'You can borrow a pair of my socks to fill them up,' he offered, stooping to help Ailsa with the second pair of boots. 'How do they feel?'

'Comfortable,' she admitted. 'They're more or less a perfect fit.'

'I've made some coffee,' he announced. 'Thought you might be ready for it.'

'Oh, we are!' Flora declared, stepping into the shallow tank of disinfectant which guarded the farm. 'We've had nothing since breakfast.'

Laughing, Tom glanced at his watch.

'Two hours is a long time,' he teased. 'It's a wonder you had the strength to get here at all.'

'You know what I mean,' said Flora. 'Walking is a thirsty business.' She was looking about her as if in search of something. 'Where's Fergus?' she demanded.

'I wish I knew,' Tom said. 'He hasn't shown up yet. Must have something else to do,' he muttered into his beard, 'but it's not like him to be late, especially on a Monday morning.'

'He'll turn up sooner or later, I suppose,' Flora decided, walking towards a large caravan parked behind the sheds. 'I hope you've got enough milk for the coffee.'

'If there isn't I've got a tin or two in reserve.' Tom stood back to let Ailsa walk in front of him. 'I live here,' he told her, looking towards the caravan. 'You'll have to excuse the clutter. It's the office as well as my home.'

Flora had reached the caravan door.

'It's not like Fergus to make a promise and fail to keep it,' she said. 'He did say he would be here to show us round.'

'You'll have to be content with me,' Tom suggested. 'I know quite a lot about fish.'

'We know you do, but a promise is a promise,' Flora pointed out. 'I wonder what could have happened to him.'

Tom opened the caravan door.

'He'll turn up,' he said briskly. 'In you go!'

The caravan accommodation was surprisingly adequate, the front section comprising a sizeable office with a desk and two filing cabinets set against the wall, and Ailsa noticed a telephone which evidently hadn't rung during the morning to explain Fergus MacNair's unexpected absence. Fleetingly she wondered why he hadn't contacted Tom or even the Lodge to explain, telling herself immediately that perhaps she was asking too much of him in the circumstances. On everyone's admission he was a busy man and no doubt he had other more important things to do than show two curious females how to breed fish. Why then should she feel so disappointed, even a little let down? It was quite ridiculous, she told herself, even though Flora seemed to feel the same way but for a different reason. She was almost sure now that Flora must be in love with Fergus, which would be quite natural when they had known each other for so long.

Without a doubt, it was a situation which would please Martha Birch, affording her the enormous satisfaction she so obviously sought, and Fergus himself had said how 'right' Flora would be for the glen.

Why did she keep remembering that? Flora back in Glen Truan bearing his children, perhaps, compensating him in part for his most grievous loss. He would never be able to repossess the Lodge, but at least he would be sure of continuing the family name even if it was only in a remote cottage in the glen.

Once more she was conscious of guilt, of possessing what should have been his, and once again she thrust the nagging feeling aside, telling herself that she could do nothing about it.

They drank their coffee, speaking about the glen but not about Fergus, and when an hour had passed Tom glanced again at his watch.

'We'll go through the sheds,' he suggested. 'It's eleven o'clock.'

They followed him to the open door of the first shed where the sound of the waterfall made it necessary to shout.

'We need fresh water,' he explained, 'and it never fails. The falls have been here for as long as anyone can remember, apparently, and it's an ideal site.'

'Do they belong to the estate?' asked Ailsa.

He nodded, looking down at her as if about to ask a question and then deciding against the impulse. Perhaps he was afraid that she might cut off their water supply if things went wrong between them, Ailsa thought, dismissing the idea immediately. Why would she do such a thing when she knew how much it meant to them? She had come to Truan to be a good landlord, not a stumbling block.

Flora and Tom were bending over the nearest tank.

'Come and see!' Flora invited.

Tom made room for her on the raised wooden platform surrounding the tank.

'I had no idea they would be so tiny!' Ailsa exclaimed as she looked down into the tank where dozens and dozens of small, perfectly formed trout milled around a pipe just above the water level.

'Watch this!' said Tom, tapping the pipe with a strong forefinger. 'They're hungry little beggars at any time of the day.'

A fine supply of food came down through the pipe at his touch and immediately the tiny fish responded, coming up to feed. It was all so interesting that they didn't notice the man who had appeared at the open doorway and was standing there looking in at them with an odd expression in his grey eyes.

They moved between the tanks.

'When they get big enough for tank number three they have learned how to reach up and tap the pipe for food,' Tom explained, 'so we have to make it harder for them and put it out of reach.'

'I've never thought of frustrated trout,' Ailsa laughed. 'They're much bigger here, aren't they?'

'They're about ready to go into the loch.' Once more Tom glanced at his watch. 'If you've time to walk down there I can show you the traps.'

They turned, seeing Fergus for the first time. He was still at the open door looking as if he was almost reluctant to join them.

'Where on earth have you been?' Tom demanded, seeing his dishevelled state. 'You look as if you've slept all night on the hill.'

'It was almost as bad as that.' Fergus moved aside to let them pass. 'One of the ewes had a difficult birth. She dropped her lamb and then passed out on me. There was nothing else I could do.'

The tension in his face spoke volumes; he was tired and bedraggled and certainly in no mood to entertain visitors.

'Fergus, what about the lamb?' Flora asked urgently. 'Is it alive?'

'As fit as a fiddle,' he assured her, looking for the first time in Ailsa's direction, 'and more than hungry.'

'Let me look after it,' Flora offered quickly. 'I've done it often enough before.'

'You haven't the time,' he pointed out. 'You'll be back in college in a couple of weeks.'

'Could I take it?' Ailsa heard herself asking. 'I could learn a lot from Flora in two weeks, don't you think?'

She saw him hesitate, as if the idea was distasteful to him for some reason, but Flora, all enthusiasm now, answered for him.

'What a brilliant idea! It will give Ailsa something to do apart from reorganising the Lodge.'

Ailsa saw the shadow that passed in the grey eyes still looking into her own.

'I had no idea you were so busy up there,' he said harshly. 'I can cope with the lamb—it isn't exactly a major issue.'

Flora was persistent, however.

'You have other things to do,' she pointed out. 'I'll take over and Ailsa can make a final decision about it when I've gone. She's not *dismantling* the Lodge,' she added, 'just opening up a few of the rooms to make it look more like a home again.'

Oh, Flora! Ailsa thought, you've said quite the wrong thing! You're rubbing salt into the wound which hasn't begun to heal yet and may never heal at all.

'If you're absolutely sure,' Fergus was saying, 'you know I'll be grateful.' He was speaking to Flora now, not even looking in Ailsa's direction. 'It's something of a task, and your mother may not like the idea.'

'We'll have to talk her round,' Flora decided. 'I'll say you were absolutely at your wits' end wondering what to do with a motherless lamb when you have so many fish to attend to!'

'That won't cut any ice,' said Fergus. 'A lamb about the house is no joke, especially when it begins to grow.'

'We'll cope,' Flora assured him blithely. 'What do you say, Ailsa?'

'I'd love to help.' Ailsa wanted the lamb very much. 'It will be a new experience for me.'

'And Fergus will be greatly in your debt,' Tom put in, leading the way back to the caravan.

Which was the very last thing Fergus would want, Ailsa decided, following in his wake.

When it was time to leave Fergus escorted them to the road while Tom answered a telephone call.

'Are you walking back?' he asked, seeing no sign of Ailsa's car. 'I could give you a lift as far as the drive.' He glanced towards the Range Rover at the side of the loch. 'I'm going that way.'

But only as far as the entrance to the Lodge, Ailsa thought—no farther than that.

'We like to walk,' Flora was saying, 'and it isn't far. We'll be in lots of time for lunch at one o'clock.' Impulsively she put her hand on his arm. 'Don't worry!' she added gently. 'I'll take care of the lamb.'

That little touch spoke volumes, Ailsa thought, expressing understanding and concern and, surely, love.

When they reached the Lodge Martha Birch was waiting for them.

'The post has come,' she announced. 'Alex has just come up.' She handed Ailsa a bundle of letters which had no doubt been well scrutinised. 'They're mostly from Canada,' she added, 'though there's one from Oban too.'

Her mother had written, Ailsa noticed with delight, and a friend from Toronto whose handwriting she recognised. The Oban letter would probably be from her uncle's solicitor. Flora stood hesitating in the doorway.

'Mother,' she began, 'could we do with a lamb? The ewe decided it has to be bottle-fed.'

'I'm sure we couldn't "do with a lamb", as you put it,' Martha Birch retorted. 'They're far too much trouble as well as being dirty around the house.'

'But it needs care,' Flora protested, a hint of tears in her eyes. 'It's just new-born, and if we don't have it up here it might die.'

'Who put that idea into your head?' her mother demanded.

'It wasn't Fergus; you know he would never have asked,' said Flora. 'As a matter of fact, I offered.'

Martha Birch looked about to capitulate.

'Since it was Fergus,' she said, 'that makes a difference, but I hope you remember you'll be in Glasgow in two weeks' time and bottle-feeding a lamb takes far longer than that.'

'Oh, Ailsa will take over after I've gone,' said Flora, delighted. 'She offered.'

'Indeed?' The housekeeper's brows drew together in a quick frown. 'I fancy Miss Mallory will have enough to do about the estate without feeding a lamb several times a day. She can't have any idea what it entails in the beginning.'

'When I've watched Flora for a couple of weeks it won't be any problem,' Ailsa turned to assure her. 'It can't be all that difficult.'

Mrs Birch tossed her head.

'I'll see to it myself,' she decided, 'once Flora has gone.'

'She's very fond of Fergus,' Flora explained as they went indoors. 'She would do anything for him.'

CHAPTER THREE

THEY collected the lamb the following morning, going to the foot of the glen with the car to Fergus's cottage where the door lay open and the lamb stood bleating in a corner of the garden.

'Fergus won't be here,' said Flora, 'but the bottles and teats and everything will be ready in the kitchen for us to collect. Don't worry about the bleating,' she added. 'Lambs are always hungry.'

Ailsa hesitated at the back door.

'Come in,' Flora invited, 'and watch your head!'

The lintel was very low, the cottage older than Ailsa had expected, but its stout stone walls and small, deeply set windows would defy any winter blast coming angrily down the glen. She could well imagine Fergus having to stoop considerably to enter his temporary home, for surely he longed to be out there at the Keep with the sea at his back door and unlimited space to stretch himself in the gift of his mother, who had been 'a MacKinnon of Nant'.

'He looks after himself, I understand,' she said as her eyes became accustomed to the dim light coming in through the scullery window.

'Most of the time,' Flora agreed. 'Nan McCall—she's a Glasgow woman married to one of the Forestry boys—comes in to clean once a week, but otherwise he's alone.'

The feeding bottles Ailsa sought had been laid out on the scullery bench, and she packed them carefully into the basket they had brought from the Lodge. Through the open door which led into the kitchen she could make out a brightly polished grate and an armchair drawn up to the hearth, while a square, scrubbed table occupied the centre of the floor on an island of carpet surrounded by stained boards worn a little at the communicating doors and obviously as old as the cottage itself.

'Come on in,' Flora said, 'while I collect the sheepskin.'

'Do you think I should?' Ailsa still hesitated. 'I've a feeling that Fergus might take it as an intrusion on his privacy.'

'We're doing him a favour, for goodness' sake!' Flora protested. 'Fergus doesn't mind who comes up here. It's open house to a lot of people in the winter, especially the Forestry boys. In the summer,' she shrugged, 'nobody has much time to be indoors.'

Ailsa looked about the low-raftered kitchen.

'How much more is there?' she asked.

Flora considered.

'Two bedrooms upstairs and a parlour through there that is never used.' She found a folded sheepskin on the armchair beside the hearth. 'Will we make a cup of tea?'

'No, I don't think we should.' Ailsa turned back to the scullery door. 'If that bleating is genuine we owe the lamb a meal,' she decided.

Flora gave the kitchen a final glance of inspection as she hurried out after her.

'It's not too satisfactory, is it?' she reflected. 'A man living on his own like this and working hard all day and having to fend for himself when he comes in at night.'

'He may like it that way—for the moment,' Ailsa pointed out.

The lamb was no problem. He snuggled up to Flora as they drove away, his small black nose close against her cheek, and only when they reached the Lodge did he start to bleat again.

'What are we going to call him?' asked Ailsa, enchanted by their new acquisition. 'He's adorable!'

'George, I think,' Flora decided.

'Why George?'

'Because I've got to G in the alphabet. He's the seventh lamb I've bottle-fed in my time.'

'All for Fergus?'

'Good gracious, no! I've taken them in from all over the place,' Flora explained. 'This is the first lamb Fergus has really had to worry about. He's been lucky. They're a bit of a problem, you know, especially if they don't take kindly to the bottle.'

George certainly 'took kindly' to his artificial feed, and Ailsa was amazed at how strongly he pulled at the teat.

'He'll do,' Flora decided as her mother came to view their unexpected boarder.

'He'll have to stay in the wash-house,' she announced. 'I can't have him running all over the place, no matter how much Fergus needs our help. Hamish has fenced off a stretch of grass at the back and he can wander about there.' Martha stood frowning at the unfortunate George. 'They make a terrible mess around the house.'

So George was more or less accepted, and mostly because he belonged to Fergus.

'I'll have to swot this afternoon, since I've been out all morning,' Flora announced when lunch was over. 'What will you do? It's a lovely day.'

Ailsa considered her question.

'I think I'll go for a walk. It's really warm, isn't it? It will be really lovely on the other side of the loch,' she said.

'Don't go too far,' Flora advised. 'Tomorrow, if it's still warm enough, we can have a swim.'

Ailsa walked briskly round the head of the loch. She had changed out of her heavy skirt and woollen pullover into a lighter T-shirt and cotton skirt, conscious of a sudden freedom as the sun beat down on her shoulders with a warmth in it which she had not expected. It was April and the sky above her was clear and blue with the promise of more good weather to come, and this was how she had pictured Loch Truan from her uncle's descriptions. This was what she had looked forward to all those weeks ago when she had first decided to leave Canada and take up the inheritance he had left her. Even then it had been something of a challenge to her, the opportunity to prove that she could succeed on her own. If Russell Forgreave's defection had something to do with it she had tried to overcome that, keeping her heartache to herself.

On a day like this she could even dismiss it, as she came to the bend in the shore road where the pines stood back to reveal a first glimpse of the Keep out there on the loch. How lonely it looked, she thought, but perhaps that was because the tide had come in and it stood on an island again.

Walking slowly, she absorbed the beauty of the backdrop to the lonely tower where so much had happened in the past, wondering what the future held for the man who now possessed it. It was certainly an outlet for Fergus's energy, but perhaps it also served as a vent for all the frustration he must feel at being deprived of his true inheritance by a stranger, a girl from Canada who had taken what should have been his by right. She had opened the letter from Oban before she had left the Lodge, and in it her uncle's lawyer had confirmed her ownership of Truan and also a considerable sum of money which he proposed they should discuss at an early date.

It didn't seem to matter about the money; it was Truan that counted most.

Gazing across the loch, she was alerted by what she thought to be a seal, the dark head just visible above the water, but when she looked again it was still there, and seals had a habit of backing down beneath the surface whenever they thought themselves observed. After a moment or two she saw that it was a sheep, one of the black-faced breed which Fergus grazed along the shore. It was swimming round and round in circles, obviously distressed and too far from the land to achieve a solid foothold.

She called and called, hoping to attract its attention or even the help of a passer-by, but there was no response. The unfortunate animal seemed unable to direct its frenzied attempt at survival towards the shore, continuing to swim round and round in ever-widening circles, exhausting itself with every effort it made. Quite soon the weight of its waterlogged fleece would pull it under and it would drown even as she watched.

That wasn't going to happen, she decided quickly, discarding her cotton skirt on the beach as she waded into the sea. She knew she would have to swim and even the lightweight skirt would have been a handicap in that event, but she hadn't reckoned on the coldness of a Scottish loch in early spring. The water was icy, and when it finally reached her chin it took her breath away as she struck out towards the unfortunate animal. Being the girl she was, however, she persisted, reaching the drowning ewe at last, and trying desperately to direct it safely towards the shore. Two moist, pitiable eyes regarded her more in sadness than in fear.

'You'll have to swim the other way,' she found herself saying, grasping desperately at a protruding horn. 'Swim—for the love of heaven, swim!'

The weight was almost more than she could drag through the water, but the stricken animal responded in one last effort at survival as she pointed its head towards the causeway where the stones were just beginning to appear above an outgoing tide. They were going to make it, after all!

She looked towards the shore where a man was standing with her discarded skirt in his hand. It could only be Fergus, she thought.

At that moment the ewe touched bottom, struggling frantically towards the causeway where green grass was already beckoning above the stones, and when she got to her own feet Fergus MacNair was wading towards her, the checked cotton skirt still in his hand.

He didn't speak as he helped her out, draping the wide cotton skirt about her shoulders with a hand so gentle that she could have cried. Her teeth were chattering and she felt drained of all the energy she possessed.

'I didn't think it would be so cold,' she managed to explain.

'It was a damned silly thing to do,' he told her. 'You could have drowned!'

'I'm a strong swimmer,' she defended herself. 'I couldn't have let the sheep just go round and round in circles till it finally sank.'

'We lose sheep like that quite often.' There was a glint of anger in his eyes. 'It was a big risk for you to take.'

'You can't mean you don't care about the ewe,' she protested. 'A dumb animal!'

'Of course I care about the ewe,' he answered brusquely. 'Apart from everything else, it would have been a financial loss I can't afford, but now we have you to think about. You're soaking wet and colder than you've ever been before, I should imagine.' He seemed to be concerned and irritated at the same time. 'We'll have to dry you out.'

Ailsa glanced up at the Keep with its stoutly forbidding walls standing starkly above them.

'I can easily go home,' she suggested. 'It isn't all that far to the Lodge.'

'It's out of the question,' he told her abruptly. 'Where did you leave your shoes?'

'On the shore quite near my skirt.'

'We'll find them later,' he decided. 'I'll help you across the stones.'

She remained where she was, hugging the cotton skirt about her with a sudden sense of the ridiculous. What did it matter about shoes when you were standing in your pants and a wet T-shirt trying to retain a dignity you didn't have?

'I'll come quietly,' she agreed, 'and I can cope with the stones.'

Fergus led the way to the Keep, reluctantly, she thought with a sudden spark of anger.

'I'm sorry about this,' she apologised, 'barging in where angels would fear to tread, and if you really want to keep your ivory tower inviolate I can dry off on the shore.'

'And catch your death of cold,' he suggested. 'Do you want me to help you up the steps?'

'I'll manage,' she assured him, 'although they're steep enough. Perhaps they were built that way to deter the intruder on the landward side, like the curtain-wall.'

He refused to rise to her bait while he unlocked the wrought-iron outer door which he had called a yett.

'No one in their right senses would ever try to break in,' she remarked as he inserted a key in the lock of the wooden door. 'It would be like——'

'Yes?' he asked, turning to look at her.

'I was going to say "like banging your head against a brick wall", but this is stronger than brick, isn't it?'

'It had to be,' he agreed, using the past tense much to her surprise. 'And you have no need to bang your head against anything.' He opened the door. 'Go in and I'll try to find you a towel. There's one about some- where, and I can even offer you a drink.'

'I think I could do with one,' she said, shivering.

The door led directly into a spacious hall with half the roof open to the sky.

'That's why I need the boxes of slates,' said Fergus, looking up through the rafters. 'It's more than half complete.'

The grey slates she had helped him to carry from the dinghy were still in their boxes, but the wood had all been utilised.

'I'll light a fire in a couple of minutes,' he offered, leading the way to a second door at the far side of the draughty hall. 'There's plenty of logs.'

Ailsa followed him cautiously, her bare feet making damp prints on the stone floor as little rivulets of water ran down her thighs, but there was no carpet to spoil, and she felt relieved.

The inner room was a complete surprise to her. Raftered and stone-walled like the hall they had just passed through, it was lighter and far more intimate than she had expected. Long embrasured windows let in the light while a deep, alcoved fireplace took up most of the space along the far wall.

'It's big enough to roast an ox,' she remarked, smiling.

A fire had been set between the iron dogs ready for an emergency—a man coming in wet off the hill, perhaps—and Fergus bent down to put a match to it while she stood in the centre of the room, waiting.

'I'm dripping all over the place,' she acknowledged as the flames leapt up between the logs. 'Your loch is very wet!'

He laughed. 'I'll get you the towel!'

When he came back he was carrying an outsize woollen pullover as well as the promised towel.

'Put this on after you've stripped,' he commanded, 'and we'll try to dry your underwear.' He looked at her keenly. 'Then we'll just about be ready for that drink.'

'Yes, thank you.' She took the towel, waiting for him to go. 'I can feel the warmth from the fire already.'

He went out and she stripped to the skin, towelling herself vigorously before the fire until she was almost warm again before she pulled the outsize woolly over her head. It was several sizes too big, as she had expected, but it was softly comforting against her skin and long enough almost to cover her knees. Standing there against the leaping firelight when he came back into the room, she must have looked an odd sight, with her bedraggled hair and her long legs appearing beneath the pullover whose sleeves wholly concealed her hands.

'Roll up the sleeves,' Fergus suggested. 'It might make you feel better.'

Ailsa towelled her hair while he put a couple of beakers on the stone window-seat nearest the door.

'You look like a water-kelpie straight out of the sea,' he observed.

'Do you believe in water-kelpies?' she asked, rolling up the sleeves to above her elbows. 'No, I don't think you do,' she added before he could reply. 'You're far too practical for that.'

'I have to be.'

'Yes, I suppose so. Fergus,' she added, 'how long is it going to take you to finish the tower?'

He held out one of the beakers.

'Most of my life,' he told her. 'I can only do it bit by bit because everything has to be exact. I'm following an old plan we found among my mother's possessions at the Lodge.'

He had mentioned Truan without too much effort, and she was glad about that as she took the beaker from him, warming her hands on it as she began to drink.

'I wish I could help,' she suggested impulsively, 'but I don't suppose you would agree to that—not in a lifetime.'

He turned to pick up his own drink.

'It would be out of the question,' he told her. 'Truan and the Keep are separate units, and Truan no longer belongs to me.'

She sensed the resentment in him and thought she could understand it.

'I know how you feel,' she said foolishly. 'You must think I have no right to be at Truan, that you're being deprived of your true home, and I can sympathise with that.'

Fergus turned to the window, looking out across the courtyard to the encircling curtain-wall, and when he looked back at her his face was tense with emotion.

'How can you sympathise, or even understand?' he demanded. 'You have never been without a home, never had to look back in anger at what might have been.'

'That's true,' she agreed, 'but I had hoped——'

He moved closer, the beaker clenched in his hand.

'That you might make amends?' he suggested. 'No one will ever be able to do that—no stranger.'

He was close enough for her to hear his sharply-indrawn breath and to see more than anger in his eyes.

'I can't argue with you,' she told him, 'and I have no constructive suggestions to make. I hoped for your co-operation at Truan, someone to advise me what would be best for the estate, but I see now that I'll have to look elsewhere. I'm sorry, Fergus, if I've made an enemy of you, and I can't understand why. All I have done is accept an inheritance and a good deal of money which I hoped would benefit the glen.'

'All the money in the world wouldn't make any difference now,' he said harshly. 'I accepted your uncle's offer to save Truan and I suppose it did, but that was never the main issue. No doubt it's difficult for you to understand that there has been a MacNair up there at the Lodge for over three hundred years and I am the last of them.' He put the beaker down on the hearth. 'Whatever that sounds like to you,' he added almost gently, 'it rings in my ears like a knell. Even if I had a son, I've sold his birthright before he was born.'

'I'm sorry,' Ailsa faltered.

'Don't be. I knew what I was doing before I made the decision to sell. I did it in bitterness and hatred for someone I had once loved, so how can I expect sympathy, of all things?'

'But understanding?' she protested.

'No one could ever understand how I felt in that moment.' He caught her arm in a grip like steel. 'No woman.'

Ailsa sank to her knees on the raised hearth and he released her immediately.

'I'm sorry,' he apologised in his turn. 'Finish your drink and we'll dry your clothes.'

'And then you can send me back to where I belong.'

He looked down at her where she sat curled on the stone hearth, her long legs beneath her, her drying hair crisping into fiery tendrils on her brow.

'I wonder how long you'll feel you belong at Truan,' he said. 'You have a lot to learn, but I don't think it will daunt you.'

'It won't,' Ailsa assured him stoutly. 'I wasn't born and brought up in Canada for nothing.'

'Your uncle regarded it as a second Scotland,' he mused, 'but he always knew he would come back here. I recognised that when we first met and he came up here to look at the estate. He felt that his roots were firmly planted here, although he had made the bulk of his money abroad.'

'We tried to persuade him to stay in Canada, but he wouldn't, even though he could have lived anywhere. Certainly he could never have been happy in Toronto, but there were plenty of other places to choose from. Ontario is vast and very, very beautiful,' she assured him, her eyes suddenly misted by a memory.

'Will you miss it?' he asked.

'Of course! It's my native land, remember, although my mother was a Scot. She never really forgot Scotland and her childhood here, and it was what made me so sure about coming. That and——'

'Yes?' he encouraged, prodding a dying log with his foot. 'There must have been something else.'

'I imagined myself in love.'

Why had she said that? Why had she allowed this man to open the wound again? When she looked round at him his brow was dark.

'"Imagined"?' he repeated. 'Surely you must be sure about that sort of emotion?'

'Not when you're—hurt so badly by it that you feel your life has been shattered beyond repair.'

'Ah,' he said, 'that makes a difference. Do you think running away will make it any easier for you to accept?'

She looked up at him, seeing the little flames of fire-light moving in his eyes.

'I don't know,' she confessed. 'I've made up my mind to forget the past—to try again.'

'It's an uphill road,' he warned, picking up her empty beaker. 'Don't go to sleep. I put some whisky in your coffee.'

'I thought it tasted pretty awful!' she laughed, gathering up her clothes which she had spread on the hearth to dry. 'Where can I change?'

'In here beside the fire,' Fergus said on his way to the door. 'I'm going to take a walk round the curtain-wall to make sure that no more sheep are out for a swim!'

For a moment they were on common ground, and she watched him go with a warmer feeling in her heart. They had both faced emotional trauma, although perhaps not quite in the same way, but she had been spared the bitterness he had suffered afterwards. 'Someone he had once loved', he had said, and it had all been bound up with Truan and his lost inheritance.

When she had dressed Ailsa walked slowly towards the door leading to the outer hall. Fergus would be waiting for her to go, and all the warmth of the firelit inner room was suddenly extinguished. Short of another emergency, she would probably never come here again. Looking back towards the fire, she saw the logs flare up and subside into a pool of grey ash as forlorn-looking in the dark cavity of the hearth as the thoughts that had stirred in her heart.

'Ready?' Fergus was standing looking into the room, and she handed him the borrowed sweater. 'If you want to keep it on for extra warmth,' he offered, 'you can return it to the fish farm next time you're down that way.'

'I'm all right,' she said. 'I'm warm enough, and the sun is still shining outside.'

He walked back to the hearth, crushing out the last of the fire with the heel of his boot.

'No use asking for trouble,' he said. 'I may not be back for a day or two.'

He locked the stout oak door behind them, padlocking the iron yett on the outside before he turned to help her down the steps.

'The last one is quite tricky,' he warned.

Hard, strong fingers fastened over hers, guiding her down while she remembered the bitterness in his voice as they had discussed the past, but the moment for confidences had passed, hurried away by his desire to keep his lonely tower inviolate.

At the end of the causeway he halted.

'I can manage on my own, now,' she offered, 'if you're busy.'

She saw him smile half-ruefully, his mouth turning up at one corner as he considered her.

'I'll see you as far as the village,' he said. 'And, Ailsa—thanks for all you've done, rescuing the sheep and so on.'

'It was pretty mad of me,' she acknowledged, 'plunging in like that when you were probably near enough to do the job yourself.'

He continued to look at her.

'That's just the point,' he said. 'I wasn't. I didn't realise what had happened till I saw you in the water trying to steer the ewe towards the shore. I knew you had no idea how strong an animal in distress can be, and sheep are no exception.'

'She struggled like mad, trying to get away. That was ingratitude for you!'

'Or just plain panic. Do you always take the bull by the horns on impulse?'

'Quite often,' she agreed. 'But this wasn't a bull, was it? It was a terrified ewe, and I had to try.'

Fergus led the way up the pebbled beach to the narrow shore road.

'I'm grateful,' he said. 'More grateful than you apparently think.'

They walked together as far as the village, causing heads to turn and curtains to stir at cottage windows as they passed until Ailsa was forced to say:

'Don't feel you have to come any farther with me, Fergus. I'm almost home.'

'I'll see you as far as the gates.'

But no farther, she thought. Nothing—not even gratitude for a rescued animal—would induce him to go through these gates and on up the winding drive to his former home.

Well, she could understand that too, although she considered that the bitterness would never pass until he was able to do just that.

When she reached the house she was aware of a mild commotion in the back garden. George had managed to find a way out of his enclosure and was gleefully exploring the flower-beds with an eye to scaling the rockery at some future date. Neither Hamish nor Mrs Birch had been able to deter his joyful progress and Flora was nowhere to be seen.

'Can I help?' asked Ailsa, her voice full of laughter as George evaded Hamish once again, bringing that worthy to his knees at the edge of the burn where the rockery went down into deep brown water gurgling over stones. 'He's very sure-footed for anything so young.'

'If he didn't belong to Fergus he wouldn't be here,' Martha Birch declared. 'They're a bigger nuisance than you think.'

'I'm sure Fergus will be suitably grateful. As a matter of fact,' Ailsa admitted, 'I've just come from the Keep.' She thought it best to tell Martha Birch personally something she would be sure to hear in the village on her very next visit to the post office.

'The Keep?' The housekeeper turned to look at her, eyes narrowed and mouth compressed. 'What were you doing there? Fergus doesn't encourage visitors.'

'It was more of a rescue attempt than a visit,' Ailsa confessed. 'I plunged into the loch to help a ewe and Fergus very kindly fished me out. I suppose it was a mad sort of thing for me to do,' she acknowledged, 'but it worked, and afterwards Fergus had to be polite and dry me out at the Keep.'

'I never heard the like of it!' Mrs Birch declared. 'No one has been in that tower for over a year, not even Flora,' she added pointedly.

Ailsa made an attempt to waylay George, who had decided to make for the house and a necessary rest in the comfort of the kitchen where he would expect to be fed.

'I didn't force my way into the Keep, Mrs Birch,' she said as George escaped between her knees. 'There wasn't much else Fergus could do when I'd saved him the loss of the ewe. It would have drowned, apparently, once its fleece got thoroughly soaked.'

Martha Birch made a final attempt to catch George as he gambolled past her.

'You've certainly made your mark on the glen already,' she observed. 'What with one thing and another.'

'I was only being neighbourly,' Ailsa pointed out. 'I think that's what we need.'

'Some people might call it interfering,' the house-keeper retorted, 'forcing your way to a friendship with

Fergus which he doesn't want. His life is quite full here—
you can take my word for that—and he can't want any
contact with the Lodge as things are. He never put a
foot over the door while your uncle was here, and there
will be no difference now. I know him far too well to
believe otherwise.'

Ailsa bit her lip.

'It's foolish,' she declared, 'holding a grudge like that,
but I must admit he did seem reluctant to see me farther
than the gates.'

At that point George decided to call it a day, walking
up to her with absolute confidence and a knowing bleat.
Ailsa took him quickly into her arms, carrying him into
the sanctuary of the house with her cheek against his
warm fleece.

'George,' she murmured, 'you and I need a quiet spell
to consolidate our defences. We've both been in the dog-
house this afternoon, through no fault of our own!'

A wet black nose touched her cheek.

'Was that a token of sympathy?' she laughed. 'Or just
plain cupboard love? George, you're absolutely
gorgeous, and I think you understand!'

Martha Birch had very little to say on the subject of
Fergus or the Keep for the remainder of the day, but she
did express curiosity about the mail Ailsa had received
the day before.

'I noticed you had a letter from Oban as well as the
two from Canada,' she remarked when they had finished their evening meal. 'It would be from your uncle's
lawyer, no doubt, about the estate.'

Ailsa suppressed a smile.

'It was,' she acknowledged. 'You must be psychic, Mrs
Birch.' She glanced at Flora, who was taking a respite
from her studies for the remainder of the day. 'I'll be
going down to Oban tomorrow. Would you like to come
with me, Flora?'

'I wish I could.' Flora looked dejected. 'But I've got
a lot to do before the exams. A whole day would be
impossible. Besides,' she added, 'there's George.' She
waited, looking in her mother's direction.

'You took on the responsibility for that animal
knowing quite well what it would involve,' Martha Birch

told her. 'It will cost you a trip to Oban, and that might be a lesson to you.'

'I thought you liked the idea of helping Fergus,' Flora protested.

'I do, but not to the extent of having a lamb in my living-room,' her mother returned. 'He was on the fireside table when I went to look for him a few minutes ago, so you can clean up the mess he's made in there tomorrow instead of gallivanting off to Oban. There's plenty of furniture polish,' she added obligingly.

'Oh, George!' Flora groaned.

'I'll be right back,' Ailsa promised. 'It won't take more than a couple of hours to get there.'

'You don't know what the lawyer might have to say to you or how long it will take,' Martha Birch pointed out, reasonably enough.

'The letter mentioned something about a final settlement,' Ailsa agreed. 'I don't know what that will mean, but surely it will only be a matter of signing a document or two.'

'That could be so,' said Martha. 'You will have to wait and see.'

In the morning Flora waved her goodbye with George in her arms.

'I really don't want to leave him,' she said, 'but hurry back!'

On her way past the fish farm Ailsa saw Tom Kelvin standing by the roadside.

'Going south?' he asked. 'I was trying to hitch a lift.'

'Where to?' asked Ailsa, happy enough to oblige as she bent across to open the passenger door. 'I'm on my way to Oban.'

'It's all the way, then!' He got in beside her. 'Fergus is using the Range Rover this morning, so I decided to hitch-hike. This is a pleasure!'

'You mean the car, of course,' she laughed. 'I thought Range Rovers were quite comfortable.'

'They are,' he conceded, 'but when you haven't got one it's something of a problem.'

'You could have gone tomorrow,' she suggested.

'Never thought of that.' He looked round at her, his blue eyes twinkling. 'Besides, this is a bonus. I was wondering when I would see you again.'

'You must have known you would meet up with me someplace,' she pointed out.

'Yes, I did. I heard you were at the Keep yesterday,' he added.

The abruptness of his unexpected remark sent a vivid colour into her cheeks.

'Who told you that?' she asked.

'Fergus.' He smiled broadly. 'It was quite an adventure, apparently. I bet there's never been a bra and pair of pants drying on the hearth at the Keep for a hundred years!'

'There really was nothing comical about it.'

'I apologise, but I wish I had seen Fergus's face when he pulled you out of the loch!'

'Never mind about that,' she said almost sharply. 'Where do you want to go in Oban?'

'To the Highland Crofters to put in an order for more wire and then to the bank.' Suddenly Tom was serious. 'We're running the farm on a shoestring and Fergus has put all he has got into it.'

'Are you saying it doesn't pay?'

'Oh, it pays all right, but it would do much better if we could expand here and now. We're both pulling our weight, but it's capital we need.'

'Is that why you're visiting the bank?'

He laughed.

'I'm going to bail myself out. I have a small overdraft.'

'Then you'll borrow.'

'I don't know. Fergus is totally against borrowing unless we can see our way clear to pay it all back in the shortest time possible. He's very proud.'

'I gathered that.'

They were driving south by the way Ailsa had come less than a week ago, but she found it hard to believe that all this had been new territory to her then, a new beginning, something to call her own, somewhere to work beside others of like mind. She believed that she could have found all that at Truan if the glen hadn't been beset by complications, but certainly Tom would be an asset. She liked this big, rough man who sat by her side appreciating all he saw, although the glens must be wholly familiar to him by this time.

'You're prepared to stay here?' she asked.

Clear blue eyes contemplated her for a moment before he said, 'Where else would I go? This is the place where I want to be.'

'I'm glad.' She slowed down a little to enjoy the view with him. 'I feel we could be friends, and you could give me a lot of good advice about Truan.'

'Just love it,' he answered unexpectedly, 'and do all you can for it.'

'I'll do my best. Do you want to drive for the rest of the way?' she asked.

He shook his head.

'I'm perfectly happy as I am.'

'I thought you might have your doubts about women drivers.'

'Not me!' He sprawled out lazily in the seat beside her. 'I'm the ideal passenger,' he declared, 'especially on a day like this.'

'I hadn't intended to come south quite so soon,' she confided, 'but I have to see my uncle's lawyer. Something to sign, I expect.'

'He was a great fellow, that uncle of yours,' Tom informed her. 'Always interested in what was going on and always ready to help if you asked him.'

'Did you ask him about the fish farm?' Ailsa enquired, anxious to know if Truan had played a part in its conception.

'He gave us the land. Fergus wanted it on a lease, but your uncle wouldn't hear of it, and in the end Fergus had to agree. Mind you,' Tom added thoughtfully, 'I had to point out that the land wasn't worth much anyway since it's mostly bog and rock, but it suited our purpose because it was so near the waterfall.'

'You were lucky in that respect.'

'Tremendously lucky. Otherwise we would have been looking for a spring to find enough fresh water. I think you enjoyed yourself at the farm the other day,' added Tom.

'I certainly did, and I hope I can come again,' Ailsa said.

'When you do you'll have to bring your own wellies!' he laughed.

'I'll buy a pair in Oban as soon as I get there!'

Tom was the easiest of companions, regaling her with anecdotes and tales of the surrounding countryside as they sped along.

'You'll have to get out and about more,' he said. 'Visit Mull and see Morvern. All these dark mountains will make you believe in the legends of the glens and the strange characters who once inhabited them.'

'Have we a legend at Truan?' she wanted to know.

He hesitated.

'All right,' she prompted, 'I can take it—even if it's a headless ghost.'

'It's nothing as gruesome,' he promised. 'In fact, if you ask me, it's no more than an idle tale.'

'So—you can tell me. I won't run the car into the ditch or rush off screaming!'

'It's not worth repeating,' he suggested.

'You can tell me, all the same.'

'Well, it's said that a second son will never inherit Truan, and one never has.'

There was an odd, pulsating silence between them in which the tyres seemed to beat out a rhythm on the sanded road. 'Never. Never!'

'And that has happened now,' Ailsa acknowledged quietly. 'It happened when my uncle bought Truan and handed it on to me.'

'I wouldn't worry about it,' said Tom.

She bit her lip.

'No, worrying won't help, I guess,' she agreed. 'Neither will saying "I'm sorry". If I could do something about it I would.' She took a firm hold on the steering-wheel. 'I'd do anything to repay that debt.'

'You mustn't hold yourself responsible,' he said, 'and I shouldn't have mentioned that silly legend. There always has been an heir to Truan.'

'The first son,' Ailsa said. 'Are you going to tell me what happened to Ewan MacNair?'

'He was drowned—out there on the loch. It was before I came here, so I don't know the details, but Fergus never got over it. It scarred him, in a way, made him seem remote when I first got to know him, and then gradually we became friends. The fish farm was my idea, but he cottoned on to it and we made it pay. Now, when he thinks we're ready to expand, I can't help him—even with money, anyway.'

'You wouldn't—leave him in the lurch?'

'What put that into your head?' He turned to look at her. 'We're close in a good many ways, though we argue a lot,' he said.

She felt reassured, looking at this big, practical man sitting beside her admiring the scenery as he discussed his hopes for the future.

When they came in sight of their destination she pulled the car in to the side of the road.

'I had my back to all this coming north,' she explained, looking across the silver expanse of water to the high mountains rising against the horizon. 'I suppose that's Mull over there beyond the long island, and Morvern of the dark mountains, as my uncle used to say.'

Tom nodded. 'I wish I could take you over there,' he said regretfully, 'but there's no time. Some day, perhaps, we will go and walk through the deep glens and sit by the water on the other side where Iona and Staffa lie against the sunset.'

'You talk as if you've come to love everything about Scotland, as if it meant a great deal to you,' she mused.

'I could never live anywhere else, not after this. It has a great beauty and a great freedom.' He gazed out beyond the island. 'It is all I need.'

'And all Fergus needs, I think.'

'That is true,' Tom agreed, 'but for Fergus it is home.' He continued to gaze out across the firth. 'I can't see him anywhere but in the glen.'

'What about the Keep?' she asked.

'Oh, he'll go on restoring it until he can live there in reasonable comfort. It's going to take years, but that won't daunt him because he's made of sterner stuff. It's hard work the way he's doing it, but he won't cut corners.'

'Perhaps—if he married he might think differently,' Ailsa suggested.

There was a long silence in which her companion seemed to shut her out and she thought that he half resented her intimate suggestion.

'There was a time when he said he would never marry,' Tom answered at last. 'A time of great bitterness, but that could be passing now. Fergus doesn't often speak about the things that are closest to his heart.'

She could not tell him of that conversation at the tower when they had spoken of the past and she had realised that the bitterness still remained in Fergus. He could hide it from Tom, who was his friend, yet he had not sought to hide it from her up there in the lonely Keep. It had surged to the surface like a hidden spring, dark and strong, warning her not to intrude, to keep her distance if they were to remain friends.

She drove the rest of the distance to Oban in silence.

'Where's your appointment?' asked Tom as they wound down the steep hill with the lovely seaside town beneath them.

'Argyll Square. I have the address here.' She indicated her handbag on the seat beside her. 'Where can I drop you?'

'The square will do fine.' He hesitated. 'How long do you think you'll be?'

'Hard to say. Perhaps an hour.'

He looked at his watch.

'I'll drop you and park the car for you,' he offered. 'Then I'll have an excuse for taking you to lunch.'

'You told me you were broke!' she smiled. 'Why don't you let me take you to lunch?'

'Couldn't be done! I have my pride, irrespective of how I look.'

'In an hour, then.' She slowed up at the kerb. 'Take good care of the car, won't you? It doesn't belong to me. I hired it at Prestwick when I landed, but I'd really like to keep it now. Do you think I could buy it from the hire people?'

'You could try,' he agreed. 'If not, there are plenty of car showrooms in Oban only too willing to sell you one, I should think.'

He took her place behind the steering-wheel, waiting until she had found the address she was looking for and saluting her gravely as he drove away.

The offices of Duncan, MacCallum and Neil were on the first floor with four windows overlooking the square, and a bell on a desk said 'Ring', which she did. Almost immediately a small, bald-headed man with bright, inquisitive blue eyes came from an inner room to answer her summons.

'Miss Mallory?' he said without preliminary. 'I was expecting you.'

'I was going to get in touch,' Ailsa told him, 'but I've only been at Truan a week and time has gone like the wind. I'm sorry if I should have contacted you sooner, but I didn't think there was much more to be done.'

His smile broadened.

'Only a few signatures,' he said. 'Everything else has been taken care of. There has been a lot to clear up, you understand, but I think you will find it has been done to your satisfaction—and your advantage,' he added importantly.

'I feel the advantage has been very much on my side, Mr——? Is it Mr Duncan?'

'Oh, dear me, no! Mr Norman Duncan is long since dead. I'm Douglas MacCallum and I dealt with all your uncle's business while he was alive, so perhaps you will feel disposed to carry on with the same arrangements.'

Ailsa hesitated.

'I suppose I do need a lawyer, even though everything appears to be fixed now,' she agreed.

'Almost everything,' he qualified. 'There's just the matter of the legacy to clear up.'

'I thought Truan was the legacy,' Ailsa murmured.

'Part of it.' He indicated a chair in front of his desk. 'Please sit down.'

When she had settled in the chair he looked at her across the desk, opening a drawer to produce a sheaf of papers in a blue folder which he placed before him with a nod of approval.

'Your uncle did not intend you to administer the estate without him making adequate financial arrangements for its upkeep, Miss Mallory,' he announced. 'He was a very practical man, but I have to admit that the final cash benefit has surprised me. There were shares and investments made over a period of years, and after making various bequests—one of them to your mother, I see—he has left the remainder to you, some of it for the upkeep of Truan, the rest to be used at your own discretion. It is quite a handsome amount,' he added, 'and I must congratulate you. You are now a considerable heiress.'

He passed a slip of paper across the desk.

'That is the exact amount,' he beamed. 'More than you expected, I gather.'

'It's—too much!' Ailsa heard herself saying. 'What can I possibly do with all that money?'

'Spend it on Truan, if you will,' he smiled. 'Otherwise, on yourself. You are not married, but you may wish to be, and this is a nice little nest-egg to have when the time comes. I wish you well.'

'I—haven't quite taken it in,' Ailsa confessed, drawing a deep breath. 'I knew there was some money, but—but nothing like this. It's overwhelming, Mr MacCallum!'

'You'll soon get used to it.' He pushed some papers across the desk for her to sign. 'I'm sure there must be something you want to do.'

'I want to stay in Scotland,' she returned almost automatically. 'I can't imagine going back to Canada with all this to sort out.'

He sat back in his chair to look at her as she signed two more documents.

'What do you think of Truan so far?' he asked.

'I love it! I want to keep it just as it is, as the MacNairs had it before they were forced to sell.'

'Ah, yes,' he said, 'that was indeed a tragedy, but there are many such misfortunes in the Highlands today. Old estates change hands with distressing frequency, new owners do their best and succeed or fail dismally according to the effort they put in. People come here thinking it's going to be easy and when it isn't they lose heart, so to speak. They want to go back to the city or the country of their origin, and then the old homes are back on the market again, for sale to the highest bidder, I'm afraid.'

'That won't happen to Truan,' Ailsa declared. 'I never mean to go away, Mr MacCallum. Never!'

'Well said!' He held out his hand. 'Please contact me if ever you are in doubt,' he added warmly. 'Meanwhile, a cheque has been deposited in the Royal Bank of Scotland to your account and you can draw on it whenever you wish.'

Feeling almost stunned by the generosity of the man who had left her Truan, Ailsa went back down the stairway to stand outside on the pavement in the sunshine, her thoughts scattered as the future stretched comfortably before her. She had neither expected, nor did she need, so much money, but she knew that Truan must benefit from it first of all. Truan and all the estate. It was what she owed to her uncle's memory and, in an odd sort of way, to Fergus MacNair.

When Tom finally drew up at the kerb she was still standing there as if rooted to the spot.

'What's the matter?' he asked. 'You look a million miles away.'

'Tom,' she said, getting into the passenger seat, 'I've had a tremendous shock.'

He looked up at the brass plate bearing the solicitor's name.

'Is it about Truan?' he asked.

'Yes, in a way.'

'You're not going to be able to keep it, after all?' His tone was serious and regretful.

'It isn't that. Not at all.' Ailsa looked out through the windscreen at the busy square. 'Can we go somewhere where we can talk?'

He glanced at his watch.

'Time to eat,' he decided. 'We'll go along the Esplanade and find somewhere to park. I know quite a good hotel.'

'That would be fine,' she agreed.

Still quite dazed, she was unable to believe what she had just been told, but by the time they had reached the hotel of Tom's choice some of her natural exuberance had returned. Her eyes were sparkling and two bright spots of colour stood high in her cheeks.

'I've so much to tell you,' she said when they had ordered their meal.

'I'm listening,' he assured her. 'Tell on!'

'Tom, I've been left a great deal of money, far more than I expected in the first place,' she confessed. 'I want to do so much with it, to invest it in Truan. Not in the house,' she added. 'I want to keep that exactly as it has always been, but I thought I could do something about the estate. The water supply, for instance. You know it all comes down from the lochan in the hills, and Mrs Birch said the other day that they often have trouble with it during a dry summer. The pipes that bring it down are old and need renewing, and the filters could be improved. It would be quite a task, but it could be done, and we could use local labour. Then there's all that land at the glen end of the estate. It should be cleared and put under cultivation, I think, and after that——'

She paused for breath, aware that Tom was regarding her with an odd expression in his eyes.

'Afterwards,' she rushed on, 'I'd like to invest locally.'

'Do you mean the fish farm?' he asked carefully.

'It had crossed my mind.' She leaned eagerly towards him. 'Surely you think it would be a good idea? You said the other day that you ought to expand, didn't you, so that would be something else I could do.'

'And something you would have to ask Fergus about,' he pointed out slowly.

He had meant to put an end to her daydreaming, to bring her up sharply to face reality.

'Oh, surely he couldn't refuse!' she protested. 'It would be to everybody's advantage, a big improvement all round, and the village would benefit too, with more jobs.'

'Hold on!' cautioned Tom. 'I think you should take this one step at a time.'

'Because you think Fergus might refuse—simply because it's me?'

'I didn't say that.'

'But it's what you mean, isn't it?' Her disappointment was acute. 'How could he be such a dog in the manger? I can't help owning Truan and I can't help being there in his place. If he refuses it will be out of stubborn pride and nothing more!'

'I think you are wrong there,' Tom said, gazing out through the wide picture window across the blue water of the magnificent bay. 'I think it goes deeper than that.'

'How deep?' Ailsa demanded, hurt that her plans for Truan could so easily be disrupted.

'He might want to do something for himself.'

'Well, that's pride, if you ask me!'

'I suppose it is, but it's something you could discuss at your peril.'

'Will you talk to him? Tom, you must,' she insisted. 'It means a lot to you too.'

'A great deal,' he agreed. 'I'll see what I can do, but I don't hold out much hope, to be absolutely honest.'

'That's your strong point, isn't it?' she observed. 'Honesty.' She met his blue eyes across the table. 'Why do you think Fergus dislikes me—apart from Truan, I mean?'

'I don't think he does.' Tom looked up as the waitress put his first course in front of him. 'I think things would have been different if it hadn't been for Ewan's death.'

'He can't blame me for that!'

'No, that's true, and I think your other ideas for Truan are highly commendable.'

He had steered the conversation away from Fergus, determined not to discuss his friend further, and Ailsa supposed she would have to accept his decision without argument.'

'But you will try to convince him for your own sake?' she suggested as a last resort.

'I could try,' he agreed. 'And now, eat up your salmon and enjoy the view!'

On the way back to Loch Truan they spoke mostly about Canada and the childhood Ailsa had enjoyed on lochs just like these.

'Only they were *lakes*,' she smiled. 'That's the wonderful thing about Truan. It's so much like home.'

'Will you bring your mother over later on?' he asked.

'I'd like to, but there's just one snag. My stepfather doesn't have too much leave, and she wouldn't come without him.'

'What does she think about Truan—about your uncle leaving you the estate?' asked Tom, surveying the mountains ahead with an appreciative eye.

'She was glad. She thought it was an ideal way of keeping my mind off the past.' Ailsa drew a deep breath. 'I had an unfortunate love affair and she thought Truan might heal the scars.'

'And has it?'

'Not yet,' she admitted with considerable difficulty, 'but I'm working on it. You can't walk around with your heart on your sleeve, no matter how badly you've been hurt. I wasn't really running away,' she added, remembering Fergus's opinion on the matter. 'It was over months before I knew about Truan and my inheritance.'

Soon they were driving up the hill where she had first seen 'the young laird' coming down across the heather with the two collies at his heels.

'I wonder why they call him that,' she said aloud.

'Who—and what?'

'"The young laird".'

'Because it's how everybody thinks of him,' explained Tom. 'I guess he'll always be the laird of Truan, no matter what happens.'

It was true. She knew it to be true, deep in her heart.

'You're late,' Flora accused when she finally reached the Lodge. 'What happened in Oban to keep you so long?'

'Oh, lots! I'll tell you about it later,' Ailsa promised.

'Mother will want to know right away.'

Why should she? Ailsa felt resentful for the first time. Mrs Birch was far too curious about things which didn't really concern her.

'Let's go for a walk,' she suggested, taking Flora's arm. 'I've been sitting in the car most of the day and I could do with some exercise.'

Flora hesitated.

'OK,' she conceded. 'Did you have some lunch in Oban?'

'Tom Kelvin took me to a hotel on the Esplanade after I'd seen the lawyer.'

'Tom?' Flora halted on the grassy path through the shrubbery. 'You were—together?'

'I gave him a lift. He was standing outside the fish farm hoping to hitch-hike when I passed. Quite by accident,' Ailsa added firmly because she had seen the look in Flora's eyes which spelled resentment.

'He'd be going to the Crofters for spares, I expect,' Flora guessed. 'I suppose you brought him back too.'

'Yes. We had a load of wire in the trunk and several boxes of nails, I think. I dropped him at Cuilfail. Satisfied?'

A bright colour stained Flora's cheeks.

'I didn't mean to pry,' she said. 'I just wondered——'

'If it's any satisfaction to you, it was all purely business,' Ailsa said firmly. 'Tom and I are friends—nothing more.'

'That's all right,' Flora assured her. 'I was just being silly.'

Silly or not, her eyes had been deep pools of anguish a moment ago, and Ailsa's heart lurched at the thought of Fergus and all the plans Martha Birch undoubtedly nurtured for her daughter.

'I don't know why my mother wants to give me such a good education when all *I* want is just to come back to the glen and settle down here,' Flora complained. 'I won't be happy in Glasgow teaching in a city school. It's all such a waste.'

'It could be,' Ailsa agreed, 'but you'll have to make that decision for yourself when the time comes.'

'I will,' Flora said, 'when the time comes.'

They walked on to where the gardens came down to the loch in a tangle of scrubland and high nettles which partly obscured their view.

'I've come into some money, Flora,' Ailsa said. 'I want to do a lot on the estate, like clearing up this bit of land and perhaps planting better trees.'

'You wouldn't be touching the old boat-house, would you?' asked Flora. 'It's been useful in its time, and the yacht's still in there.'

'What yacht?'

'*Kirsty of Truan.*' Flora hesitated. 'I suppose it belongs to you now. It must have been sold with the estate.'

'Let's go and see,' Ailsa suggested.

Flora hung back.

'Perhaps we should wait and ask about *Kirsty* first,' she suggested. 'Mother would know.'

'We'll have to inspect the boat-house, anyway,' Ailsa decided. 'I would love to be able to sail again,' she mused.

'Did you sail a lot in Canada?' Flora led the way along an overgrown path towards the loch. 'Had you a boat of your own?'

'Only a sailboat.' Memory carried Ailsa swiftly back to the days when Russell had been her constant companion. 'But I knew someone who had a yacht and I suppose I learned to handle it quite well. There are so many small lakes in the Algonquin that you soon get to handle a boat if you go up there often enough.'

'Perhaps you miss all that,' Flora suggested.

Ailsa took a full minute to reply.

'I haven't had much time for introspection since I got here,' she admitted. 'The days have been very full, and regret doesn't help very much once you've made a decision and tried to carry it out.'

'You'll soon grow to love Truan,' Flora predicted.

Ailsa smiled.

'I'm halfway there already,' she declared.

They ploughed on towards the distant loch which shimmered beyond the trees, the going becoming more difficult as the path narrowed and the ground became soggy underfoot.

'I forgot to buy a pair of gumboots when I was in Oban,' Ailsa commented. 'It went straight out of my head.'

'You'll need them if you visit the fish farm again,' Flora pointed out. 'Maybe you can buy a pair at the yard.'

'Are they busy down there?' asked Ailsa. 'Repairing boats?'

'Not too busy so far.' Flora was walking ahead, slashing at the nettles with a stick she had found. 'There was some talk of a marina a year ago, but the idea fell through. Fergus was interested, but it needed more backing and the Glasgow people put it all on hold for the meantime. I think we need a marina up here, or something like it. All sorts of yachts call in during the summer months and a few of them need repair.'

Ailsa filed the information away for future reference, seeing a flourishing marina at the far end of the loch at least during the summer months.

They had come to the end of the path where they could see the loch quite plainly.

'Someone's been here,' Flora observed, looking down at the trampled grass. 'Quite recently.'

Ahead of them Ailsa could see the dark outline of a boat-house with a short wooden jetty jutting out into the water in front of it.

'It looks in pretty good condition,' she remarked.

'Oh—the boat-house? Yes, it was built to last, like everything else at Truan,' Flora assured her, her thoughts evidently in the past.

'Shall we press on?' Ailsa added half-doubtfully.

'Why not? It would be interesting to know if we had a prowler, someone sleeping rough, perhaps.'

Ailsa was close behind her. 'Could they get in?'

'They could break in,' Flora agreed. 'It's easy enough with a padlock.'

There was a door at the side of the shed and double doors leading on to the loch where a sizeable boat could be launched.

'I'm quite excited about this,' Ailsa declared. 'I've always fancied a boat of my own.'

There was no answer from her companion.

'He—or she!—didn't come in this way,' Flora remarked a minute or two later as she tried the side door. 'It's quite firmly locked. Maybe we've got vandals or something.'

Ailsa looked towards the loch.

'Like the Norsemen of old, they must have come in from the sea,' she suggested. 'Flora, how far is it to the Keep?'

'Just round the Point. You can't see it from here, but it's easy enough to row round from the bay.' Flora stood quite still, listening. 'There's someone out there,' she whispered.

They could hear the splash of oars as they waited, the gentle sound of a wooden blade going into the water and out again, propelling a dinghy along just beyond the shore, but they could see nothing because of the heavy undergrowth. Then Flora said with something that could have been a sigh of relief, 'It's Fergus!'

When he came fully into view Fergus MacNair was rowing leisurely, intent on looking at something farther out on the loch, a seal, perhaps, or a fishing seabird. Gradually he came closer to the shore, passing almost in front of them.

'I wonder if he'll notice us,' said Flora.

'We can hail him and make sure.' Ailsa cupped her hands around her mouth. 'Ahoy there!' she called. 'Are you coming in?'

He was looking directly towards them, his face contorted with a ravaging emotion to which she could not put a name.

'Not now,' he called, shipping his oars. 'Have you walked down from the house?'

'We needed the exercise,' she told him. 'Flora's been studying most of the day and I've been in Oban.'

'So I understand.' He leaned heavily on the oars. 'Tom's been filling me in with the details,' he added without smiling. 'You're going to be kept very busy for a long time, I gather.'

'It's what I need.' Ailsa looked across the intervening water to where he sat in the dinghy she had last seen at the fish farm. 'I wanted to speak to you,' she added urgently. 'Could I come down to Cuilfail and see you tomorrow morning?'

There was a lengthening pause in which the bright stretch of sunlit water between them seemed to broaden and deepen so that she could make no real approach to him in his present frame of mind.

'I'm going to be busy,' he said bluntly. 'We're transferring some of the trout into the loch in the morning.'

'What I have to say won't take very long,' she assured him. 'It's something I want to get off my chest as quickly as possible, but if Tom has already told you about my idea I guess you've already made up your mind.'

'Not completely,' he said, much to her surprise, 'but I'm not ready to accept charity.'

Her face flamed scarlet.

'I might have known!' she shouted at him. 'I might have guessed that would be how you would react!'

'I think you're flying off the handle much too quickly,' he told her. 'Come to the fish farm if you must, but I can't promise you a decision immediately. I would have to think about it a while longer.'

'How much time do you need to finally say no?' she challenged, angry and disappointed that her offer could be so summarily refused. 'It'll be nothing more than your stupid pride that will make you refuse, in the end!'

'Try me!' he suggested with an odd, twisted smile. 'I won't say no to a reasonable bargain.'

Surprised out of her aggressive mood, Ailsa looked back at him as he dipped his oars again into the sea.

'Flora thinks someone has been prowling around here,' she called out to him. 'Could they break in from the jetty?'

'Not easily.' He slid the oars through the water where the evening sun caught the tiny drops falling from the blades, turning them to shining jewels. 'I've been here once or twice,' he added, 'checking up, if that's any consolation to you.'

'Oh, I'm sorry!' She was quick to apologise. 'It—kind of puts our minds at rest.' She looked round, hoping that Flora would endorse her statement, but Flora had gone. 'I'll come and see you tomorrow,' she added. 'About three o'clock, perhaps.'

'Whenever you like.'

Fergus rowed away, lost to view almost immediately as he turned the Point into the bay where the lonely Keep stood waiting, and Ailsa was left standing on the shore wondering how many times he had passed the locked-up boat-house reliving a memory. It was no way to combat bitterness, she thought, renewing it constantly like this. His brother was dead, the person he had always looked up to, but after six years surely the bitterness should have eased a little.

'We'll never really know,' she mused as Flora made her appearance among the nettles.'

'Know what?'

'About Fergus. Whether he's going to live part of the time in the past, colouring his life darkly.'

'I'm glad he's been able to come here,' Flora returned unexpectedly. 'At least, it's better than worrying about vandals as far as we're concerned.'

'We haven't taken a look at the yacht,' Ailsa pointed out.

'Another time,' said Flora. 'We don't want to get Mother in a tizzy by being late for our dinner.'

Coming down to the small sitting-room a good ten minutes before Flora, Ailsa found Martha Birch busy setting the table for their evening meal.

'Let me do that,' she offered. 'Flora will be down in a minute, I guess.'

'She's been busy with that lamb.' Mrs Birch frowned. 'I knew it would prove a nuisance, running all over the place and breaking things. I should have put my foot down when it was first mentioned.'

'George will grow up one day and be no bother at all,' Ailsa predicted. 'He's quite a lad, I admit, but he'll improve with time. He's beginning to follow Flora all over the place. I think he looks real cute!'

'Nothing looks more foolish than a fully grown sheep lumbering after you,' Martha Birch decided. 'We'll have to get rid of him as soon as we can. Were you down at the village just now?' she ended on her usual note of enquiry.

'No, we went the other way, to the far end of the paddocks,' Ailsa told her. 'As a matter of fact we went as far as the old boat-house down on the shore. Flora tells me there's a yacht in there, though we weren't able to examine it. Would you know exactly who owns it, Mrs Birch, because I'd dearly like to make an offer for it if it didn't really come with the estate?'

Martha Birch drew a deep breath before she answered.

'I'm thinking it will belong to you now since all the rest of the estate is yours,' she said carefully as she laid out the cutlery with her usual precision. 'It went with the house when your uncle bought the place, although he never sailed it. He was a man who liked to have his feet on solid ground, I'd say, but if you're sailing mad like all the rest of the young people around these parts you'll probably find a use for it.'

'I can hardly believe it!' Ailsa cried. 'My own boat! What incredible luck!'

'It will need seeing to after all those years,' the house-keeper warned her, 'but it was a good stout boat in its time, clinker-built and well equipped to sail in these dangerous waters. You'd be wise to seek professional advice about any repairs,' she added, her voice suddenly harsh. 'It was Master Ewan's boat and he died sailing it out there among the islands. It was found drifting in the loch, as if it had come home afterwards.'

'How dreadful! But surely that must mean it now be-longs to Fergus?' Ailsa suggested.

The housekeeper took her time about arranging the final place setting, her eyes as hard as flint, her mouth compressed into a narrow line.

'Can you imagine him wanting to sail that boat after such a tragedy?' she demanded. 'He never has and he never will. At one time he couldn't bear to mention *Kirsty of Truan* or even look at her.'

'And since then?' asked Ailsa. 'Surely after six long years he's beginning to forget?'

'It depends how you look at it,' Martha Birch told her. 'Fergus is the most loyal person I know. As well as his brother, his fiancée was drowned out there that wicked day. They went together, the girl he was going to marry and the brother he idolised. It was a cruel moment for him.'

Stunned, Ailsa digested the truth, which was almost a repetition of her own sad affair, love, forlorn and un-dying, unable to see beyond grief to any hope in the future. But now she had a new life and all her former bitterness had gone. Here, at Truan, she had something worthy of her tremendous enthusiasm and drive, and it was helping her to put the past behind her. Surely Fergus could do the same?

'I'll ask someone at the yard to look at the yacht, Mrs Birch,' she said uneasily. 'We can't just let it rot there for want of attention. After that I shall probably sell it,' she sighed. 'I couldn't possibly sail it in the bay with Fergus at the Keep.'

'You must do what you like with it,' said Mrs Birch, 'but sailing it down the loch can't make much difference after all this time, I'm thinking.'

Perhaps not, Ailsa thought, but how would she feel if Russell Forgreave were suddenly to appear on her horizon again to renew all the memories and all the heartache of the past which she was trying to forget? If he had married someone else that would never happen, of course, but the hurt still remained.

CHAPTER FOUR

THE following afternoon Ailsa made her way to the fish farm, walking down through the village in a thin mist of rain that clung to her anorak, starring her hair beneath its enveloping hood with diamond drops of moisture as she hurried along. It was exactly three o'clock when she reached the sheds, to find them deserted. Fergus and everyone else must still be down at the loch.

Walking quickly, she reached the shore to find a small knot of men standing on the low stone pier where the traps were launched to be anchored in neat rows in the shallow water at their feet. Fergus was one of them, but he allowed Tom to reach her first.

'Have you come for the pow-wow?' Tom asked. 'Fergus said you would be here at three o'clock.'

'It was three at the fish farm,' she informed him, 'but I suppose half an hour one way or the other doesn't matter too much in this part of the world.'

'We had trouble with one of the traps. I apologise for both of us,' he smiled.

'Tom, did you explain to Fergus how I feel about—helping out with all this?' She waved her hand to include the traps and equipment on the pier. 'We could do so much more—you said so yourself.'

'Granted, but I told you it would be entirely Fergus's decision.'

'Yes, I know,' she acknowledged. 'I saw him on the loch last night and he told me he would think it over and give me a final decision this afternoon.'

'Well, that's just what he will do,' Tom said. 'I'll walk with you back to the sheds while Fergus sees to the nets,' he offered. 'We have to cover the traps to protect the young fish from a marauding heron who lives hereabouts and from the odd seal on the prowl for an easy meal, to say nothing of the terns from the far side of the loch. It's murder sometimes while we're stocking the traps.'

Glancing in Fergus's direction, Ailsa was almost reluctant to leave.

'He'll be right behind us,' Tom promised, leading the way from the pier.

'Tom,' she asked, 'do you know what he's going to say?'

'Honestly—no. He had a lot to think about.'

'Especially his pride!'

'Don't bring that up again! He says pride doesn't come into it.'

'He mentioned something about charity.'

Tom stroked his bearded chin.

'He won't take anything for nothing, that's for sure, but you'll have to wait and see what he proposes,' he told her.

'OK! Just let's wait and see, then.'

'Why are you so afraid of a simple business deal?' he demanded.

Ailsa paused to look at him.

'Is that what it is to be?' she asked. 'Well, I ought to be satisfied.'

'But you're not, are you?' he suggested. 'You'd prefer something nice and cosy, like an outright gift to reconcile some of your guilt over Truan.'

'Oh, Tom,' she breathed, 'you know that isn't true! I've no real reason to feel guilty.'

'Neither you should. Did you buy a pair of gumboots at the yard?' he demanded, changing the subject abruptly.

'I haven't been down there yet.'

'Yet? Are you meaning to go?'

'I need some advice about a yacht.' She wasn't going into details about the forlorn occupant of the boat-house. 'I'd like to buy one in the near future because I love to sail.'

He gave her a quick, penetrating look.

'Hold your horses!' he advised. 'I'll see what I can do.'

'I don't know why you're so kind to me,' she said, feeling grateful.

Tom paused at the disinfectant trough to look down at her from his great height, touching her rain-cooled cheek with the back of his hand. 'The Lady of Truan!' he said. 'It's quite something to live up to, but I think you'll manage.'

Instantly she smiled back at him. 'I'm trying very hard,' she acknowledged.

When they had stepped through the trough he unlocked the door of the caravan.

'I'll make some tea,' he suggested.

'Let me do it,' she offered. 'I'm quite good at making tea!'

'Nice and strong,' he directed. 'Man's stuff!'

'Do you want the spoon to stand up in it?' she laughed.

'Is there a spoon?' he joked. 'Usually it's in the toolbag.'

'Tom,' she asked, searching for the spoon, 'do you ever think of getting organised—setting up a more conventional office, for example?'

'Mm!' he said, regarding the chaos around them. 'Might be an idea, but the trout have to come first, y'know.'

'I understand that,' she agreed, 'but you have two empty sheds at the far end of the site standing there doing nothing and the fish lorries come in that way to pick up your stock.'

'Never thought of it like that,' he returned, 'but if we did have a pukka office we'd need somebody permanently there, and that could be a problem.'

Ailsa thought of Flora, but Mrs Birch would never agree to her daughter working in an office shed after the education she had been given.

'Things don't work out evenly all the time,' she mused.

'How come?'

'Oh, it was only a thought.' She couldn't possibly involve Flora without talking it over with her first, and that might be Tom's task, in the end.

Fergus splashed through the shallow disinfectant tank a few minutes later.

'Sorry you've had to wait,' he apologised, throwing his green anorak over a convenient stool. 'We had a big order this morning from London, so there was quite a lot to do. Is that tea you're making?' he asked.

'Hot and strong,' Ailsa assured him. 'Do you have sugar?'

'When there is any.'

Tom offered him a half-empty bag.

'There are no refinements down here, as you can see,' he said to Ailsa. 'Everything comes steerage!'

'I'll have to get used to all this nautical talk!' she laughed. 'The milk will be out of a can, I suppose.'

'Oddly enough,' said Fergus, 'it's fresh. We get it from a local farm.'

Tom made room for her to sit down on the cluttered bunk while he perched on a convenient bench, holding up his mug of tea.

'Cheers!' he said. 'This is a bit of a celebration, I suppose. We've been hoping for this London order for some time.'

'It's going to make quite a difference,' Fergus agreed. 'If we can throw in a few salmon every time the lorries collect they would be about the best customers we have.'

Tom drank his tea.

'Duncan Carmichael would pull in the salmon,' he reflected. 'He has nothing else to do.'

Ailsa glanced at Fergus, seeing the light of enterprise in his eyes.

'We could think about it,' he agreed.

Tom slid to his feet.

'Have to go,' he announced. 'There's all that fish to pack before five o'clock tomorrow morning.'

'We'll be employing more labour shortly!' Fergus laughed.

'It might not be such a bad idea.' Tom paused at the door. 'See you!' he said.

Ailsa gathered up the mugs and the teaspoon, looking round for a basin in which to wash them.

'There isn't one.' Fergus came to stand beside her. 'We need all the available buckets and basins to carry the fish. You'll just have to rinse them under the tap.'

She imagined a warmth in the atmosphere which had been completely lacking in their previous encounters, so perhaps they were beginning to understand each other a little better. Never being one to beat about the bush, she put her proposition to him immediately.

'Fergus,' she said, 'I've just come into more money than I originally thought, and—and I'd like to invest some of it locally.'

She waited, but he refused to help her, standing with his back turned.

'Of course, anything Truan needs must come first,' she went on, not quite sure how to phrase her daring request, 'but Tom says you're ready to expand and the only snag is that you're short of the necessary capital. What would you say if I offered to help?'

He turned, at last, regarding her with a half-smile.

'I'd say you were completely irresponsible—even out of your mind,' he told her. 'We have very little collateral—a few fish tanks and several locally-made traps down on the loch—and a handful of potential customers in Glasgow and Edinburgh and now this one in London.'

'Which is wonderful,' she suggested with characteristic enthusiasm. 'It's enough to build on—more than enough. It's all right being careful, but you have to take a chance, sooner or later.'

'And you think your offer of help is "sooner"?'

'Yes.' There could be no more beating about the bush, she decided. 'I have this money lying idle and I want it to work for me as well as boosting a local business. I'd thought of the boatyard, but it's more or less established and Tom said you had plans for expansion in the future.'

'Tom has been very busy,' he reflected.

'He's completely honest,' she countered, 'and he knows I want to help.'

'Why should you?' Some of the coldness had crept back into his voice. 'You don't owe me anything, nor Truan either.'

'You're wrong there,' she argued. 'Truan is my responsibility now, but that's beside the point. I know what I want to do with the estate. It's the fish farm we're talking about. Community enterprise, if you like, and—and a bit of loyalty. I want to belong up here, Fergus, to feel I'm part of the glen, but I can't do that unless I'm allowed to help. I don't know a lot about your way of life, but I'm willing—willing and eager to learn. If you refuse me you'll be turning me away empty-handed with nothing else to do with my uncle's money but spend it rashly.'

'I can't imagine you doing anything so unproductive.' He was looking deeply into her eyes now. 'You're something of a business tycoon, aren't you?' he laughed. 'Are all Canadian girls as ruthless?'

'Generally we know what we want and go after it, within reason,' she conceded.

'You almost convince me,' he said. 'What is it you want to do down here?'

'First of all, I don't want to interfere with what you and Tom are doing now.' She drew a deep breath. 'What is it the Big Boys say? I want an interest in an ongoing business which affects the glen apart from the Lodge. I'd like to see the fish farm grow and prosper, and I'm sure Tom looks at it in the same way.'

'While I appear to be the only stumbling block,' Fergus added, walking to the door of the caravan to look out. 'How much do you want to invest?'

If this was capitulation she could hardly believe it.

'I thought—about twenty thousand at first,' she suggested.

'You'd be taking a risk,' he warned. 'Tom should have told you that.'

'We—didn't go into details.' She crossed the floor to his side. 'Please, Fergus, don't think we've been planning something behind your back, because we haven't. Tom got to know about the money because we were in Oban together and I was surprised and excited about it. I've never had a lot of money, and it gave me a feeling of——'

'Power?' he suggested. 'Was that what first struck you?'

'In a way, but not power as you see it,' she said. 'I don't think I felt that I could get anything I wanted just because I had this amazing windfall. I wanted to use it carefully and to the best advantage, so if that's being a business tycoon then I suppose I am one.' She looked over his shoulder to the broad, shining expanse of water between Truan and the Morvern hills. 'If it must be strictly business, Fergus, what are your terms?'

His steel-blue gaze challenged hers.

'A percentage of the profits according to your investment,' he answered slowly. 'Nothing more, nothing less.'

'But you and Tom will be doing all the work,' she protested.

'We'll take a salary if it bothers you too much,' he suggested. 'A small one at first, and then, if things go well, a more substantial share.'

'Why are you doing this?' she asked, unable to believe that he had given in so easily.

'Because I can't very well refuse.' He turned back into the caravan. 'I'm a realist, you see, and I feel this would be good for Tom and me. It would inject new blood into our efforts and make it a lot easier for us to expand.'

Ailsa felt a sudden, irrational disappointment, as if he had taken some of the excitement out of their joint venture, as if the sun had gone in with an abruptness which had left her cold.

'How do we go about it?' she asked.

'It's simple enough.' He crossed to the bench which was obviously used as an office desk, picking up a sheaf of papers on his way. 'If you would like to look at these I'll try to explain.'

When he had spread out the papers on the bench she recognised some of them as architects' plans.

'These were drawn up when we first started,' he explained. 'They're the rough design of what we wanted to do and what we could add to eventually. Here are the original sheds and the one that was built on.' His long brown forefinger travelled across the outline which she recognised as the present fish farm. 'Over here, where you see the dotted outline, is what we had hoped to achieve in a year or two.'

'So this is me!' Ailsa put her own finger on the dotted outline of three more sheds. 'When can we start?'

'There's quite a lot of work to do before we can even hope to build,' he explained. 'Foundations to clear and a new way in from the road. We'd come in here, I think, to make turning easier for the lorries—in one way, out the other.' Suddenly he turned to look at her. 'But that's for another day,' he said. 'We'll have to contact our lawyers in Oban and get down to the nitty-gritty first.'

Their heads were very near, bent over the future of a joint project which would eventually draw them closer together, and suddenly Ailsa felt a tremendous elation which had nothing to do with their business success. A faint pink colour rose slowly into her cheeks as her pulses quickened to his nearness. It was a completely physical attraction which unsteadied her, blurring her vision for a moment as she stared down at the plan he had spread out before her.

'I—when will you go to Oban?'

She hadn't said 'we' because there was Tom to consider too. They already had a partnership.

'I'll get Alan Hadley on the phone tomorrow,' Fergus promised. 'He'll draw up something for us to sign and pass it on to your lawyer. It's Duncan, MacCallum and Neil in the Square, isn't it? He negotiated for your uncle when he bought Truan.'

It was said without bitterness this time, an accepted fact which he had learned to live with over the difficult years.

'Do you want me to contact Mr MacCallum?' she asked.

'Oh, Alan will get in touch with Doug,' he said. 'Nothing is very conventional in these parts because we've all known each other from infancy, but you needn't worry about the agreement. It will all be legal and above board, I assure you.'

'I wasn't thinking about that,' she said. 'I know we've got to trust each other and—and I'm only glad it has come about so easily.'

Fergus paused on his way to the door, rolling up the plans.

'Believe me, it hasn't been easy,' he said. 'It's gone against the grain because my pride wouldn't stand for it at first, but I had to think of Tom, and progress, and what might be best for the glen. I'll consult you, of course, over any major decision we might have to take, but otherwise things will go on very much as they are. Would you like to talk it over with Tom?'

Already Ailsa was beginning to feel shut out again, only part of a merger which would benefit them all and bring added prosperity to the glen.

'I don't expect Tom to need much persuading,' she answered. 'He loves the life up here, Fergus, because it offers him the freedom he has always wanted and he's also very loyal. I don't think he would go against any decision you made unless it was completely incomprehensible.'

'Which is Tom in a nutshell!' He stood aside to let her go.

She met Tom before she reached the main road.

'Are we flushed with success or just exasperated?' he enquired, noticing the high colour in her cheeks.

'Success, I think.'

'You have to be sure.'

'Well, I am, then. Fergus has agreed to accept my money.'

'Unconditionally?' He looked amazed.

'Oh, no, there are plenty of conditions.' Ailsa smiled as he turned to walk beside her. 'I'm to be a sort of partner providing you're willing.'

'You know I am. Did you need to ask?'

'I suppose not.'

'What were the other stipulations?'

'No interference during working hours!'

'That should be easy enough. Who wants to smell of fish!'

'Tom,' she smiled, 'I'm trying to be serious. Fergus has decided I'm not to interfere, which I wouldn't have done, anyway, but I guess the partnership clause is just to salve his conscience about taking my money. He wants everything to be fair and square—"legal and above board", I think the phrase was—but I'm not really part of Cuilfail. I'll have a long way to go before I have any real say in the running of the fish farm, but I'm not quarrelling with that. I only want to feel as if I— belonged.'

'Fergus ought to know that.'

'Tom!' She caught his arm. 'You won't repeat what I've just told you?' she begged. 'You won't let Fergus know how I feel about all this?'

'There's no reason why I should.' He looked down at her with a curious expression in his eyes. 'Or is there?'

The colour deepened in her cheeks, causing her to turn her head away.

'None that I know,' she said.

They walked a few paces in silence till they came to the road.

'What is it with you?' asked Tom. 'Are you already in love with Fergus MacNair?'

Ailsa looked back towards the loch, to the yachts moored in the bay and the sun gilding the hills on the far side of it, thinking how still everything had become, waiting for her to answer the most momentous question of her life.

'I can't tell you,' she admitted, not yet sure of her feelings. 'I came to Scotland promising myself that I wouldn't fall in love a second time, determined I would never care for anyone in the same way I did for Russell Forgreave so that I would never be hurt so badly again, but now——'

'Truan has changed all that,' Tom suggested.

'I don't know. How can I say after so short a time?'

'This Canadian—this man you were in love with— what was he like?'

'A very attractive person. I believed most of the things he said, and then he walked off as if it had never mattered to him at all. He had to take on the responsibility of a family business and he hadn't time for anything else. I felt rejected, cast aside, and then I felt proud and determined not to care, all the negative emotions you go through when you're hurt beyond anything you've ever felt before. Perhaps that was why I came here in the first place,' she acknowledged. 'To get away—to find my feet again.'

'And your heart? Or have you really left that behind in Toronto?' he asked.

'No,' she said, albeit uncertainly. 'It was a clean break—or I hope it was.'

'What did Mr Perfect do for a living?' asked Tom.

'He's in the fur trade—his father's business. He was responsible for the European market and I suppose he still is.' To change the conversation she asked, 'What about you, Tom? What made you come to Truan?'

'There was this job and the promise of freedom. It means a lot to me. I met Fergus at university and we thought up the idea of the fish farm because the sheds and some of the land belonged to the Keep.'

'Were you here when Ewan was drowned?' she heard herself asking.

He shook his head.

'I came shortly afterwards, and maybe that was what cemented the friendship between us.' He paused to look down the loch. 'Deirdre was drowned that day too. She went with Ewan because Fergus was late getting back from Oban, and I think Fergus blamed himself for that. They were childhood sweethearts, and he must have been very much in love with her, because it seemed that he could never mention her name again.'

A hard knot of emotion fastened in Ailsa's throat, keeping her silent. The thought of Deirdre—'Deirdre of the Sorrows'—had taken possession of her, and it seemed to explain a good many things about Fergus MacNair which she had been willing to understand, but six years was a long time to mourn. He had picked up the pieces afterwards, but obviously he could not forget the brother he had idolised and the girl he had loved.

'Were they engaged?' she asked.

'Not officially, but it was always understood, apparently. Deirdre Buchanan was a local girl, and I guess they must have been made for each other, as people say.'

All the way back to the Lodge Ailsa thought about their conversation, picturing Fergus and his first love here in the glen where they had been brought up to appreciate the same things and share the same pursuits, enjoying halcyon days on the loch or among the hills until evening sent them back to their respective homes, tired and happy, with the prospect of other blissful days to come. These must have been perfect days, she thought with a strange constriction in her throat again. To be loved by Fergus MacNair! Surely that must have been a heart-stopping experience.

Shattered, she tried to adjust her thoughts, telling herself that she could not possibly have fallen in love again in so short a time. She had known Fergus for only two weeks, two crowded, confusing weeks filled by so many conflicting experiences and impressions that she had scarcely been able to sort any of them out. There had been Truan and Fergus's first vague antagonism, and Mrs Birch and her almost open hostility, and Flora's vague unhappiness with a future which offered her nothing but frustration in the end, and there had been Tom's friendship which Ailsa valued now more than she fully realised. Otherwise, she knew very little about the glen itself or the people who lived there. She must have neighbours apart from the villagers and perhaps the Buchanan family was one of them, mourning a daughter who had been drowned so cruelly with 'the rightful heir' to Truan by her side.

With the thought of friendship in her mind she approached Martha Birch the following morning.

'What should I do about getting to know my neighbours?' she asked as she sat down at the breakfast table. 'Do I have to sit around and wait for them to make the first approach? In Canada it's much easier. We just go and say "Hi! I'm your neighbour and I'd like to know you", but it might be different here.'

Mrs Birch stiffened.

'You have to wait till you're asked,' she said, 'but I've a notion it won't be long before you're invited somewhere. People here like to give a stranger time to settle in.'

She had emphasised the word 'stranger' which touched Ailsa on the raw.

'I'll never be anything but a stranger if I don't get to know people,' she pointed out. 'Surely, after six years in the glen, my uncle must have made some friends.'

'Only a few,' Martha Birch said. 'He was a quiet man who didn't entertain much. He liked to fish and shoot, but he never gave parties, if that's what you're meaning.'

'What does happen up here in the way of entertainment?' asked Ailsa.

'Oh, there's plenty of that!' the housekeeper told her. 'People think nothing of driving twenty or thirty miles to a *ceilidh* after a day's sailing or a hard day's work.'

'Do we have these—*ceilidhs* very often?'

'All the time in the winter; in the summer not so often, but that's something you'll have to ask Flora about. When she's here during the winter she seems to be away at one every week.'

'You must tell me what to do,' Ailsa said. 'I don't want to ask anyone to come to Truan unless they really wanted to.'

She was thinking about Fergus but wouldn't say so.

'Have no fear of that,' Mrs Birch assured her with a tight-lipped smile. 'Curiosity will bring them, if nothing else. They'll come to see what you have done with the Lodge and to pass judgement. They're a calculating crowd, but it gets them out of their gumboots and jerseys and does no harm.'

Two days later the first invitation arrived.

'It's from a place called Lettercairn.' Ailsa looked across the sitting-room at a waiting Mrs Birch who had brought in the mail. 'Someone called Struthers.'

The housekeeper looked impressed.

'You'll be going, of course,' she suggested. 'It's a very big farm at the head of the glen.'

'Will Flora go?'

'I expect so.' Mrs Birch looked towards the kitchen where her daughter was busy feeding the lamb. 'You can ask her,' she said.

Flora seemed delighted to be included in the invitation.

'The Struthers are fun,' she declared, 'and it's my last night before I go back to Glasgow. Which means you will be responsible for this!' she laughed, tugging against the lamb's affection for the empty bottle. 'He's getting sillier every day! George, give up!' she implored. 'There's no more left!'

'What do I wear?' Ailsa asked.

'An overall or a pair of dungarees!'

'I didn't mean about feeding that ridiculous lamb,' Ailsa smiled. 'I meant for the party.'

'Oh, anything goes, usually. I wouldn't overdress, if I were you, but I wouldn't go in jeans or a sweater either. The Struthers are friendly, but they're quite particular.'

'How many will be there?' Once again Ailsa caught herself thinking about Fergus. 'They'll all be locals, I expect.'

'Mostly. Although sometimes people come from Oban or the canal if they have been sailing down there. The Struthers are very well known.' Flora pushed George out into his garden pen, rolling down her sleeves. 'Are you going back to the boat-house?'

They had been working on the yacht, anti-fouling it at a great cost to hands and clothes, and it would soon be time to take it down the loch to the boatyard. The engineer at the yard had come up to overhaul the engine and assess the need for repairs to the hull in general, expressing surprise at the little craft's general seaworthiness after lying up for so long.

'Is the swotting over?' Ailsa asked.

'More or less.' Flora sighed. 'I've been packing my books ready to go at the weekend. Mother thinks I could come back once or twice during term time, which is quite a concession on her part and it will help as far as I'm concerned. I love it here, Ailsa; I don't want to go away—ever!'

They were good companions now, trudging towards the boat-house through the long grass, and Ailsa knew she was going to miss Martha Birch's daughter very much in the days to come.

'Let's take the yacht out,' she suggested impulsively. 'Just for a trial sail.'

Flora looked up at the cloudless sky.

'Why not?' she agreed. 'We've dried out the sails we found in the locker and there's just sufficient wind.' A quick flush mounted her cheeks. 'This is something else we have in common,' she said. 'You sailed a lot in Canada, didn't you?'

'On the lakes. Oh, yes, we were up there most holidays and even at weekends occasionally. I was getting to be quite an expert!' Ailsa boasted.

'Sailing on an inland lake can be different,' Flora pointed out. 'We have squalls here coming out of the blue because of the glens and the mountains, but don't worry. There won't be anything like that today.'

They had worked so hard on *Kirsty of Truan* that they both considered they had earned a break.

'I wonder why there's only one set of sails,' Ailsa mused as they checked the rigging. 'Usually there are two.'

Flora remained silent, the flush gone from her cheeks. After a moment she explained, 'Fergus didn't replace the other set. They were ripped to pieces that day when *Kirsty* was found. This is the spare set. I don't think it's ever been used.'

For a moment they stood beside the yacht, silenced by a memory.

'How old were you when it happened, Flora?' asked Ailsa.

'Fifteen. And like everybody else I thought Ewan was wonderful. I might even have been half in love with him, but I know now that I wasn't.'

Ailsa didn't ask her why, because a cloud already seemed to be settling on their bright and sunny day.

'We'll have to push her out,' she said, looking at the little yacht that had carried Ewan MacNair to his death. 'Unless—suddenly you don't want to go?'

'I'm not like that,' Flora declared. 'I don't believe in an ongoing jinx. I think *Kirsty*'s safe enough in normal weather. It would have to be another freak storm to capsize her a second time.'

Unwilling to pursue the subject, they manoeuvred the yacht to the water's edge, sliding her down the slipway till her keel touched bottom and she floated clear.

'There's nothing wrong with her,' said Ailsa, elated. 'Not even a bucketful of water in the bilges!'

'We'll try the pump again once we get the engine going,' Flora decided, 'then we can hoist the jib and go down to the yard in style!'

'Your pride will be the ruin of you,' Ailsa laughed, 'but I think I know how you feel. It's always a bit shameful going anywhere on the engine, even though it's only as far as the yard!'

When they turned the Point they could see the Keep standing silent guard above the bay, but the tide was in and there was no dinghy waiting at the causeway. Fergus was not at home.

'It's a sort of lonely place for a man to be thinking of living for the rest of his life,' Flora reflected as they sped past. 'Too remote, and difficult to get to in an emergency.'

'Perhaps Fergus will change his mind once he has completed the restoration,' Ailsa suggested.'

'It's going to take him a lifetime at the rate he's going now,' Flora prophesied. 'He'd need a lot of money to speed it up.'

'It's liveable-in even now,' said Ailsa.

'Of course, you've been there!' Flora was checking the set of the jib. 'We used to go over there and play "barons and Vikings" when we were kids, and it all seemed so romantic and brave, and nobody wanted to do anything about it till Fergus took over. It belonged to his mother—but he must have told you that.'

'Yes, he did.' Ailsa was remembering the expression on Fergus's face as they had spoken about the past. 'I don't think he'll ever part with it.'

Rounding the Point, they were met by a fresher breeze than they had expected. It filled the sail and *Kirsty* responded to it immediately. Sitting in the cockpit looking up at it, Ailsa was aware of the exhilaration to which she had responded so often in the past, with the wind in her hair and spray tossing up from the prow. Flora shut off the engine, smiling at her in that inexplicable moment when nature takes over from mechanical propulsion and a yacht runs free. There was no sound now but the whisper of the sail and the faint hiss of water running along the hull as they sped forward with their faces turned to the sun. It was a magical silence which

Ailsa remembered from long ago and would remember always. She turned her head to look back at the Keep, thinking that Fergus need never be lonely while he lived there so long as he had a boat to sail.

'We'll go as far as the yard and back,' Flora suggested, 'and then we can check the bilges. I don't think she's taking in more water than she should do after being laid up for so long.'

They passed the village and the bay, running down close to the shipyard where they could see the fish farm down by the shore.

'They'll be working like mad over there,' Flora gloated. 'I'll bet they envy us!'

No one seemed to be on the shore to observe them, however, as they tacked expertly to speed back across the loch.

'Should we hoist the mainsail?' wondered Flora.

'I don't think we need it,' Ailsa decided. 'We've got enough wind as it is.'

'It's always tricky going up the loch,' Flora said. 'We'll stick to the jib.'

They lay back in the sun with Flora's hand firmly on the tiller and the sheets wrapped round Ailsa's fingers as she watched the sail.

'This is glorious!' she declared. 'We must come out again—often.'

Flora treated her to a wry smile.

'You can, whenever you like,' she pointed out, 'but I'll be in Glasgow pounding the pavements at Jordanhill. I envy you!'

Unexpectedly they were caught by a gust of wind which came down between the hills to send them careering towards the twin islands which dominated the centre of the loch, but Flora had been ready for it in the subconscious manner of all good seamen, who never really relax at the helm.

'Whew!' she gasped. 'That was tricky, but didn't *Kirsty* do well?'

Ailsa had drawn in a swift breath of surprise, but now she was able to relax.

'I'll have to learn about your Scottish lochs and the squalls that come down between the hills,' she acknowledged.

They made for the shore.

'Well, we've done it!' Flora rejoiced as they rounded the Point. 'Taken *Kirsty* for her first voyage after all these years! It's been quite an achievement, hasn't it?'

'A very minor one,' Ailsa allowed, suddenly conscious of being observed from the shore.

'It's Fergus,' said Flora. 'He must have seen us from the Keep.'

The watching figure disappeared, striding quickly along the causeway as they turned into the bay.

'We'll let the sail down now and ease her into the landing-stage. Pity you haven't a buoy,' Flora remarked.

'All in good time!' Ailsa assured her. 'I'll ask them to put one down next time we go to the yard. Then *Kirsty* can spend the summer out here in the bay.'

They busied themselves with tackle and sails, stowing them away and tidying up in the cabin before they closed down the hatch.

'I've enjoyed myself so much,' Ailsa declared as she turned with the keys in her hand.

'I'm glad,' said Flora, 'for I don't think we're going to enjoy ourselves much longer. I know that look on Fergus's face from long ago!'

Fergus was standing at the end of the jetty waiting for them to step ashore, his face ashen, his hands tightly clenched by his side.

'Oh, dear!' said Flora as they walked towards him.

Ailsa was at a loss for words. She had never seen such anger mingled with despair as he took her roughly by the shoulder to demand:

'What in heaven's name are you thinking about going out in a boat that's been lying in a shed for six years without repair? You must be mad—out of your right mind!'

The hand that held her captive was like a vice, and she thought he would have shaken her if Flora hadn't been there.

'You risked your life,' he went on. 'Both of you!' He seemed to be aware of Flora now. 'Surely you could have said something? Told her how dangerous it was?' he demanded.

'We tested everything and we've been working on *Kirsty* for over a week,' Flora protested. 'We weren't in any danger, Fergus, not like——'

She couldn't finish the sentence, looking into his eyes.

'I'm sorry,' said Ailsa. 'I didn't know you felt so badly about it, although perhaps I should have known.'

He continued to hold her.

'You should have known about the sea and an unreliable boat,' he said with icy calm. 'You could have been drowned!'

'Yes. Well, I'm sorry. There's nothing else I can say.'

He stood looking at her for a moment, his eyes deep wells of conflict as he seemed to conjure up a scene from the past.

'Don't do it again,' he said, 'until you have everything overhauled and doubly checked. I suppose you took it for granted that the yacht was yours, since it was here when your uncle bought the estate,' he added grimly. 'It was never mine, anyway, though I was willing to see it rot in the shed rather than set eyes on it again.'

'Oh, Fergus,' she whispered, 'I'm sorry! I'm truly sorry. I should have known better; I should have understood how you felt.'

He released her abruptly.

'How could you understand?' he said. 'You were not here.'

Flora put out her hand, touching his arm as she had done once before.

'We're both sorry,' she said, 'and we *do* understand.'

Fergus turned to help them with the yacht, mooring it securely to the jetty as Ailsa picked up the sailbag.

'If you don't want me to use *Kirsty* again, I won't,' she said. 'It's all been a ghastly mistake. I understood from Mrs Birch that it was mine—part of the estate when my uncle bought Truan. I would never have taken it out otherwise.'

'There was no agreement,' he said. 'It was there for anyone to take.'

'Strictly speaking, Fergus, it's yours.'

Fergus shook his head, not looking at her.

'Use it,' he said harshly, 'if you will.'

She walked along the jetty by his side. 'Dan Craig fixed the engine for me yesterday and I've booked in at the yard for a complete overhaul, but I can easily cancel that,' she offered.

'Why should you?' He turned to look down at her, his eyes as cold as steel. 'You don't have to ask my permission about *Kirsty* or anything else. You're mistress of Truan now, and *Kirsty* goes with the house as far as I'm concerned. Just make sure you don't take any more risks.'

When he had gone, striding off in the direction of the causeway to return to the Keep, Flora looked after him with a curiously disturbed expression in her eyes.

'He was concerned about us,' she said. 'I know he was. Fergus would never let his anger show.'

'It looked very much like anger to me,' Ailsa returned, 'but maybe I should excuse him. Seeing us out there on *Kirsty* must have brought back all the agony of the past, the memory of the dreadful accident when he lost the girl he loved. It was for ever, Flora. It wasn't as if they had parted in anger or anything like that.'

Flora didn't answer. Instead she traced a little pattern on the jetty boards with the toe of her canvas shoe, looking down at it with bleak indecision in her eyes.

'There's a lot you don't know,' she said as they walked towards the boat-house, 'but it wouldn't be fair to Fergus to uncover the past. I thought he had put it behind him a long time ago, but now it seems he can never forget.'

They walked slowly back to the Lodge over the rough ground where Ailsa had planned to grow new trees, but suddenly it seemed less important now if everything she attempted to do was going to go wrong.

In the morning, however, she determined to put her first big mistake behind her and go back to the fish farm, where she found Fergus mending nets down on the shore.

'I thought I'd better check up on our partnership,' she began when he looked up from his absorbing task. 'Have you contacted your lawyer friend to ask what he thinks about it?'

He put the net he was working on aside, getting up to meet her.

'Look, I'm sorry I bawled you out yesterday,' he apologised. 'I didn't mean to be so brash, but the fact that you were out there on the loch took me by surprise. I should have remembered Canada.' His lips twisted in the one-sided smile which had endeared him to her in a very short space of time. 'It must have been the chauvinistic male in me thinking that a woman couldn't handle a boat in an emergency as well as a man. You'll forgive me?'

'Certainly.' A great weight of doubt fell from Ailsa's shoulders. 'Flora and I deserved to be ticked off for not checking properly with the yard before we ventured out at all.' She stood looking down at the traps for a moment. 'Fergus,' she said, 'if we're going to work together even in a small way we'll have to trust each other. I don't want to go blundering round making mistakes all the time, and you can help me, if you will.'

'It will be in our mutual interest,' he returned drily. 'What do you want to do now?'

'I thought we might equip a decent office,' she suggested. 'If we expand, as we're sure to do, we can't make do with just the caravan. Everything is all over the place.'

'We can agree on that, for a start,' he said, the smile reaching his eyes. 'Do you want another trip to Oban to buy office furniture?'

'There you go!' she declared. 'You think I'm not settled, not really willing to stay put at Truan, but I am. I've even started to clear that rough pasture down by the boat-house to plant trees, and I'd like to re-surface the drive up to the Lodge. It's full of potholes and terribly bad for the springs on my car.'

'It should have been done years ago,' he acknowledged briefly, 'but your uncle didn't use it much. He went straight on to the hill by the back road up to the lochan where he liked to fish.'

'The lochan's another thing,' she remembered. 'Where can I contact someone to renew the water pipe down to the house and the other outlet for the village?'

'You can fix up with a contractor from Oban or Fort William,' he told her. 'You *are* being a new broom, and no mistake!'

'Fergus, I want to do this,' she protested. 'The new water supply is essential and you can call the trees a whim, if you like, but I think they're necessary too, and they'll pay for themselves in the end.'

'You could even take up forestry!' His smile deepened. 'I know what you're trying to do and I appreciate it, although it's no affair of mine. What we have in common is an interest down here.' He glanced towards the rows of wooden traps floating a few yards away. 'Want to come and see?'

Ailsa followed him willingly, eager to learn about their 'common interest', as he had called it. The fish here in the loch were almost fully grown and as they negotiated the floating walkways he put out a hand to steady her.

'There's an art in it,' he said.

'Talk about walking the plank!' she laughed. 'I had no idea the fish would be so big.'

'They eat well.' His fingers tightened over hers. 'This next section can be a bit tricky,' he warned, 'so hold on!'

She clutched his arm as the plank seemed to buckle under her, and then suddenly he was holding her close, her head against the roughness of his chin as he sought to steady her again. For a moment they stood there while the same feeling of inevitability swamped her, making her unable to draw away. If she had been looking for sanctuary surely she had found it here in this man's arms.

Abruptly Fergus drew away, and she looked down at the swarming fish at her feet, unable to see them clearly for a moment because her vision was suddenly dimmed.

'We take them out according to size as the orders come in,' Fergus was explaining. 'In the last tank they are fully grown.'

'There must be thousands and thousands of them,' she said vaguely. 'We should make a fortune!'

Trying to make light of that moment when he had held her in his arms was an effort, and she refused his outstretched hand when they walked back to the more stable surface of the pier.

'Have you been invited to the *ceilidh* at Lettercairn?' she asked casually. 'Flora says the Struthers are very nice.'

'More than that,' he said. 'They'll make you welcome.'

'You haven't said whether you'll be there or not,' she reminded him.

'Everybody will be there,' he smiled. 'The Struthers never do things by halves. Tom has been talking about the *ceilidh* ever since we got our card through the post the other day. He'll teach you how to dance a reel or two—he's the expert.'

He had still not committed himself, and Ailsa was too shaken to press the point while all she could remember was the touch of his hand on her hair. He had recommended Tom as a partner, but not himself.

'I must go back,' she said. 'Flora goes to Glasgow on Sunday, and she's looking forward to the *ceilidh* nearly as much as I am.'

Fergus walked with her to the road and she watched him go on to the hill. It was how she had first seen him, coming down across the heather with the dogs at his heel.

CHAPTER FIVE

THE evening of the *ceilidh* was cool and clear.

'We'll walk,' Flora suggested. 'It isn't very far, and we're sure to get a lift back.'

Was she thinking about Tom? Ailsa wondered, remembering how Flora blushed at the sound of his name. And what a disappointment that would be to Martha Birch who wanted her daughter to marry 'the young laird'!

They walked part of the way beside a brown burn gurgling over stones, and under beeches where the mast of the year before lay thick on the side of the road like a bronze carpet to cushion their feet. The smell of wet earth after rain rose up to meet them, a nostalgic reminder of Canada.

'Do you miss Toronto?' Flora asked idly.

'I miss Canada, which isn't quite the same thing,' Ailsa told her. 'I was never a city type. Whenever we could we would go to the lakes or climb among the mountains.

It was so much like it is here that perhaps I shouldn't miss Canada at all.'

'Someone in Canada, then?' Flora queried. 'Were you ever in love, Ailsa—really in love?'

'I don't know.' Ailsa kicked through the red mast. 'No doubt I imagined I was, but there must be something apart from giving all the time.'

'Was that how it was?'

'I think so. Perhaps that was why I was so shocked when Russell told me it was all over. I'd given so much— trust and fidelity and most of my time.'

'You'll meet someone else,' Flora predicted. 'You'll see!'

Ailsa smiled. Had she met in Fergus MacNair a man who could compensate for all the hurt and disillusionment of the past and, if so, wasn't she courting disaster to love for a second time when she knew how badly he had been hurt in his turn?

The road started to climb, taking them away from the burn and the shelter of the trees on to the moor where there was only heather and a few windblown birches grouped above the now cascading burn which had carved a deep channel in the hillside. They could hear the rush of the water as it plunged down over rocks, and once or twice they caught a glimpse of it framed in flowering mountain ash which took Ailsa's breath away.

'It's lovely!' she exclaimed. 'Really beautiful!'

'Wait till you see the rowans in October,' Flora advised. 'They're like a flame all along the burnside. I wonder what will have happened to us between then and now,' she mused.

'It's a long way ahead. Anything could have happened by then.' Ailsa stood quite still on the upland road. 'Listen! Do you hear the sound of pipes?'

Flora seemed unimpressed.

'That will be Duncan Carmichael,' she said. 'He likes a practice blow before he goes down to the house. He'll be playing for the reels when we start to dance. You're going to enjoy this, Ailsa—I'm sure you will!'

For a moment longer they listened to the lone piper on the hillside, but it did not seem to be a dance he was playing. The music sounded wild and abandoned before it sank, in the end, to a note of lament. Ailsa drew in a deep breath.

'Do they always sound like that, as if they wanted to tear your heart out?' she asked.

'Duncan practises all the time—marches, dances and laments. There's nothing so poignant as a lament, especially when it's played out in the open like this. We're an odd lot, we Highlanders,' Flora concluded. 'We live on our emotions, although we wouldn't dream of admitting it.'

'Hence the bagpipes.'

'I suppose so.' They walked on. 'You should understand that, when you are half a Scot yourself.'

'I'm beginning to realise that there's more of my mother in me than I suspected,' Ailsa admitted. 'I want to put down roots here, Flora, though I think it might be difficult.'

'Because of Fergus?'

'In a way.'

'Give him time,' Flora advised. 'He won't come running half-way to meet you, but he'll recognise what you're trying to do. Especially what you will do for Truan.'

'He gave me the impression that he has no further interest in Truan,' Ailsa said.

'That isn't true. He loves the place,' Flora declared. 'It's part of him—has been ever since he was knee-high to a grasshopper. Funny phrase, that,' she added thoughtfully. 'I wonder where it originated.'

'Probably in America,' Ailsa suggested. 'You don't have too many grasshoppers here, I wouldn't think.'

'Not a lot. We have plenty of midges, though, and they're terrible!' Flora grinned. 'They try to eat you alive in August, even up here among the hills.'

Ailsa laughed, breathing in the moist, cool air and thinking that she was happier than she had ever been in all her life before. This was a new adventure; this was something she had been waiting for!

They came to Lettercairn unexpectedly. Where the hills clustered more closely, coming down to meet each other, a large house stood in the last of the sunshine, its whitewashed walls forming an open-ended square at the end of a long drive. At first glance it seemed to be surrounded by sheep, but soon Ailsa noticed the heavy iron fence which kept them from straying on to the drive or damaging the gardens which were already ablaze with rhododendrons and azaleas in full, magnificent bloom. Other sheep grazed the hillsides in all directions, their bleating loud in the quiet air.

'It's a big farm,' Flora explained, 'but there are two sons to help run it. You'll like Pa Struthers; he's a poppet! Always teasing. And you'll like Alex and Graham. They appear to be shy, but they're not really once you get to know them. Just a bit slow about making new friends.'

'No daughters?' asked Ailsa

'No. That's why Mrs Struthers likes to give big parties like this.'

'Hoping for a daughter-in-law?'

'Perhaps she is, but I think she just loves having young people around. She's very good-looking,' Flora added.

They were approaching the door where a tall, handsome woman with bright red hair stood waiting to receive them.

'Surely you haven't walked all the way!' she exclaimed as she shook hands first with Flora and then her companion. 'You must be Miss Mallory?' she guessed.

'The girl from Toronto!' laughed Ailsa, suddenly sure of her welcome in this obviously happy household. 'I've been given my label already!'

'We'll want something more personal than that,' Naomi Struthers told her. 'Ailsa, isn't it? Welcome to Glen Truan, Ailsa. We're glad you could come.'

They were ushered into a large and noisy hall where tall, kilted figures shamed the scattering of girls in party dresses which were neither new nor fashionable. There was much chatter and wholehearted laughter as friend greeted friend after a long, cold winter.

'Everyone is ready to play a little after the lambing season is over,' Naomi Struthers observed. 'Come and meet my sons.'

Alex and Graham were both over six feet tall with bright red hair like their mother's and vividly blue eyes.

Their skin was clear and fresh, evidence of a life spent mostly in the open air, while they wore their kilts with grave dignity and a sort of shy pride.

'Are you liking Truan?' asked Alex. 'Do you think you might take to life up here once you are properly settled in?'

At least he was allowing her a period of adjustment. Ailsa smiled at him.

'I came prepared to like it,' she told him. 'My first two weeks have been hectic, there was so much to do, but I'm sure I'll get the hang of things in the end. This is a bonus,' she allowed, looking up towards the rafters where a gallery ran round three sides of the hall. 'Have you always lived here?'

'For five generations,' Graham acknowledged. 'That's including Alex and me. There's something special about it. Have you a big family back in Toronto, Miss Mallory?'

'Only my mother.' Ailsa was looking around the hall in the hope of seeing another kilted figure she knew, but there was no sign of Tom, or Fergus either.

Alex brought her a drink which he had rescued from a large, fat man carrying a tray. He also wore a kilt which, in spite of his considerable girth, hung splendidly on him.

'Why does everyone look splendid in Highland evening dress? I can't think of anything more flattering,' Ailsa declared.

'It isn't meant to flatter,' Graham assured her seriously. 'It's traditional, and we keep it up because it's sort of second nature to us. It's far from being fancy dress.'

Ailsa's gaze still lingered on the door where more and more guests were arriving, much to his mother's delight.

'I'm sure half the countryside must be here by now,' she smiled.

'More than that!' Alex agreed. 'The MacDougalls have come up from Oban and the MacDonalds have just arrived from Inverness. Come and meet them,' he invited.

After his first few introductions it was difficult for Ailsa to remember who was who. Flora had disappeared in the crowd, laughing as she greeted people she hadn't seen for months, but Ailsa was prepared to stand on her own two feet and become one of them. After all, she would be living here for a very long time and she would need neighbours.

'We'll be dancing in a minute,' Alex told her, 'but first of all, come and eat!'

A buffet supper had been set out in the adjoining dining-room whose windows framed a picture of the hills, and before they had gone very far a handsome elderly man came to greet her.

'Well, Ailsa Mallory, how are you enjoying Truan?' he asked. 'I hear you are performing wonders at the Lodge already.'

'This is my father,' Alex introduced them. 'Beware of him, because he'll dance you off your feet if you're not careful!'

'Which is more than can be said of my sons!'

James Struthers' lean, weatherbeaten face was dominated by a long, high-bridged nose and two mischievously-twinkling eyes which suggested a never-failing sense of humour and perhaps something more. Behind them Ailsa detected a genuine friendliness which she was eager to embrace as she looked back at him and smiled.

'Everyone should learn to dance,' she said. 'It's part of the joy of life, but it's going to take me a while to learn about reels and things!'

'They're not too difficult once you get the hang of them, and the music helps,' he encouraged her.

'Bagpipe music! We heard someone playing as we came up the glen,' she told him. 'Flora said it would be Duncan Carmichael getting in some practice before we started to dance.'

'Well, she was wrong,' James told her. 'Duncan was down here shifting tables. It would be Fergus you heard. He often brings his pipes with him when we're having a *ceilidh*.'

'Fergus MacNair?' Ailsa could hardly believe what she had just heard.

'The very same,' he agreed. 'Didn't you know?'

'I had no idea. What he was playing wasn't dance music,' Ailsa remembered. 'Flora said it would be a lament.'

'He could be playing anything,' said James, 'just to keep his hand in.'

'It sounded—terribly sad. Much more so up there on the hill,' Ailsa reflected.

He took her arm, leading her towards the buffet.

'Fergus is worth his weight in gold,' he said. 'You'll find that out in next to no time.'

Had she found it out already? Ailsa took the plate he offered with the deep conviction that she had.

She was standing beside one of the long, embrasured windows when Fergus came in, magnificent in his kilt as she had imagined him, with Tom carrying a set of bagpipes under his arm.

'Fergus must have been giving him a wee lesson,' James decided. 'Tom's keen to learn, even though he is a Lowlander and will never be able to play with passion in his touch.'

'Is that what it takes—a passionate reaction to life and how it should be lived?' asked Ailsa.

'You could say that,' her host agreed, 'but I wouldn't call Fergus a passionate man in the ordinary way. He cares about things and I suppose he can feel deep emotion like the rest of us, but he isn't an angry man, nor would he bear a grudge for very long. He'd come to terms with it, if you ask me, and after that he would try to forget about it.'

'Which might not be so easy to do.' Ailsa was watching Fergus as he approached, walking tall and straight towards her through the crowd. 'He must have come here many times in the past in happier circumstances, Mr Struthers.'

'That he did,' James agreed. 'Year after year when the boys were young. He was like a second son in the house and my wife's favourite. Of course, we liked them all—Ewan and Deirdre Buchanan and her mother—but Fergus was the special one.'

The special one! Ailsa could see how true that was as the two men shook hands, clapping each other on the back, and then Fergus turned to look at her and her heart stood still.

'Did you motor up?' he asked. 'We didn't see you on the road.'

Ordinary words, but they lit a torch in her eyes, sending a wild colour into her cheeks which she could not control.

'We walked,' she told him. 'We heard you playing on the hill.'

He looked beyond her.

'You must blame Tom for that,' he said. 'He's determined to master the pipes, but I think he should stick to the chanter for a while.'

'It wasn't Tom playing like that,' she said with absolute certainty. 'Flora told me it was a lament.'

'There are thousands of them,' he answered with seeming indifference, 'and they're all good practice. You must ask Tom to play for you.'

He had referred her to Tom quite deliberately, but she was determined not to let it disconcert her.

'I hear you'll be playing for a reel or two,' she said, 'and I'm determined to dance.'

Fergus reached for a plate, filling it with tempting savouries as she watched.

'Tom will see that you enjoy yourself,' he assured her. 'I'm not much of a dancer, although I can generally stagger through an eightsome reel.'

'Is it very difficult?' she demanded.

He hesitated.

'Why don't we try it and you can make up your mind afterwards?' he suggested.

The colour would not leave her cheeks. He must see that she was delighted.

'I'd like that,' she agreed. 'I'd love to be able to say I could dance an eightsome reel.'

'When you return to Canada?' he asked.

She met his eyes squarely in the light from the wall sconces.

'Fergus, I'm not going back to Canada,' she said. 'I'm here to stay.'

A dance band had gathered in the gallery above the hall and gradually Naomi Struthers' guests filtered out there, drawn by the first strains of a waltz.

Fergus put his arm about Ailsa's waist.

'Don't condemn me too quickly,' he said. 'Once I was quite good at this.'

'I suppose a waltz is thought old-fashioned these days,' Ailsa said, her hand cool in his.

'Not a bit of it! The waltz will never die.'

'Nor a reel?'

'I should hope not,' he said. 'We've been dancing them for centuries.'

They circled the room while their host and hostess watched them from the door.

'They make a bonnie pair,' James Struthers reflected. 'I wonder——'

'Don't let it go to your head,' his wife advised. 'You know what happened the last time you paired Fergus off with the perfect woman. It ended in disaster.'

'This could be different,' James argued, 'and it would mean a MacNair back at the Lodge.'

'You're daydreaming,' Naomi accused him with a look in her eyes which suggested she could be wrong.

Fergus circled the floor with Ailsa in his arms, aware that he had not danced like this for many a long day.

'You get out of the way of it,' he said, 'and it's not so easy to step back once you've got a reputation for providing the music. We used to come to Lettercairn at least once a week and there was generally a *ceilidh* somewhere else in between. Have you ever been to one before?'

'No,' Ailsa confessed, 'but I've heard all about them from my mother.' She felt a new warmth in her heart. 'She had a wonderful singing voice and often entertained at our local concerts. Old ballads were her favourites, and I can almost hear her singing *The Rowan Tree* at this moment.'

'You'll sing it for us?' he suggested. 'We all do our piece, and Tom will play for you. It's part of the tradition.'

'Oh, I couldn't,' she protested. 'It would be too—presumptuous of me.'

'You can sing, can't you?' He held her at arm's length, looking down at her with the one-sided smile she would never forget. 'We don't expect anybody to hide their light under a bushel at a *ceilidh*.'

'I thought I would only be dancing,' she protested.

'A *ceilidh* is more than that,' he informed her. 'It's poetry and readings and songs and tall stories if you've got one to tell. Robin Carmichael is very good at the stories, and Tom has been known to use his fertile imagination on more than one occasion too, so I'll put your name down for a song.'

'Please—no!' begged Ailsa. 'I couldn't do it.'

'You could try.' The dance had ended, but Fergus stood with his arm still round her, willing her to agree. 'I can't imagine you not having a go.'

'This is different, Fergus.' Her lower lip was caught between her teeth. 'It's my first appearance in the glen and I don't want to seem—bold.'

'Who would think that?' he demanded. 'Certainly not the Struthers family. They like you.'

'In that case I can't offend them by singing out of tune! Please let me stay quiet and enjoy myself.'

'I'd like to have heard you singing *The Rowan Tree*,' he said.

'Perhaps another time.'

He led her to where Tom and Flora were standing just inside the door.

'Now for a reel!' said Tom. 'You'll be playing, Fergus?'

'Not this time,' Fergus answered. 'I'll be taking a leaf out of Ailsa's book and dancing instead.'

They chose their partners, forming a square, and Ailsa found herself next to Tom.

'It's easy,' he said. 'Follow me!'

It was far from easy, Ailsa thought, but there was an exhilaration about the reel that flushed her cheeks, adding to the sparkle in her eyes as they wheeled and circled in time to the piper's tune. Duncan Carmichael was in his element, blowing away with all his might as he tapped out the rhythm with a practised foot. When the reel was over Ailsa collapsed into the nearest chair.

'I'm completely exhausted!' she gasped. 'How many eightsomes can you really dance in one night?'

'Three or four at a neat guess,' Tom returned, 'quite apart from Strip the Willow and a few others! You managed pretty well, may I say? We'll make a Highlandwoman out of you eventually!'

Ailsa held Fergus's gaze.

'I'm going to make sure of that,' she said.

The evening progressed with amazing rapidity and all too soon it was time to go.

'Do you need a lift?' asked Tom.

'We'd be grateful, as you can well imagine!' Flora answered. 'My feet have been trodden on all evening and I can hardly walk!'

'Traitor!' grinned Tom. 'You know I had on the wrong shoes. I meant to bring my best dancing pumps, but I must have used them for some other purpose.'

'You know you haven't got a special pair of dancing shoes,' Flora laughed. 'Truthfully, I half expected you to turn up in your wellies!'

'For that you'll sit in the front of the Rover all the way back,' he told her as they moved to say goodnight to their host and hostess.

'Come again,' Naomi Struthers invited spontaneously, while her husband suggested artlessly, 'Fergus could bring you. It's far too long since we saw him up this way.'

'Thank you,' Ailsa said, waiting for Fergus to walk with her to the Range Rover where Tom and Flora were already climbing into the front seat.

It was a fine night with a moon already high above the hills and sound carrying a long way, a fitting conclusion to a wonderful party, Ailsa thought, settling down in the back of the Range Rover with Fergus by her side.

'I think you enjoyed yourself,' he said.

'Who wouldn't?' she answered. 'The Struthers are so kind.'

They lapsed into a comfortable silence, sitting no more than a heartbeat away, and she wished the journey would never end. Tom and Flora chatted happily in the front seat, their voices muted, until Flora began to sing.

> Far over yon hills of the heather sae green,
> And down by the corrie that sings to the sea,
> The bonnie young Flora sat sighing her lane,
> The dew on her plaid and the tear in her e'e.

She looked at a boat with the breezes that swung
Away on the wave like a bird of the main,
And aye as it lessened she sighed as she sung,
Farewell to the lad I shall ne'er see again...

Why had she chosen that old, tender song with its
ever-haunting memory? Ailsa could hear her mother's
voice singing as she played her own accompaniment on
the piano in that far-away house in Blair's Landing where
she had been born. It was the song she remembered best,
but she could not sing it with Flora now because, suddenly, her voice was full of tears.

When they reached the foot of the glen Tom drew up
as if at some unspoken command.

'We'll drop you here, Fergus,' he said. 'No point in
you coming all the way and back again.'

Fergus's cottage was no more than a stone's throw
away, but Ailsa knew that he was also shielding his friend
from the hurt of making that well-known journey up the
drive to Truan Lodge.

'We'll see you soon,' said Flora as Fergus got out.
'I'm off to Glasgow on Sunday, but it won't be long
before I'm back again. Meanwhile, good luck with the
fish!'

Tom set them down at the side door to the Lodge.

'I think Fergus enjoyed tonight,' he said. 'I know I
did.'

'There will be other *ceilidhs*,' Flora said wistfully.

Ailsa led the way into the house. It was two o'clock
in the morning, but a light still burned in the small sitting-
room where Martha Birch was waiting for them. She got
to her feet as they reached the door, looking directly at
Ailsa.

'There's been a telephone call for you,' she announced with an odd sort of satisfaction. 'From Paris.'

'Who could be phoning me from Paris?' Ailsa wondered. 'I've never been there.'

'It was a Mr Russell Forgreave,' Martha enlightened
her importantly. 'He is on his way here. He's been in
Paris selling skins for his company and he would like to
see you.'

'I can't believe it!' gasped Ailsa. 'I never thought of Russ——'

'I told him to come, of course,' Mrs Birch went on. 'I said you would be pleased to see an old friend from Canada.'

Confused and surprised, Ailsa was aware of a rush of sudden anger as she returned her housekeeper's un-wavering gaze.

'You had no right to invite him here without—without me knowing about it,' she objected. 'He could have phoned tomorrow morning to check. I'm afraid you've exceeded your authority, Mrs Birch.'

For the first time she recognised antagonism in Martha Birch's eyes.

'I don't think so,' the older woman said coldly. 'He described himself as a very old friend—your former fiancé, as a matter of fact—and he was leaving Paris tonight.' She glanced at the clock ticking away the minutes on the mantelpiece. 'Or should I say *last* night? It is nearly two o'clock in the morning,' she pointed out with a glance in her daughter's direction which Flora chose to ignore. 'He will be in England by now.'

'Did he give you an address?' asked Ailsa, feeling as if she was clutching at straws. 'Somewhere where I could contact him before he comes all this way?'

Mrs Birch favoured her with a brief smile.

'I didn't think of asking him for a London address,' she said slowly. 'I gathered that he did not want to stay in London for long and would prefer to come straight here. He asked if you could meet him at the airport and I said I was sure you would.'

'Glasgow!' Ailsa exclaimed. 'It's half a day's journey!'

'Surely,' Martha Birch suggested, seeing her con-fusion, 'you will be wanting to make an old friend welcome.'

'Yes.' Ailsa took off her velvet cloak, laying it over the back of a chair. 'I'm sorry I was sharp with you just now, Mrs Birch, but I was very much surprised. Russ was the last person I expected to hear from, and I had no idea he was in Paris.'

'He sounded a very nice young man.' Mrs Birch turned to the door. 'I've set a tray for you, so I'll say goodnight.' She turned to Flora. 'Did Fergus bring you home?' she asked.

'No.' Flora looked uneasy. 'It was Tom. We dropped Fergus at the foot of the glen—at his cottage, because it seemed pointless bringing him all the way through the village when he would just have to go back again. Tom was going to the fish farm, anyway.'

'I wonder he doesn't get tired of living in that caravan,' Martha sniffed, 'but perhaps he prefers it. I've no doubt living rough like that will appeal to his gypsy instincts!'

Flora turned to inspect the tray her mother had prepared for them.

'Tom isn't like that at all,' she said. 'He's a highly intelligent person with a degree in Engineering, only he isn't using it at the moment.'

Martha paused at the door. 'Dear me!' she remarked. 'The things you hear if you live long enough!'

When she had gone Flora unscrewed the top of the flask.

'Cocoa?' she asked. 'You look as if you could do with a nightcap.'

Ailsa sat down in the nearest chair.

'I've had a bit of a shock,' she admitted.

'About Russell Forgreave?'

'Well, about him turning up out of the blue like this.' Ailsa gazed into the dying fire. 'It's something I hadn't reckoned on.'

'Did you invite him to come before you left Canada?'

'No—we'd parted long before I knew about Truan. It was a very long time ago.'

'Mother said you were engaged to him.'

'Yes. We were engaged for nearly a year before he broke it off,' Ailsa admitted flatly.

'I'm sorry!' Flora poured the steaming beverage into one of the mugs on the tray. 'Does it still hurt?'

Ailsa continued to look into the fire where the logs were almost burned out.

'I don't know,' she said slowly. 'I won't know until I've seen Russ again.'

Confronted by the past, she knew that she must face the issue of her long-lamented love, and it would not be easy. Her heart had raced for a moment at the sound of

Russell's name, her pulse-beats quickening, but under-
neath it all was confusion. Face to face with her past
love, would she find it to be as strong and demanding
as ever, or had it died a natural death in the months
between?

'I've no alternative,' she decided slowly, 'but to bring
him to Truan.'

That was what Mrs Birch had achieved in her own
devious way when she had failed to ask Russell for a
London address and had only taken his flight number
and the time of his arrival at Glasgow airport.

'I have to go and meet him,' said Ailsa, taking the
mug from Flora with a sense of the inevitable. 'Will you
come with me?'

Flora hesitated.

'No,' Ailsa said quickly, regretting her impulse immediately, 'I shouldn't have asked that. You have enough
to do, packing to go back to Glasgow. I was being a bit
of a coward because I know quite well I have to go alone.'

'I'll be leaving on Sunday,' Flora said, 'and I'd like
to say goodbye to Tom.'

'Of course!'

They drank their cocoa, crouched in front of the fire
which was no more than a pile of embers now. I have
to go, Ailsa thought; I have to make quite sure that it's
all over between Russ and me.

'It's time we went to bed,' Flora said, 'if you are to
be up early to go to Glasgow. I thought we might have
gone somewhere special today, but we'll have to wait till
I get back. Unless—— ' She paused, not knowing how
to put what she was going to say. 'Unless you go back
to Canada.'

'With Russ?' Ailsa put her mug back on to the tray.
'How could I leave at a moment's notice, even with Russ,
when there's so much to do here and at the fish farm?
I've asked for a stake in Fergus's business, so it would
involve him, and Tom too. I couldn't just cut adrift after
all I've promised to do.'

'It depends how much you're in love,' Flora said
quietly. 'You might decide to abandon everything and
not even consider Truan. Sometimes love is like that.'

'Oh, Flora,' Ailsa sighed, 'why must we be faced with so many decisions? Different decisions,' she added as she turned to the door. 'Do you think your mother has fed George?'

'She must have done.' Flora carried the tray towards the kitchens. 'There hasn't been a bleat out of him since we came in. I bet he's sound asleep and dreaming of milk in the morning.'

When morning came the mist was down on the hills, obliterating the view across the loch. Was it an omen, Ailsa wondered, that the day would not be fair?

'It could clear up long before eleven,' Martha Birch said when Ailsa went down to the small sitting-room ready for her unexpected journey. 'It generally does at this time of year, and Glasgow isn't often fog-bound. Your friend will be on time, I'm quite sure.'

'Mrs Birch,' Ailsa pointed out, 'if Russ comes back with me it means that he'll have to stay here, at least for the night.'

'That won't be any trouble.' The housekeeper seemed even glad of the extra work. 'It will be nice to have a few young people about the place for a change. If—your friend decides to stay maybe you could do some entertaining,' she added. 'After Lettercairn it will be expected of you.'

Ailsa could not look back to Lettercairn without the memory of Fergus intervening, remembering how happily they had danced the evening away while Duncan Carmichael had played his pipes and song and story had sped the hours until well after midnight, but coming home through the glen with only the light of the moon to guide them had been the true magic, while Flora sang in her sweet soprano voice the songs Ailsa already knew from her Canadian childhood.

'We'll think about entertaining later on,' she decided. 'Perhaps when Flora comes home again.'

Martha Birch came out to stand on the terrace as she drove away.

'Have a pleasant journey,' she said. 'I'll hold the dinner back till eight o'clock and prepare a room for Mr Forgreave in the main wing.'

'Anywhere will do,' Ailsa responded. 'He may not stay more than one night.'

The morning mist had lifted before she reached Connel Ferry, but it was down again as she negotiated the winding shore of Loch Lomond where she could scarcely see the surrounding mountains. Blinded by it for a moment, she thought how much it resembled her present frame of mind, grey and impenetrable, without any hope of seeing clearly until she had steered her way through it and come out in the sun again.

The sun did come out as she crossed the Erskine Bridge and soon she was heading for the airport with plenty of time to spare. As the minutes ticked away towards her meeting with the man who had been her first love, her sense of confusion only deepened as she wondered how they would meet and what they would have to say to one another.

Better to leave it to the impulse of the moment, she decided, parking her car without difficulty before she mounted the double stairway to the concourse and looked at the clock. An hour to wait! It seemed a very long time to be left wondering what would come of this meeting, with her heart pounding at the very thought of it and her hands unsteady as she put her car keys into her pocket, turning finally to the restaurant on the second floor where she ordered a meal.

The light salad with prawns which was placed before her only sent her thoughts winging back to Truan and the fish farm on the shore, to Fergus and Tom who would very soon be her partners in a new enterprise which she hoped would stabilise her position in the glen. If it all worked out as successfully as she expected, it would bring extra vitality to the village and renewed hope to a small community which had dwindled for lack of work in the past.

She paid her bill, powdered her nose in the ladies' room, and walked determinedly towards the arrivals gate. If this was to be her Waterloo she would know in the next few minutes!

The London plane was already in. She had watched its arrival through the wide glass windows where other travellers waited for other flights seated on benches along the wall, and now her heart was beating steadily, neither in panic nor anticipation. Just waiting, she thought. She could feel nothing as the first few passengers came through the gate, and then she saw him. Russell pushed his way ahead of his fellow-travellers with the same arrogance which had characterised him in the past, coming towards her immediately.

'Ailsa!' he exclaimed, sweeping her into his arms. 'It's been a long time!'

She could not return his greeting immediately, standing there with his arms about her experiencing all the old surge of emotion which she had felt so strongly in the past, although this time it was tempered with a certain amount of caution.

'I wish I'd known you were coming—known sooner,' she admitted, drawing away from his spontaneous embrace, her breath held as if to give herself more time, her eyes desperately searching his. 'It was a very big surprise, and I had no idea who could be calling me from Paris.'

'It was too near for me *not* to call you,' he said as he led her away from the gate, 'and I didn't have a lot of time. We've built up quite a business with the Paris couture houses and I had to do the rounds. Otherwise I would have phoned you earlier. I might even have asked you to fly over to Paris so that we could meet.'

'That would have been impossible,' she said, going with him to collect his luggage. 'I've been very, very busy since I got here. There's been so much to do.'

'Tell me about Truan,' Russell asked when he had claimed his grip and a rather large leather suitcase. 'Did it come up to expectations, or were there none?'

'Everything happened so suddenly,' Ailsa explained. 'One minute I was wondering what to do with myself in Toronto, the next I had the chance of building a new life in Scotland. I've found it very beautiful at Truan and very stimulating.'

'A Highland estate,' he mused. 'What could possibly interest you in that?'

'A great many things,' she told him. 'You'll have to make your decision about them once you've seen Truan.'

'You sound as if you intend to stay there,' he suggested incredulously as they crossed to the car park, 'but I can't imagine you wanting to opt out of things to that extent, knowing you as I did.'

'It wasn't much different in Canada,' she pointed out. 'We went to the Algonquin when the snow melted in the spring to sail on the lake just as they do at Loch Truan, although there you can sail all the year round if the spirit moves you, and there are parties there too, Russ, for our amusement, as well as hard work. I was at one last night, as a matter of fact, when you phoned. My first party in the glen! It was quite a revelation to me!'

'You sound quite sentimental about it,' he observed, putting his luggage into the back of the car. 'What's the Lodge like?'

'Part of it has been shut up for a long time, but I'm working on that,' she admitted. 'I want it back to its former glory, I suppose, because it's been neglected for a long time.'

'It belonged to your uncle, I hear.' He came to stand beside her, offering the couturier's box he had carried from the plane. 'This is for you,' he said, 'because it will soon be your birthday. Funny how I remember,' he added, stooping to kiss her on the lips.

'I couldn't take it—whatever it is!' Ailsa drew back as much from the casual kiss as from the present he had offered.

'Oh, but you don't know what it is yet!' he smiled, tossing the offending box on to the back seat. 'You'll change your mind when you see it, my love. I have immaculate taste, as you were so fond of telling me not so long ago!'

She turned to look at him, her pulses racing.

'Russ,' she asked, 'why have you come?'

'Why not?' he countered. 'I wanted to see you again. Isn't that reason enough?'

'I don't think so.' She swallowed hard. 'I've started to make a new life for myself.'

'Are you asking me to go straight back to Canada,' he challenged, 'without even seeing your miraculous inheritance?'

'I wouldn't suggest anything so uncivilised,' she answered. 'You're welcome to come to Truan, of course, now that you've travelled so far, and I'll make you welcome for as long as you want to stay. Mrs Birch— you spoke to her on the telephone—has prepared a room for you.'

'She was far more welcoming than you appear to be, my love,' he said tersely. 'Who exactly is Mrs Birch?

'She was my uncle's housekeeper for the past six years and before that she was housekeeper to the old laird.'

'A laird!' he exclaimed. 'With all the trimmings—kilt and all?'

'He's dead,' Ailsa said quietly. 'There's only his son left.'

'And why isn't he at Truan Lodge?'

'It's—a long story. He was only the second son and he had to sell the estate almost as soon as he inherited it—because of debt, maybe. I haven't asked for the details. One doesn't in a place like Truan.'

'In case you hurt their pride,' he suggested. 'Does it really matter now that you're in charge?'

Ailsa drove out of the car park.

'It matters a great deal,' she answered slowly, 'but you have to understand these people. You have to know exactly how they feel giving up something as precious to them as an old family home which has been theirs for several hundred years. You have to think about it like that, all those years under one roof, loving the place because it's truly part of them—and then having to go, having to give it all up and still remain there seeing a stranger in their place doing the things for the estate that they were never able to do.'

When she paused to draw breath Russell said without consideration, 'It sounds like damn bad management to me. When a place is run into the ground like that it must be somebody's fault, but I guess they'll be crying "hard luck" and moaning about fate or whatever they call it in the Gaelic.'

Ailsa felt the colour mounting to her cheeks and a hard anger gathering in her throat.

'It isn't like that at all,' she protested, 'and I don't really want to discuss it. How did you find out where I had gone?'

'I read all about it in *The Times*,' he said. 'We were quite impressed—I suppose that's the word I want. Then I phoned your mother and got your address.'

'Oh, I see!' It would have been easy enough for him to trace her when they had both lived in the same city for so long. 'How is Toronto?' she asked.

'Flourishing, as usual. There can't have been many changes since you left. Why do you ask?'

'I suppose,' she said, driving through the city which would soon be as well known to her, 'because it was the conventional thing to do.'

'Not from sudden nostalgia?'

'I don't think so. I'm very content as I am.'

'You were always independent, my love, but time could change all that.'

Ailsa didn't answer him, giving her full attention to the traffic and the way ahead. She wanted to show him Scotland at its best, but by the time they reached Crianlarich the mist had come down again, wrapping the Grampians in a white shroud which obscured their majesty and made visibility a hazard even on the road.

'Apart from the legendary Loch Lomond,' asked Russell, 'is there anything else?'

She bit her lip, looking around her at the shrouded countryside.

'There's a whole world of beauty everywhere,' she explained. 'What we should be seeing is the great peaks of the Grampian Mountains—Ben Ledi, Ben Vorlich and Ben More—and after that Cruachan, but perhaps it will clear as we go farther west. I hope so, because I would like you to see Scotland as it really is.'

'Surely the mist will rise in a day or two,' he suggested. 'I have a week to spare.'

'A week?' she repeated almost in dismay. 'I thought—knowing you, I thought you'd only be able to stay overnight.'

'I've surprised you, in that case!' he laughed. 'Your delightful Mrs Birch said you'd be pleased to have me stay for as long as I liked.'

'Yes—yes, of course. I didn't mean to be rude, Russ, or—inhospitable, and I suppose Mrs Birch was just being polite.'

'She sounds like a charming old dear,' he mused. 'I suppose she *is* old?'

'Fiftyish, I shouldn't wonder. She has a twenty-two year-old daughter.'

'Your age,' he said. 'Are you friends?'

'I hope so.'

'What about the men about the glen?'

A high colour sped back into her cheeks.

'Most of them are farmers, and we have a thriving trout industry in the village and a boatyard at the head of the loch.'

'It sounds promising,' he agreed. 'Boatyards I've seen before. Who breeds the trout?'

Ailsa hesitated.

'Tom Kelvin, who came up from Glasgow University and decided to stay, and Fergus MacNair who once owned Truan before he sold out to my uncle six years ago.'

'The dispossessed one!' he said, watching her closely. 'How does he feel about you?'

'Not very happy, I expect, though he would never show it.' Ailsa steered the car towards the Pass of Brander, looking down at the dark trough of water running between the mountains as if she might see into the darker places of a man's soul. 'It must have been difficult for him at first.'

'And Tom Kelvin?' he asked.

'Oh, Tom has become a friend. Nobody could help liking him,' Ailsa declared, 'and I'm sure he would never let Fergus down.'

'If Fergus MacNair came courting that would solve all his problems,' Russell suggested drily.

Her hands tightened their grip on the steering-wheel till her knuckles showed.

'Courting me, do you mean?' she said harshly. 'That would never happen, Russ, not for the reason you're suggesting.'

'OK!' he laughed. 'I stand condemned. Fergus MacNair is too strong, too noble a type to marry for

what he could get out of it. Point taken! But I still don't
see why it should upset you so much.'

'I'm not upset!'

'Distressed, then. You were very quick to leap to his
defence,' he pointed out.

'Can we not talk about it?' she suggested. 'If we could
see clearly, Cruachan is just above us on the right,' she
added more calmly. 'The whole mountain has been hol-
lowed out to make an electric power station. I believe
there's a lochan up there on the mountainside that sup-
plies the water and it's pumped back after it's been used
to produce the electricity.'

He smiled at her effort to interest him in their surroundings, still intrigued by the thought of Fergus
MacNair. Somehow her friendship with Tom Kelvin
seemed irrelevant.

When they reached Connel Ferry the whole magnificent panorama of Mull and the islands lay before them.

'I'm glad it's cleared,' said Ailsa. 'I wanted you to see
it at its very best.'

'I must admit,' said Russell, 'it's quite something. Is
that Mull over there?'

'Mull and Kerrera, and the mountains across the sound
are the Mountains of Morvern, which we also see from
Truan.'

'Dark and unfathomable,' he suggested. 'They'll make
you morbid if they're always like that.'

'They're not. When the sun shines on them they're
magnificent, and even on a bad day they have a certain
majesty.'

'I take your point,' he said. 'How far have we to go
from here?'

'Not very far now. You'll love it at Truan, Russ,' she
declared on a sudden rush of enthusiasm, 'and I'll show
you as much of the Highlands as I can while you're here.
You'll fall in love with it all, as I did.'

When they came to the hill which plunged down to
the village she looked up to the moor as if she half
expected to see a man and his dogs coming down across
the heather, but the moor was bare and uninhabited for
miles. Or so it seemed, yet somewhere up there sheep
would be grazing with their lambs and a herd of red deer

might be watching their progress, frozen into immobility by the sound of the approaching car.

'You won't see Truan till we've turned the next bend,' she told her companion, 'but it's there, all the same, hiding away at the head of the loch.'

'I could do with a drink,' Russell said abruptly. 'Is there a local hostelry, or doesn't Truan run to one?'

'Oh, yes, there's the hotel, but that's beyond the entrance to the Lodge.' She glanced at her watch. 'It's only five o'clock.'

They were on the brow of the hill, looking down on the loch now, and she drew in her breath as the sun burst from the lifting shroud of mist to bathe it in a tender glory.

'This is it?' he asked. 'I must say it has a certain attraction, but it isn't very big, is it?'

He had summed up Truan in a dozen condescending words, and Ailsa was suddenly angry.

'That's just the point,' she said. 'It's small and intimate and caring. Everybody knows everybody else for miles around and they would go out of their way to help if it was needed. It's a community, Russ, in the fullest sense of the word.'

'Do we pass the trout farm?' he asked.

'Yes. It's down there beside the loch.'

'Let's call in,' he suggested with unexpected enthusiasm. 'I'm very interested.'

Ailsa hesitated.

'We could go down tomorrow,' she said.

'Why not now? You said it was only five o'clock.'

'I'm not sure if anyone will be there,' she explained. 'Fergus is often on the hill or at the Keep and Tom could be out at the traps,' she hurried on to explain. 'They put the trout into salt water when they're old enough and select them from there for sale.'

'Let's go see!' suggested Russell. 'If there's no one to show us round we can come back tomorrow.'

Fergus was locking up the caravan when they pulled up at the gate.

'I—wondered if we could have a look at the fish,' Ailsa asked, 'but if it's too late we can come back in the morning.'

'There's no reason why you shouldn't come in now.' Fergus was looking beyond her at her companion. 'I heard you had gone to Glasgow to meet a friend. Flora told me,' he added, 'when she came to say goodbye.'

Russell had got out of the car, smiling broadly.

'This is Russell Forgreave from Toronto,' Ailsa introduced them. 'Fergus MacNair, Russ. He owns the fish farm.'

The two men measured each other with an odd hostility in their respective glances, but Fergus was first to hold out his hand in greeting.

'Did you have a pleasant flight?' he asked. 'The mist was fairly bad here this morning.'

'I only came from Paris,' Russell told him. 'I phoned Ailsa last night to let her know I was on my way, but apparently she was enjoying herself elsewhere.'

'You'd have to witness one of our *ceilidhs* to realise how much!' Fergus said. 'Are you staying for long?'

'About a week, unless Ailsa can persuade me otherwise,' Russell returned. 'She ran away from Toronto very quickly without giving us a chance to dissuade her, so I'm sure anxious to see what the attraction was.' He looked about him. 'Do you hope to expand?' he asked. 'I dare say there's quite a market for trout these days, especially in the cities. We don't have that problem in Canada. Our rivers are full of fish produced naturally.'

'You're very lucky,' said Fergus, 'but I can assure you there's very little difference in the quality of the trout. We get them naturally here too, but not in sufficient quantity to satisfying a growing market. Hence the farming. We're also doing it with salmon and even mussels.'

'This I have to see!' Russell decided. 'Do you mind?'

'Not in the least.' Fergus unlocked the gate. 'I'll get you some gumboots.'

'What in heaven's name are the gumboots for?' Russell demanded as Fergus disappeared. 'The ground isn't wet, but maybe he feels I won't want to spoil my fancy Paris shoes.'

'It isn't that at all,' Ailsa told him. 'It's to prevent infection to the fish. We have to walk through a trough of disinfectant before we can go into the sheds because the tiny trout are so vulnerable to disease.'

'What a palaver!' Russell commented, taking off his shoes.

Fergus was gravely attentive, showing them round while he explained the various stages of growth and the method of feeding to his unexpected guest, yet Ailsa was immediately conscious of a reserve in him which had not been there the evening before. At Lettercairn in the company of his friends he had been a different person, responding to the lighthearted gaiety which she had so much enjoyed, but now he appeared to be holding back, weighing up the situation now that Russell had appeared on the scene to swell their numbers.

When they had toured the sheds he suggested that they might go down to the traps in the loch where Tom was still working. Ailsa glanced at her watch.

'It's almost six,' she said. 'Mrs Birch will be wondering what's happened to us. Perhaps we can come back tomorrow to look at the traps.'

'Any time,' Fergus agreed. 'Tom is sure to be somewhere around.'

When she was re-seated behind the steering-wheel Ailsa looked up at him.

'We'd like some of the end product if you have them to spare,' she suggested. 'Russ is very fond of trout.'

Fergus drew back, as if to consider her request.

'Mrs Birch has already been on the phone,' he said, 'and Flora confirmed her order when she was here an hour ago. By the way,' he added, 'I've been in touch with Alan Hadley and our two lawyers will sort out our contract when you are ready to sign.'

'Oh, thank you, Fergus!' She could think of nothing else to say. 'Will you let me know?'

'You'll get a letter from Doug MacCallum in due course,' he told her, standing back. 'It shouldn't take long.'

'What contract?' asked Russell as they drove away.

'It has to do with the trout farm.' Ailsa was almost reluctant to discuss her private affairs with this man who had once been her closest confidant. 'I've invested some money in it because they're ready to expand and haven't enough capital to do all they want to do. It won't be too much of a gamble,' she assured him confidently. 'Just—a helping hand.'

'Watch how you go in that direction, all the same,' he warned. 'MacNair didn't strike me as being much of a businessman, and he didn't make a great success of the estate when he had the chance, did he?'

The car almost left the road.

'That's preposterous!' Ailsa exclaimed, changing gear rapidly. 'He *didn't* have a chance. I thought I'd made that reasonably clear.'

He turned in the passenger seat to smile at her.

'What you've made clear, my love, is the fact that you're greatly impressed by this man who only has to lift his little finger to have you running in his direction with an open cheque-book in your hand.'

'Russell, that's just not true!' she exclaimed. 'I never imagined Fergus would agree to let me invest my money in the first place, and I suspect it was only after Tom talked him round that he did. Fergus is tremendously proud of this effort they're making, and I won't be pouring my money down the drain, if that's what you think,' she added proudly. 'I've acquired a lot of good, honest common sense since we last met, Russ, and I think I'm using it wisely investing in Truan.'

'Depending how long you mean to remain here,' he stipulated.

'I don't understand you,' she protested. 'As far as I'm concerned, I'm here to stay.'

He laughed briefly, getting out to open the Lodge gates for her.

'I thought we were expected,' he said.

'Flora must have closed the gates without thinking,' Ailsa returned. 'Sometimes the deer stray in if we're not careful and do a lot of damage.'

When they approached the house Martha Birch was standing at the main door to greet their first official visitor.

'Russ, this is Mrs Birch whom you spoke to on the phone,' Ailsa said.

'Mrs Birch, I'm delighted to talk with you again, and I want to say how glad I am that we came to that agreement!' Russell exclaimed.

'Oh, that was nothing,' Martha Birch assured him. 'I couldn't have a friend of Miss Mallory turned away when you were so near. Had you a pleasant flight from Paris?'

'Excellent.' Russell took his grip from the back of the car and walked towards the open door. 'You can bring the box, Ailsa,' he added. 'It's for you, as I explained.'

The housekeeper's gimlet eyes were already on the silver and mauve striped box on the back seat.

'Let me carry it for you,' she offered as Ailsa hesitated. 'It's nice to be getting a present from Paris, isn't it?'

Ailsa walked ahead of her without answering because there was something about Mrs Birch's apparent good humour which was decidedly out of character.

The transformation the housekeeper had made in the hall was also surprising. A welcoming log fire burned cheerfully on the stone hearth between the ancient and-irons, and bowls of freshly-gathered rhododendrons and azaleas brought life and colour to the darker corners beneath the staircase whose wide sweep dominated the whole scene. The broad red carpet had been brushed and the handrail polished till it shone, while the striped dust-covers had been removed from the furniture around the walls.

'You've been working very hard, Mrs Birch,' Ailsa acknowledged. 'It's quite a transformation.'

'It's how it ought to be,' the housekeeper returned. 'How it was in the old days. I've put Mr Forgreave in the Oak Room because of the view.' She led the way towards the staircase. 'If you'll come with me I'll show you the way.'

Russell followed her up the stairs, appreciative of all he saw, especially the portraits.

'These paintings will be of the former owners,' he supposed. 'What an army of kilted splendour! I guess you know all their names, Mrs Birch. I guess you could tell a tale or two about the past!'

'That I could,' Martha Birch assured him, 'but I would never betray a trust by talking about them. I worked for the old laird, helping him to bring up two sons, and I hope I did my duty by them.'

'I'm sure you would, Mrs Birch,' Russell agreed as he followed her along the upper corridor, 'and I'm sure everything you did would be duly appreciated, just as Ailsa must be glad of the help you're giving her now.'

He was exerting his considerable charm on a woman who had rarely been complimented in the past, and Martha succumbed to it as easily as a child would have done except for the fact that she knew she was being used for a purpose.

'You're in here, Russ,' said Ailsa when they reached the open bedroom door. 'I hope you'll be comfortable. If there's anything else you need I'm sure Mrs Birch will get it for you.'

'I feel I have only to ask!' Russell went on into the room. 'Mrs Birch, you're a gem!'

Smiling, Martha Birch went on along the corridor to deposit the silver-striped box on Ailsa's bed before she retreated down the back stairs to the kitchens where Flora was waiting for her.

'What's he like?' asked Flora. 'Ailsa's ex-fiancé?'

'I don't think he'll be ex for very long,' her mother told her. 'He's a really charming young man, and she'd be a fool not to take up with him again if he asked her.'

'And supposing he doesn't?' Flora asked.

'We'll not suppose anything of the kind,' her mother said. 'I don't think he came this far just to say "hello!"'

Ailsa walked slowly along the corridor to her own room, aware of uncertainty and an odd feeling of alarm. Something was happening to her that she could not understand, and the fact that Russell had come back into her life was only a part of it. The rest was like a dark tide surging around her like the waves breaking against a lonely keep. Fergus! she thought, but she could not place him in the wild clamour of her heart.

Automatically she crossed to the bed where Martha Birch had put the silver and mauve striped box on the sprigged counterpane, feeling resentment even before she opened it. What right had Russell to come bearing an expensive gift when he had rejected her love so finally so short a time ago?

Slowly she undid the silk cord which tied it and lifted the lid, to be confronted by a foam of tissue paper and the gleam of fur. Lifting the sable wrap, she held it out in front of her. It was exquisite. The delicately beautiful skins dripped through her fingers, falling on to the bed as a man's figure blocked the doorway.

'Well,' asked Russell 'what do you think of it?'

She turned to look at him.

'It's beautiful,' she said, 'but you know I can't take it.'

'Why ever not?' He came to stand beside her. 'I thought it was just you, and I meant it to say sorry for the past.'

Ailsa returned his look as steadily as she could.

'It may have been "just me" when we were going out together, Russ, but it wouldn't be any use to me now,' she said firmly. 'When and where could I wear it up here among the mountains?'

He put his hands on her shoulders, looking into her eyes.

'You won't always be here,' he said. 'I can't see you wasting your life in a place like Truan. You'll come back to Canada, sooner or later. I know you will.'

He stooped to kiss her on the lips, but she turned her head away and his kiss fell on her cheek.

'I have no intention of coming back,' she told him. 'You must understand that. Russ, I'm here to stay, and nothing you can say or do will change that.'

'It may be how you feel at the moment,' he said, 'because it's all new to you.'

'It's how I'll always feel.'

'I think I can make you change your mind,' he said with overwhelming conceit. 'Meanwhile, you can show me Truan and what you mean to do with it.'

'I'll do my best.'

For the next two days he held her to her promise. They took Flora to Oban where she joined the Glasgow train, driving on south to the Mull of Kintyre in warm sunshine before they returned by Loch Awe in time for an evening meal. Mrs Birch had excelled herself, producing fresh salmon and a succulent joint of prime beef, followed by chocolate éclairs smothered in cream, which they walked off by inspecting the rough land at the loch end of the estate where Ailsa proposed to plant the new trees.

'What's that over there by the loch?' asked Russell, seeing the boat-house between the bushes. 'Have you some sort of sailing craft?'

'It isn't there any more,' Ailsa told him hastily. 'It's at the boatyard having a complete overhaul.'

'Maybe we could take it out if it's ready,' he suggested. 'This must be good sailing country, I guess.'

'Repairs aren't done at the drop of a hat up here,' she said firmly. 'It's a very small yard, and—and I'm not in any hurry to sail someone else's boat.'

'I thought it was yours,' he said. 'Who does it belong to?'

'Fergus MacNair. I think it's his by right, although he doesn't press the point. It was in the boat-house when my uncle bought the estate, and Mrs Birch assumed it was now mine. I think she made a mistake. I feel it really belongs to Fergus, though I don't think he'll ever use it.'

'Not fond of the sea, perhaps,' he mused. 'Mrs Birch is a very astute lady, I would say.' He paused, waiting for her to express an opinion. 'She must be useful to you.'

'She's been here for a very long time.'

'I gathered that. Feels she owns the place in a subtle sort of way, I suppose, like most old servants who have been too long in a post.'

'I need her, Russ.' Ailsa turned back towards the house. 'She knows all there is to know about Truan, and I'll be working blind, in a way, when I come to make major decisions about the house.'

When they reached the Lodge it appeared to be deserted.

'Everyone gone to bed?' he asked. 'Do we lock up?'

'Mrs Birch will be around somewhere,' Ailsa decided. 'She likes to lock up herself. A nightcap?' she suggested.

'A splendid idea!' he agreed.

She followed him into the small sitting-room where a decanter and glasses had been placed ready on a side table.

'Whisky?'

'What else in the land of the malt!'

Mrs Birch came to stand at the door.

'If you're in for the night I'll lock up,' she said. 'After that I'll be away to my bed. I have an early start in the morning.'

They wished her goodnight, sipping their drinks beside the dying fire.

'This is very civilised, I must say,' Russell observed, stretching out his legs across the hearth. 'It would make an ideal holiday get-away-from-it-all.'

Ailsa stiffened.

'It was never meant to be a holiday home,' she returned. 'It never could be. Truan has to be lived in and cared about and full of family all the time. That was why it was built, and that's what it has been for several generations up till now.'

He got up to put his empty glass down on the tray.

'That sort of thing changes all the time,' he said. 'Houses like Truan have become hotels or they're divided up into time-share flats, which would be good business as far as you're concerned.'

She looked at him askance.

'I wouldn't dream of doing anything like that with Truan,' she told him firmly. 'I'm not in this to make money, Russ. I'm not a businesswoman.'

'You're a very desirable one, all the same.' He moved to put his arm about her, drawing her close. 'You've— matured, I think that's the word I'm looking for. You're different, somehow.'

'More experienced, perhaps.'

He smiled as she walked purposefully towards the door.

'I'll follow you up,' she suggested, but she found him waiting for her at the foot of the stairs.

'All these ancestors,' he remarked, looking up at the portraits on the wall above them. 'They're quite a responsibility, don't you think? They would make me uneasy, to say the least.'

'I should say you would have to be born to that sort of responsibility,' Ailsa answered. 'Recently I've come to understand what it must mean.'

'For MacNair, I suppose you mean. Well, there's nothing much he can do about it now, short of marrying you and moving back in.'

She turned at the head of the staircase, looking down at him.

'It's the very last thing Fergus would do,' she said with utter conviction. 'He's not like that.'

'I wouldn't be too sure,' he said, following her along the corridor to her open bedroom door, where they were suddenly confronted by the gift he had brought her from Paris.

'I want you to keep this,' he said, walking towards the bed to pick up the sables. 'No strings attached,' he added, smiling down at her with all the old charm. 'You can't disappoint me.'

Ailsa stood back, refusing to take the sables.

'I wish it had been that way when we were in Canada,' she said. 'No strings attached, Russ. We might have come out of it with less trauma if we hadn't been engaged to be married.'

For a moment he appeared to be disconcerted, but only for a moment.

'We can forget about that,' he said, taking her in his arms. 'We can start again.'

'Oh, Russ.' For a moment she put her head against his shoulder. 'You know it wouldn't work.'

'Who says so?'

'I do. I seem to have—grown away from all that in the past few months. I don't want to feel that way ever again.'

'Are you saying you don't want to be in love for a second time?'

The question startled her.

'That wasn't what I meant. I was thinking about all the pain and disillusionment, all the self-questioning that came afterwards, and the sleepless nights and long, empty days wondering where we'd gone wrong.'

He held her close, pressing her head against his shoulder.

'It was all my fault,' he admitted. 'Giving in to family pressure like I did. My father has always been a hard taskmaster, but now he's retired I'm my own master at

last. I can do as I like with the company and my own
life.'

'Russ,' said Ailsa, 'I don't think we can ever turn back
the page. I've changed; I know I have, and probably so
have you.'

He said without conviction, 'I don't think I'll ever
change. I've always been in love with you.'

Over his shoulder Ailsa saw movement at the open
door.

'Oh, excuse me,' Martha Birch said. 'I was wondering
if there was anything else Mr Forgreave might be
needing.'

Russell released Ailsa as he turned towards her,
smiling.

'Nothing, Mrs Birch, thank you,' he said. 'I have
everything I want for now.'

CHAPTER SIX

FOR the next few days Ailsa tried to entertain her unexpected guest as best she could, driving him around the
Highlands and taking him to Skye, which really did impress him. They were good companions in a great many
ways, exchanging memories of the happier past when
they had first met, but always Ailsa was conscious of
an underlying tension, a holding back within herself
which had to do with Truan and the way she wanted to
live her life. More and more she realised that this sleek,
sophisticated man of the world was out of place in her
Hebridean paradise where only a man like Fergus
MacNair really belonged.

The thought startled her, because it could never be
anything more than a pipe-dream, one she had imagined
for herself. Fergus was no more in love with her than
Tom was.

As they travelled to and from Truan on their various
excursions she began to see Russell as shallow compared
with Fergus and the people she now counted as her
friends. It was all about sincerity and a different kind
of love.

When they returned to the Lodge late one evening Fergus had been there.

'He came with some papers for you to sign,' Martha told her, 'so I asked if he could leave them for you. They are in the study on your desk.' She stood waiting, as if she had something to say. 'I was pleased when he stayed for a while looking at what we've done with the house,' she added deliberately. 'It's the first time he's been here for several years.'

'I'm glad he came,' Ailsa answered. 'I'm glad he doesn't feel he should stay away because of me.'

'Why should he feel that?' Martha wanted to know. 'I made him welcome, and we spoke of old times—and Flora.'

'Yes. Yes, I understand.' Ailsa was far from understanding, but it was not the sort of thing she could let Mrs Birch see. 'Did Fergus say when he wanted the contract back?'

'He said perhaps you could leave it at Cuilfail when you were passing, if it wasn't too much trouble in the circumstances.' Martha looked at their guest across the breadth of the hall. 'You've had another nice day, Mr Forgreave. I trust you've enjoyed yourself.'

'Very much, Mrs Birch.' He smiled into her calculating eyes. 'And now I'm sure I'm going to enjoy a perfect dinner just as much. I'm more or less starving!'

Smiling with satisfaction, Martha Birch turned away. 'It's my pleasure, I'm sure,' she declared.

'You flatterer!' laughed Ailsa. 'You could charm a bird off a tree!'

'I haven't been able to charm you into becoming engaged to me again,' Russell pointed out, 'but I'll keep on trying.'

She paused on her way to the study to pick up the contract Fergus had brought for her to sign.

'Russ,' she said, 'I'm trying not to be cruel, but that's all over. I think we both know it,' she added gently, 'so why pretend? I couldn't marry you now—not ever—because I know I've changed. I want you to go back to Canada feeling sure about that and without any hard feelings—if you can.'

'Is this tit for tat?' he asked, pulling her round to face him. 'Are you giving me a taste of my own medicine just to get even?'

'No.' She drew away. 'Please don't think that, because it's just something I wouldn't do. You'll go back to Toronto and go on with your work and forget all about me, and very soon you'll meet someone else. Someone more suitable than me.'

'You think so? Well, we'll see.' He didn't look too pleased with himself. 'Are you going to give me a farewell party? Mrs Birch says you ought to be inviting people in, returning hospitality, and I've already met a few of your men friends, so you could make a gesture on that account, at least.'

'Why not?' she shrugged, relieved that he was now prepared to go. 'It will have to be something unconventional. We haven't a lot of time.'

He smiled as he recognised his swift dismissal.

'How about a barbecue?' he asked.

'It would rain and put out the fire!'

'Talk about putting out a fire,' he said coolly, 'would you invite Fergus MacNair?'

Ailsa flushed. 'And Tom Kelvin, and the Struthers family from Lettercairn,' she said. 'You met them yesterday when I took you up the glen.'

'The Dominant Matriarch and the Sheep Farmer! Yes, I remember. Would they come?'

'It would be short notice, but I think so. I'd also like to ask the district nurse and one or two other people I know.' The sorrow in Ailsa's eyes changed to enthusiasm. 'We'll try a barbecue and bother the weather!' she decided.

Mrs Birch, when consulted, thought an out-of-doors meal was tempting fate, but she ordered the steaks, all the same, leaving the building of the barbecue itself to their guest.

'It's like smoking kippers,' she commented when she saw his handiwork with some bricks and an iron grill. 'We'd be better with a buffet in the hall, like it used to be.'

'We can think about a buffet as a standby,' said Ailsa, 'provided it isn't too much work for you, Mrs Birch. I'll help with the sweets,' she offered. 'I'm quite up on trifles and chocolate gateau!'

'You're wishing me away,' Russell said with a grimace, 'but I still think you'll change your mind about marrying me!'

Ailsa signed the contract Fergus had left for her, making Russell's work on the barbecue an excuse to go to Cuilfail on her own the following afternoon. She had phoned Lettercairn during the morning and received an instant acceptance, and also one from the district nurse and Moira Cameron at the post office, and Mrs Birch could be relied upon to invite the others.

'I wish Flora could be here,' she said on her way out. 'She would enjoy it.'

Ailsa reached the fish farm as Fergus and Tom came up from the lochside.

'Hello!' she called to them. 'I've brought back the contract.'

'Duly signed, sealed and delivered!' Tom laughed. 'How do, pardner!'

'I'm only a third partner,' she said, looking at Fergus. 'I'm so sorry I was out when you came,' she added. 'I'd promised to show Russ the Highlands.'

'So Mrs Birch explained.' He allowed Tom to take the signed document from her. 'There was no great hurry for your signature. Tom and I have already signed.'

'Do you think this might call for a celebration?' she asked diffidently. 'I'm giving a small party at the Lodge on Saturday. It's supposed to be a barbecue, weather permitting. Would you come?'

'Haven't been to a barbecue in years,' Tom remarked. 'Of course I'll come!'

Fergus hesitated. 'I'm collecting some sheep from Perth,' he said. 'I could be there all day.'

'Ailsa is talking about the evening,' Tom pointed out. 'You've time enough to get to Perth and back by six o'clock.'

'Please come,' said Ailsa. 'It's my first effort at entertaining.'

'I'm sure you'll do very well.'

'But will you come?' she persisted. 'With Tom?'

'I'll see that he does,' Tom promised, moving towards the caravan with the signed contract. 'Leave it to me.'

Ailsa drew in a deep breath.

'Have I spoken out of turn?' she asked. 'I know coming to your old home must hurt, Fergus, but you were there yesterday. You've made the break.'

'Yes,' he agreed, 'and I didn't find it so very difficult after all.' He looked down at her, his eyes stormy. 'Mrs Birch made it easy, up to a point, but making a habit of it might be a different matter.'

'Surely you were made welcome,' she protested. 'Mrs Birch is very fond of you.'

'There could be no doubt about Mrs Birch's welcome, but she is hardly the mistress of Truan,' he pointed out. 'I came to see you, much against my will, but you weren't there. Perhaps I should have waited for your formal invitation.'

'Fergus, you know you'll never need to wait for that,' she assured him. 'You're welcome to come to the Lodge at any time, and I'm truly sorry I wasn't there yesterday, but I had to entertain Russ as best I could. He's a very old friend.'

'Yes, Mrs Birch thought so.'

A deep colour rushed to her cheeks.

'She's been—speaking out of turn!' She paused for a moment, wanting to tell him the truth. 'If you have to know, Russ and I were engaged once. We were childhood friends in Canada, but it all came to nothing. We parted months before I came to Scotland. It was all over a long time ago.'

Fergus continued to look down at her, only half believing.

'I didn't go to the Lodge to ask you about the past,' he said slowly. 'I went with the odd idea of making you feel that you were not resented. I lost Truan, fair and square, and I think I would rather see you there than anyone else. These things are hard to say,' he looked down at his boots, 'but I've got to say them, all the same. If you stay here, Truan will take on new life, and that means that I can't resent you any more.'

Ailsa looked into his darkened eyes.

'I know how you must have felt, Fergus, when I first came here,' she began, 'seeing a stranger in possession of your old home, but believe me, I do mean to try at the Lodge—and knowing you don't resent me personally will make a big difference. I thought when we made the bargain about the fish farm that we could work together without acrimony, and perhaps we can. I don't mean to be an absentee landlord, you can rest assured about that, but I'd like to have your opinion about a lot of things. If you don't want to visit the Lodge too often,' she added, 'I'll try to understand that too.'

'I've made the effort,' he said quietly, 'and it wasn't as traumatic as I expected.'

'I'm glad.' She held out her hand. 'We're partners, remember!'

Fergus took her fingers in his, holding them in a firm clasp for a moment before he let them go.

'Tom should be in on this,' he said lightly. 'Will you come up to the caravan for a cup of tea?'

Tom had the kettle boiling and three mugs handy on the bench when they reached the caravan.

'Not much of a celebration,' he allowed. 'We'll have to keep that for Saturday.'

'We can wish each other luck,' Ailsa suggested, taking one of the mugs as she looked about her for somewhere to sit down. 'And perhaps we could start on some plans for a decent office with a desk and a filing cabinet in it, and a chair or two!'

'All in good time,' Fergus agreed, sounding far more relaxed. 'We have to creep before we walk.'

'I'm in the mood for running,' she told him, 'but that's just my notorious enthusiasm taking over. When do you think we can start to build?'

'We'll have a lot to see to first—tenders and official permission to extend and that sort of thing,' he explained, 'but October should see us on our way.'

'As long as that?'

'The summer goes past here very quickly,' Tom said. 'It'll be October before you realise it.'

The summer would pass, month by lazy month, and they would be together as partners, at least, Ailsa thought. They would work together for a single cause, and she must be content with that.

Fergus gave her a lift back to the Lodge gates on his way home to the cottage in the glen.

'You'll try to come on Saturday?' she asked as she got down from the Range Rover.

'I'll do my best.'

He drove away, leaving her to complete the journey to his old home on foot, but she walked along the tree-shaded drive with a lighter step now, knowing that some, if not all, of his bitterness had passed and he no longer resented her.

Mrs Birch was busy in the kitchen when Ailsa went in to ask if she could help with their evening meal.

'Everything is ready,' the housekeeper informed her virtuously. 'I like to have my preparations well in hand before five o'clock at the latest.' She dusted her floured hands over the kitchen sink. 'Your friend has gone for a walk, presumably in search of you,' she added.

'Fergus gave me a lift as far as the gates,' Ailsa explained, 'but I didn't pass Russ coming up the drive. Perhaps he went the other way.'

'If you ask me, he's getting restless, eager to be off home to Canada, I would think, and perhaps he's wanting to take you with him.'

Martha paused, waiting for Ailsa's reaction to such a sensational idea.

'Mrs Birch,' Ailsa said, laughing, 'you have far too fertile an imagination! I'm not ready to go back to Canada for a very long time, and if I did it would be only for a holiday.'

'Your mother must miss you, I'm thinking.'

'In some ways I'm sure she does, but she's taken on a whole new life and a new family now that she's re-married, so she'll have plenty of other things to think about. She may come over later in the year,' she added hopefully, 'just to see how I'm getting on. Mothers always like to check on their daughters when they take on anything new!'

'I've been on the telephone to Flora,' Mrs Birch remembered. 'I thought she would like to know about the barbecue.'

'I wish she could have been here,' Ailsa said.

'She will,' Martha Birch said with some satisfaction. 'Since it's at the weekend she could be in Oban by twelve o'clock. I took advantage of what you said before you left for Cuilfail and invited her.'

'That's splendid,' Ailsa agreed. 'It wouldn't be quite the same without her, Mrs Birch.'

'She said she wouldn't miss it for the world,' Flora's mother returned, looking straight at her. 'I told her Fergus would be here.'

Turning away from that searching gaze, Ailsa thought that Martha Birch was utterly transparent in her desire to see Flora married to 'the young laird' whatever happened or however hard she had to scheme, but what she had overlooked was Tom. She hadn't taken him into her calculations at all, and Tom was a force to be reckoned with. If he loved Flora he would ask her to marry him.

Another pipe-dream! Another way of saying that everything should fit into a pattern of her own making and everyone would live happily at Truan for ever after!

The following two days were, of necessity, given over to their preparations for the barbecue. The weather was fair, with only a little wind rising in the evening to ruffle the calm waters of the loch and stir the garden trees into life as Russell put the finishing touches to what was now a very elaborate barbecue grill at the foot of the terrace steps. Steaks and sausages had been ordered from the travelling van which came up from Oban on two days a week, and Martha Birch had been baking endless rolls and buns until the kitchen bench was piled high with her handiwork.

'But what if it rains?' Russell had the temerity to ask when most of their preparations were complete.

'It wouldn't dare!' laughed Ailsa. 'Not after all the work we've put in.'

'If it rains we're prepared for that too,' Mrs Birch said. 'We'll open up the big dining-room and put tables in the hall. It's been done before, and very nice it looked too. Then if people do want to come inside they can sit in comfort.'

In spite of all the things she had to think about, Ailsa found herself wondering about Fergus. He had promised

to come, but he had also said that he would be away
most of the day in Perth, buying sheep. Duty before
pleasure! It was as finely balanced as that, but the truth
of the matter might be that he didn't want to come at
all.

Tom, it was decided, would have to go to Oban to
pick up Flora, driving Ailsa's car, and Mrs Birch made
no comment about the arrangement, much to Ailsa's
surprise. So long as Flora gets here, she thought, it won't
matter who brings her.

The dining-room took longer to arrange than they had
anticipated.

'You wouldn't think I went in once a fortnight to dust
it,' Martha Birch complained as Russell helped Hamish
to move the heavy table back to the wall where they could
set it out with part of the buffet supper which would be
taken indoors, anyway.

Coming in with an armful of rhododendrons in pinks
and white, Ailsa thought how beautiful the room looked
with its high, carved ceiling and the deep rose-coloured
velvet curtains in the three window alcoves. It was pan-
elled in light pine with window-seats upholstered in the
same rich velvet as the curtains, and a fire was set, ready
to be lit if the evening turned chilly, as well it might.
Long ago it must have looked exactly like this when the
last mistress of Truan stood there waiting for her guests.
Fergus's mother! It was easy to picture her from the full-
length portrait which adorned the wall above the
staircase, easy to see her walking down those magnificent stairs with a gentle smile on her lips.

Flora arrived in a whirl of excitement.

'I never expected to be back so soon!' she cried. 'And
I have Monday off as well, which means I needn't go
back till Tuesday morning.'

'Fergus will take you through to Oban,' her mother
suggested. 'I'm sure he would have met you himself if
he hadn't gone to Perth.'

'Oh, I didn't mind Tom coming to get me!' Flora's
cheeks were stained a deep pink to match the curtains.
'We had a lot to talk about.'

'Help Ailsa with the flowers,' her mother ordered
briskly. 'You've done nothing yet.'

'Ailsa,' Flora whispered under her breath, 'I've got an awful lot to tell you!'

'Which will have to wait till tomorrow,' Ailsa said, seeing Russell at the door.

'Heavens, it's good to be home,' Flora declared, smiling at him. 'Have you enjoyed your stay here?'

'More or less,' Ailsa heard her ex-fiancé reply as she turned away.

In an hour her guests would be arriving and she had yet to change, but she stood for a moment at her bedroom window looking out at the advancing night. Would Fergus come? she wondered once again, for that was all that really mattered to her.

She knew now how deeply she had come to care for him and how much his good opinion of her mattered. It had been a swift progress from admiration to love, and her heart stood still for a moment as she contemplated all that this could mean, but whatever the future held for her she could no longer deny her love. The finality of it came to her with blinding clarity, because she had never known a love like this before. It had taken possession of her completely, obliterating everything else in its powerful orbit, shaking her physically as well as mentally as she stood there at her window overlooking the shrubbery where a thin rain had begun to fall. 'I love you! I love you, Fergus,' she whispered under her breath. 'I've never loved anyone like this until now!'

She could hear the rain, cool, life-giving rain, dropping gently on the garden trees, and somewhere on the hill the bleating of sheep and the cry of a curlew on its homeward way. It was all part of Truan and the life she wanted to lead, but what hope was there of ultimate happiness if Fergus remained aloof? She thought they had come to understand one another, but understanding was no substitute for love.

It was the thinly falling rain that steadied her thoughts in the end. The barbecue was off; they would have to hold her first party as mistress of Truan inside the house itself, which meant that Fergus, if he came, would see her in his mother's role as hostess, which might only aggravate the original bitterness he had felt. If she could have turned the whole estate over to him in that moment she would have done so without a qualm. Oh, my love, she thought, if I could only see you here as master in your old home anything I did would be far too little to achieve such an end!

'It's raining!' Flora was standing at her bedroom door. 'What rotten luck, when it's been fine all day! It means we won't be able to be outside, but they're clearing the hall and putting the small tables in the dining-room where we can eat. We couldn't find you to ask for your decision,' she added. 'My mother had to make the final choice.'

'I should have come down as soon as I realised it was raining quite steadily,' Ailsa acknowledged slowly, because she was still thinking about Fergus and what their change of plans might mean to him. 'It's all going to look very much like the house parties the MacNairs used to give when they lived here, isn't it? I didn't want it to be like that, Flora, not something that might hurt Fergus and send him back to that forlorn Keep of his to lick his wounds.'

Flora crossed the room, looking out at the drenched garden with thoughtful eyes.

'You know, I think you misjudge Fergus in some ways,' she said. 'He wouldn't hold you responsible for this or compare what you've done with the past. We had good times in those days—all of us—but this is different. He'll see it as a new era, something that has benefited Truan already, and he won't want to turn back the page. He'll admire you for what you're trying to achieve.'

'It's not his admiration I want.' Ailsa turned from the window. 'Oh, Flora, you must know that I'm in love with him! It must show as clearly as daylight, and I can do nothing about it.'

'I think I've guessed,' Flora said. 'You can't hide a thing like that—not really. I've seen you in his company quite a lot these past few weeks, and I've felt a "something" in the air.'

'But not where Fergus was concerned,' Ailsa suggested quietly.

'No—I can't lie to you. He was so grievously hurt that first time, so terribly betrayed, and you must have seen the scars it left, but even I was beginning to hope for a miracle,' Flora submitted. 'I want him to be happy, Ailsa, more than I can say, because he's been like a brother to me, a kind, gentle older brother who gave me confidence and joy. I can't thank Fergus enough for that, and I can't even begin to thank him for Tom.'

'Tom?' Ailsa repeated, knowing that she was about to hear a confession, that 'awful lot' Flora had to tell her before the weekend was over.

'He brought Tom here and encouraged him to stay,' Flora rushed on. 'I was only a kid at the time and I think I must have hero-worshipped them both, but soon it was Tom who mattered most. Fergus never teased me about him, as some brothers would have done. He recognised it as first love and he knew it was a tender thing, but Tom never told me how he really felt about me till this afternoon. When he met my train at Oban I felt it so strongly, hanging there between us, and I just had to kiss him and hug him very close.' Flora drew in a quick breath. 'Do you know why he hadn't told me before this?' she demanded, answering her own question before Ailsa could reply. 'He thought he hadn't anything to offer me.'

'But love,' Ailsa said quietly. 'If only they could accept that,' she added. 'Nothing else matters.'

'Do you know,' Flora said, 'I think I finally got that through to him. It took me from Connel right to the Lodge gates before I could convince him, but finally I did.'

'Flora!' Ailsa held her close. 'Are you going to announce your engagement tonight?'

Flora looked stricken.

'You know I couldn't do that,' she said. 'I'll have to battle it out with my mother first. She'd like me to marry Fergus.'

'I gathered so.'

'*You* wouldn't want to marry your brother, even if you had one,' Flora declared with a return of her old inconsistency.

Ailsa laughed.

'That must be the final argument in this case,' she said. 'I love you, Flora, and I wish you and Tom the greatest happiness in the world. You will come to live here?' she asked urgently. 'We need you both at Truan.'

'It may not be for a year or two,' Flora predicted. 'I'll have to teach for a while to justify all the money that has been spent on my education, but as soon as Tom sees his way clear to set up a proper home, we'll be married.'

Ailsa hesitated, but almost instantly Flora held up her hand.

'I know what you're going to suggest,' she said. 'You're going to offer us some money to get a house, and I love you for even thinking about it, but Tom wouldn't want that. He wants to do it all on his own, and you've given him a good start already. In a couple of years' time the fish farm will be flourishing, and then—and then we can have the cottage of our dreams somewhere in the glen!'

'The farm is picking up already,' Ailsa said, 'and once we get the new tanks and the offices built we'll be on our way. Orders are pouring in, not just repeats but big new customers, and we'll soon be able to take on more staff.'

'You've been good for Truan,' said Flora, 'and good for Cuilfail too. They couldn't have done it without you.'

'We'll all reap the benefit,' Ailsa pointed out. 'It will be a joint enterprise from now on.' She moved towards her wardrobe. 'And now I'd better look out something suitable to wear,' she added. 'I couldn't appear in front of my guests like this!'

'Wear that lovely blue dress you wore the first time we had a meal together,' Flora advised. 'You looked so nice in it, and Fergus likes blue.'

'Off you go!' Ailsa ushered her to the door, but she took down the blue dress all the same, laying it ready on her bed before she went to run her bath.

Her first guests were arriving as she descended the wide sweep of the staircase to greet them.

'We're always the first because we're always hungry!' James Struthers laughed, taking both her hands. 'This is a fine sight,' he added as he looked around him. 'Truan coming back into its own. How wise you were to have everything inside instead of juggling with plates in the garden!'

'I hadn't much choice,' Ailsa pointed out. 'We could hardly eat in the rain!'

'It's lovely to be back at Truan again,' Naomi declared. 'You've made the old place glow, my dear. I've always envied the Lodge its azaleas, but your uncle, bless him, always preferred to let them run wild. He wasn't a man for parties either, but we finished up being good friends.'

Other guests were arriving, younger people from the surrounding glens, always eager to attend a barbecue.

'Such a shame it's raining!'

'How disappointing for you!'

'We'll make the best of it and ask for better weather next time!'

'I've always wanted to see Truan. It really is lovely!'

All the conventional remarks she might have expected, Ailsa thought, as she mingled with the gathering crowd whose laughter and eager conversation echoed to the rafters of Fergus MacNair's old home. It had been his birthplace, the great house where he had spent his tender years, where he had grown up within a happy family learning to love the land.

Russell came to stand beside her, offering a tray of drinks.

'It's almost feudal,' he declared, 'all those kilts and big, bearded men! I feel like a duck out of water.'

'Not you!' she smiled. 'You would never feel inferior, Russ, wherever you found yourself. It's just that it's not your scene, is it?'

'I'm not convinced that it's yours either,' he said, 'although you seem to be trying hard.'

It had come naturally to her, she thought, because the Lodge was a place which should always have been a family home. Naomi Struthers had implied that when she had first come in, and the noise and happy laughter everywhere only served to accentuate the fact.

'Everybody must be here by this time,' Russell observed. 'Even the piper fellow who appeared to be blowing his brains out the other day up there on the hillside—Duncan something or other.'

'Duncan Carmichael. I asked him because I thought people would like to dance if it did rain,' Ailsa explained, 'and Hamish is a wizard on the violin, I believe.'

Not all her guests had arrived, she thought. Fergus MacNair was still missing.

Again and again her eyes sought the door, but even when it did open it was always someone else.

'I hope there's going to be enough to eat,' Flora remarked on her way to the dining-room with a tray of empty glasses. 'There's far more people here than we invited, though that's not unusual.'

'You mean we've got gate-crashers?'

'Oh, you can't call them that,' Flora said quite seriously. 'They've just been ''brought along'', which is a way people have in these parts, so you'll have to get used to it. Is Fergus here?'

Ailsa shook her head. 'Not yet.'

'He'll come. He must have been held up somewhere.'

'He could have phoned!'

'Yes, but maybe he didn't think of that. He'll be here— I feel it in my bones!'

'Flora, you're the eternal optimist!' Ailsa laughed.

An hour later there was still no sign of Ailsa's missing guest, and her heart contracted with a new pain of disappointment. Part of the drawing-room had been cleared and the strains of dance music drifted through the open doors into the hall. Soon the hall itself was empty with only Ailsa standing at the foot of the staircase. Standing waiting? She pushed her hands through her thick dark hair, about to turn away, when the heavy outer door opened again and Fergus was there. He came forward, resplendent in his kilt and neatly-brushed velvet jacket, *skean dhu* and sporran tidily in place, the lace jabot at his throat immaculate and a look in his eyes which she had never wanted to see there again.

'Fergus!' She took a step towards him, holding out her hand in greeting. 'I'm glad you've come.'

He drew in a deep breath as he looked beyond her to the line of portraits on the wall above them.

'I'm sorry I'm late,' he apologised conventionally. 'We had an accident with one of the sheep in Perth and it took me longer to get away. After that,' he smiled, 'there was all this clobber to get on!'

His smile had chased the pain from his eyes, but she knew what he must be thinking, travelling back down the years to scenes like this in his childhood when his mother had stood on the staircase where she was standing now.

'You've made such an effort,' she found herself saying. 'I know it couldn't have been easy for you, coming here like this.'

'It wasn't easy,' he admitted. 'These things never are, but I had to come some time, and now I'm glad I did.' He sat down on the bottom stair, an old habit long remembered. 'Ailsa, I'd like to talk to you,' he said.

'Here?' She looked round the empty hall.

'It's as good a place as any.'

'Yes, I suppose it is.'

Her heart was suddenly beating fast in her breast, pounding so hard that she wondered if he could hear it.

'I want to thank you for what you're doing, both here and at Cuilfail,' he said. 'You've given this place a new lease of life and the farm is flourishing.'

'The farm would have paid, anyway. It would have grown and prospered even without my help,' she suggested.

'Not in such a big way,' he assured her, 'and not nearly so quickly.'

'Is this a business talk?' She smiled up at him.

'Not entirely.' His face darkened again. 'I wanted you to know what all this means to me, seeing the Lodge returning to life, seeing it as it was before——'

Ailsa put a hand on his arm.

'Do we need to go back to that?' she asked gently. 'I know about your grief, Fergus. I know how you must have felt losing the two people who meant so much to you and then losing Truan into the bargain.

His brows came together as he looked deeply into the past.

'Losing Truan came afterwards,' he said. 'I had made up my mind to struggle on with the estate, but it didn't work out that way. Things had gone from bad to worse after my father died and Ewan——'

He seemed to find difficulty in mentioning his brother's name even now, sitting in a difficult silence till Russell came thrusting through the double doors from the dining-room. The sound of music rushed out with him as Fergus got swiftly to his feet.

'Oh, there you are, my love!' said Russell, holding out his hand. 'Come and dance!'

In a moment which seemed to last for ever Ailsa waited for Fergus to speak.

'I'll go and find Flora,' was what he finally said.

'Odd sort of guy, isn't he?' Russell observed. 'Why was he late?'

'Something about sheep,' Ailsa answered huskily. 'He's been in Perth all day.'

'I thought he might just be trying to make an entrance,' her ex-fiancé mused. 'The rightful master, and all that!'

'Fergus wouldn't even think of such a thing.' Ailsa rose to her feet. 'I don't think I want to dance just yet, Russ,' she added. 'I feel I need some fresh air.'

'In the rain?'

'It isn't raining now,' she said.

'As you desire, my love!' He opened the big main door. 'We can stroll on the terrace for five minutes and then I think you'd better return to your guests. They all seem to be enjoying themselves,' he added, 'especially the younger ones.'

They walked along the terrace with the strains of music coming out to them through the open windows laced with the laughter which amply proved his point. Her guests were enjoying themselves and Truan had come into its own, but all Ailsa could think of was the way that Fergus had hesitated over his brother's name. He had scarcely been able to utter it, and he had not spoken of his former love at all. Deirdre Buchanan's name seemed to have stuck in his throat.

'I wonder if six years is too short a time to soften a memory,' she said aloud. 'I wonder if you never forget.'

Russell turned to look at her in the light coming from the dining-room windows.

'It depends what you're trying to thrust into the background,' he said. 'If it's pain and disillusionment, that might take a long time.'

'I know.'

'You mean us, of course.' He attempted to take her into his arms. 'You know I want to forget about the past,' he said. 'I want to make amends.'

'Russ,' she said quietly, 'you can never do that. It's all over, and I want to forget about it. We were very young at the time, very emotional, but now I think we've both grown up. When you go back to Canada you'll meet some nice girl who will be the sort of wife you need, and then you'll really forget about the past.'

'You sure have it all worked out, nicely docketed with everything in its proper place. Is that what you think you've found here?' he demanded.

'In some ways,' she was bound to confess. 'I've got enough money to bring Truan back to what it used to be and enough enthusiasm to get it right, in the end. If that's all I can do,' she added quietly, 'maybe I can become content.'

'Content without love, do you mean?' Russell looked at her keenly, at the beauty he had always seen in her and the new sadness in her eyes. 'You'd never make it,' he added cruelly. 'You'd wilt here and die in the end.'

Ailsa squared her shoulders, a new, defiant light in her eyes.

'I don't intend to die, Russ,' she said. 'I mean to carry on here at the Lodge as my uncle should have done during these past six years, improving it and even adding to its amenities if I think that would be the right thing to do.'

'Taking MacNair's advice, I suppose.'

She drew in a deep breath.

'No. Fergus wouldn't want to interfere. We're more or less partners at Cuilfail—with Tom—and that's about it. But we can work together there,' she added hopefully, 'and eventually it will benefit the community as a whole, which is what Fergus must want.'

'While he remains aloof in his ivory tower?'

Her heart contracted at the thought of the lonely Keep.

'If that's what he wants,' she was forced to say.

'If you ask me,' Russell observed on their way back to the hall, 'you're at a dead end. You'll never be one of these people—they're too insular—and you'll never survive without love and affection.'

'That isn't true,' she told him with a steady hand on the door knob. 'I'm already accepted. Nobody could have been kinder than the Struthers family from Lettercairn. Surely you can see that?'

'I can see their curiosity and a certain amount of pique when it comes to the younger girls who are no doubt convinced that "the laird" will come running, in the end, if only to re-establish himself here as the rightful master of Truan with you by his side.'

'You're being ridiculous!' she accused. 'Fergus would never marry for that reason. He may never marry at all.'

'He's got a tough fight on his hands, in that case,' Russell decided. 'A man in a kilt deserves to be pursued.'

'Now you're just being silly!' Ailsa tried to laugh. 'Come in and make yourself as pleasant as you can to all these girls you think must be pining for Fergus in their spare moments when they're not studying hard or helping to run a farm.'

'You absolutely amaze me!' he said, putting his arm about her. 'But I'm still not bowing out till you're finally able to convince me about Truan and the young laird.'

His arm firmed about her waist as they walked into the dining-room, and not only Fergus but Tom seemed to see it as a sign of their continuing love.

Tom crossed the floor to dance with her.

'I thought Forgreave was going back to Canada,' he observed.

'He is—on Monday.'

'Somehow I got the idea that he might be staying on.' Tom seemed oddly relieved as they stood watching the last frantic whirl of an eightsome reel on the polished floor. 'Come and sit down.'

'I thought we were going to dance.'

'There's bound to be an interval,' he said. 'There always is after an eightsome, it takes so much energy, and the piper needs to wet his whistle before he can play again. I'll get you a drink and we can sit out in the hall.'

Ailsa glanced at the staircase where she had been sitting with Fergus so short a time ago, turning deliberately to a deep, unoccupied settee in an alcove near the drawing-room door.

'We'll be comfortable here,' she decided, 'and you can bring me a long, cool drink of lemon soda.'

'That should be cool enough,' he agreed. 'Anything to eat?'

'No, thank you, Tom, but do help yourself. I expect all these reels and Strip the Willows have made you hungry.'

He came back after a few minutes with a tray.

'I've settled for sandwiches,' he said, 'although some of the other delights were very tempting. Trifle is my ruination, as you can see!'

Two generous portions of the trifle Ailsa had made the day before adorned the tray.

'Try one,' encouraged Tom, biting into his first sandwich.

'I already have, last night when I was preparing them!'

He munched contentedly.

'This is how it all used to be, I gather,' he said after a few minutes.

'When the MacNairs were here.' Her voice was suddenly unsteady. 'I thought that was why Fergus had stayed away at first, until he explained about the sheep.'

He took another bite of the sandwich.

'Fergus has changed,' he remarked. 'It must be for the best, because he's been far too wrapped up in his grief for the past few years, far too shortsighted to believe that most wounds are healed with the passing of time.'

Ailsa sipped her drink.

'He must have been very fond of his brother,' she ventured.

Tom hesitated.

'You'd better know the truth,' he said, sitting forward with the half-eaten sandwich in his hand. 'Ewan and Deirdre had decided to go away together. They were lovers, in spite of the fact that she was about to become engaged to Fergus, and they had told him that morning. He couldn't believe it, and he swore he would never forgive them—the woman who had promised to be his wife and the brother he had looked up to since he was a child. All he had hoped for, everything he had worked towards crumbled before their revelation, and he declared he would never forgive them nor forget their treachery. He sent them away that morning to their ultimate death. They took *Kirsty of Truan* and sailed to Mull, but somewhere on the way a storm blew up. The yacht was found drifting towards the Morvern shore and the bodies were picked up next day.' Tom sat staring at the half-eaten sandwich for a moment. 'It must have been a terrible experience for all concerned,' he added, while Ailsa sat rigidly beside him, hardly able to believe what she had just heard. 'Ewan had gone off owing a lot of money,' Tom continued, 'and when Fergus was forced to sell the estate because he had no money of his own he was devastated. On top of everything else it must have been the final blow, and he found it difficult to accept your uncle afterwards as the new owner of Truan. I think he recognised the fact that *someone* had to buy the estate when he could no longer afford to run it, and he managed to keep enough sheep on the hill, but that wasn't the point. Truan had been dismembered as far as he was concerned; it was no longer one unit as it had been for generations, as it could have been if his brother had lived to work it with him.'

'Oh, Tom!' she exclaimed. 'He must have suffered terribly.'

'Without saying very much,' Tom agreed. 'He spoke to me about it once, and once only, and now I've told you.'

'Why?'

He looked up at her.

'Because I think you ought to know,' he said. 'You might misjudge him otherwise.'

'I couldn't do that,' she said, 'especially after all you've just told me. It's such a numbing thought, knowing how hard he's tried.'

'You've made it easy for him as far as Cuilfail is concerned,' he said. 'Easier for us both.'

'That's not very much when you think about the Lodge and the rest of Truan,' Ailsa pointed out.

Tom was silent.

'I thought you ought to know,' he repeated. 'It might help you to understand him better.'

'I've been trying to understand for a very long time,' she answered, 'but I had no idea how it really was. I'm so sorry, Tom——'

'Don't ever let him think you pity him!' Tom exploded. 'That would be the end!'

Ailsa rose to her feet. 'What do we do now?' she asked.

'Wait. You don't want to go back to Toronto and we don't want you to go. It would be a disaster for Truan and all of us, quite apart from the fish farm—Cuilfail could survive on a shoestring, but the glen would suffer a bitter blow.'

'Tom, you're good for me!' she smiled. 'You always will be.'

It seemed there was no more to be said, but what she had just been told only served to deepen her love, to make her certain beyond any shadow of a doubt that she could never love anyone else. When Fergus finally came into the hall to say goodnight to her her world seemed complete.

'We've had two estimates for the new buildings,' he said. 'You can look at them and the plans whenever you like and we can decide which tender we'll accept. It will be largely up to you.'

'I thought this was to be a partnership,' she objected.

'It is,' he allowed, 'in a kind of a way. Tom will have his say too, of course.'

'What's this about Tom?' Tom had come up behind them. 'What "say" do I have?'

'It was about Cuilfail,' Ailsa explained. 'We have two estimates for the work now, so I suppose we could make a quick decision and get the building in hand right away.'

'I can't see any harm in that,' Tom agreed. 'It means that the job could be finished before October and we would be all set for the winter. Working in brick-built sheds with a decent office adjacent would be my idea of heaven, especially as I would have the caravan as sleeping quarters without a typewriter and a filing cabinet threatening to fall on top of me whenever I moved.'

Fergus had reached the door.

'We can settle all that on Monday,' he said, looking round at Ailsa. 'Unless you have other things to do.'

Ailsa hesitated.

'Russ is leaving on Monday,' she explained. 'I'll be taking him to Glasgow to catch the London plane, but if we could meet later, perhaps——?'

He nodded.

'Seven?' he said. 'At the caravan.'

She had been about to suggest a meeting and an evening meal at the Lodge, but decided against it.

'Seven, then, at the caravan,' she agreed.

It seemed an eternity away, yet the following two days passed quickly enough. Since she would be driving to Glasgow anyway, Ailsa offered Flora a lift as far as Jordanhill on her way to the airport to see Russell finally on his journey back to Canada. Convinced that she had meant what she had said about remaining in Scotland, he did not press her to change her mind.

'But if you ever should realise how much happier you would be on the other side of the Atlantic, get in touch, my love, and I'll be waiting,' he assured her.

You can't wait for a lifetime, Russ, she thought, and Truan is for ever, as far as I'm concerned.

She drove quite fast on her way back to Cuilfail, arriving at the caravan to find Tom snowed up under a mound of paper.

'Whatever are you doing?' she demanded.

'Working my way through this lot.' He rose to make room for her beside the bench. 'We've been keeping old bills and old orders in utter confusion for years, but I've weeded out most of them. These are all ready to burn.' He indicated a considerable pile at his elbow. 'The rest can be accommodated in the brave new cabinets when we get them. Have a look at the plans till Fergus gets here. You're early.'

'Yes, I know, but I promised Mrs Birch to be back for supper before nine o'clock,' Ailsa said. 'I delivered Flora to Jordanhill, by the way, safe and sound.'

'She wasn't very keen to go back.' They looked at each other. 'Did she tell you——?'

'Yes, Tom, and I'm very, very pleased,' Ailsa said.

'Her mother won't be overjoyed, I'm thinking,' he observed. 'I haven't much to offer.'

'That won't be for long,' Ailsa said. 'Cuilfail will be just the beginning.'

'I hope so.'

'Tom, I'm sure of it! None of us wants to look back, and we'll have quite a lot going for us when the new tanks are installed and we have twice as many traps in the loch.' Ailsa unfolded the plans he had produced. 'It all looks pretty good to me,' she said. 'Smaller than it could have been,' she added, 'but then Fergus says we must learn to creep before we can walk.'

Their heads were still bent over the plans when Fergus appeared at the door.

'Is there room enough for me?' he asked with the one-sided smile Ailsa thought must break her heart in time. 'I didn't expect you till seven.'

'I came away as quickly as I could,' she explained. 'I promised to be back at the Lodge before nine.'

They pored over plans and tenders for the next half-hour, heads close together, ideas flowing. It will always be like this, Ailsa thought, an easy partnership, a link between us that will hold our interest, at least. Was that all she sought, all she could ever hope for now that she had heard Fergus's tragic story in full?

He took her back to the Lodge in the Range Rover for nine o'clock, driving up to the terrace, although he refused her invitation to come in.

'Some other time,' he said before he drove away to his lonely cottage in the glen.

CHAPTER SEVEN

THE DAYS passed quickly after that, slipping into weeks as May gave place to June and Flora was preparing to return to the glen once more.

For Ailsa it was a case of endless activity on the estate, clearing scrub, planting trees, organising the new water supply which came down from the lochan in the hills to carry it on to the village where for so long they had de-

pended on the burn and an inadequate spring which had
been known to dry up during long spells of drought.
Not that there was much drought in the Western
Highlands, she thought, remembering the disastrous
evening of the barbecue and the three weeks of almost
constant rain which had followed it. It was fine rain,
though, like a mist fingering the hills and leaving the
earth refreshed. It certainly didn't hinder the progress
of the new sheds at Cuilfail, and when she took time off
to go there she saw that Fergus was delighted with their
progress. He had stopped working on the Keep and was
giving all his energy to Cuilfail.

Some of her own energy had been applied to the ever-
growing problem of George. Now a lively, energetic ten
weeks old, he was hard to repress, and Martha Birch was
constantly throwing out hints about his return to the
flock.

'We'll keep him till Flora gets back but no longer,'
she decided. 'If he hadn't belonged to Fergus it would
have been a different story.'

She was still cherishing the hope that Fergus and her
daughter would eventually come together, and obviously she had not been told about Tom.

George followed Ailsa around whenever he could,
complaining with a strident bleat when she appeared to
be taking little notice of him.

'You're nothing more than a pest!' she accused one
afternoon when she found him following close behind
her with her cardigan in his mouth.

He dropped the cardigan in the nearest puddle.

'Now look what you've done!' she protested. 'It was
quite clean, and now it will have to be washed all over
again!'

He stood, forelegs apart, waiting for her to play.

'I haven't time for you,' she told him severely. 'Go
away!'

A man's laughter halted her in her tracks.

'I was coming to see you about that fellow,' Fergus
said. 'I'm sure you've had quite enough of him.'

'Some days I have.' Ailsa turned with tenderness in
her eyes and a bright flush on her cheeks. 'But don't
think I've regretted the offer to take care of him. He's

been a happy distraction when—other things were on my mind.'

He walked beside her towards the new plantation while George remained standing on the path.

'Leave him with us till Flora gets back,' Ailsa suggested. 'She'd never forgive us if he was just one of the flock by the time she saw him again.'

'I hope that's going to happen,' he said. '"One of the flock" doesn't always work.'

'Are you wishing George on me for ever?' she laughed.

'That would be a life sentence as far as you were concerned. No,' he decided, 'I'll take the pest back as soon as Flora gets here.'

'I didn't mean to call him that,' she smiled. 'It was "pest" in the nicest meaning of the word. What do you think of my trees?'

'They're a great improvement.' Fergus leaned on the dividing fence. 'It's what I had decided to do a long time ago before I realised I hadn't the money to spend on such niceties.'

'You did your best,' she said slowly. 'Nobody can do more than that, Fergus. I'm trying to do the best I can for Truan and I need your help.'

'I can't see how that follows,' he said. 'I don't have much to give.'

'You're wrong there,' she told him. 'I'll make mistakes, I'll do the wrong thing on occasion without realising it, I suppose, and it won't be fun falling down on a project if there's nobody there to pick me up.'

'You want me to do that,' he said, 'but how can I?'

'By telling me beforehand what you would have done.'

He took a long time to think it over, leaning against the wooden fence with his back to the trees and his face turned towards the distant house.

'If that is the way you want it,' he said at last, 'I'll do my best.'

'For the moment I can only thank you.' Ailsa knew a great relief. 'We've got so much going for us at Cuilfail that I'd like to do the same for Truan.'

'I see you've got the new water system working,' he reflected. 'That alone will be a help.' He looked down at her, his eyes ablaze. 'The new mistress of Truan is making her presence felt in a big way!'

'Don't call me that!' she protested. 'It's a title that doesn't belong to me—a relic of the past, if you like. I don't want to act the grand lady, Fergus, because I know I could never take your mother's place. Not for a very, very long time, anyway. She was greatly beloved here, I understand, so I have a long way to go to come anywhere near her popularity, and I don't think I'll ever achieve the dignity she had. Mrs Birch keeps telling me that I'm far too impetuous and I guess that's true enough, but it's the way I'm made. I want to get things done immediately, and up to now I haven't been able to see any harm in that.'

They were very close, standing with their backs to the fence, when Fergus reached out and drew her swiftly towards him.

'You'll do!' he said huskily. 'You're what Truan needs, and who am I to object?'

Suddenly his mouth was on hers, kissing her with a tenderness which did not surprise her. This was Fergus as he had been long ago before Deirdre Buchanan had appeared on the scene to torment him. When he drew away Ailsa felt confused and disappointed. This kiss she had longed for had been no more than a token of his regard, an impulsive 'thank you' for what she had already done.

Yet the touch of his lips haunted her for the rest of the day and far into the silent night while she lay on her bed, remembering.

Flora arrived a week later, to the absolute delight of the impetuous George.

'Heavens, how he's grown!' she cried. 'It's back to the hill for you, my lad, if all the things I hear about you are true!'

'Fergus thinks he should go right away,' Ailsa told her, 'but perhaps we could keep him for another week.'

'He recognised me,' Flora said. 'That's the sad bit, really. He's never going to be an ordinary sheep.'

Her mother frowned at her.

'There's plenty for him to eat on the hill,' she declared. 'He's been overfed here for far too long and over-indulged, but Fergus will know what to do with him.'

'He won't send him to market, that's for sure,' Flora said. 'It will be over my dead body if he does. Won't it, George?' She caressed the ecstatic lamb. 'You'll always be different!'

Tom had met the Oban train on the pretext of picking up some wire from the Highland Crofters, bringing Flora back to Truan in the late afternoon. They had looked so utterly happy in each other's company and Ailsa felt that Martha Birch must be blind not to see how much they were in love. Maybe she just won't admit it, she thought.

A week later they took George down to Cuilfail.

'We've brought you a house-trained lamb,' they told Fergus. 'What are you going to do with him?'

'No problem,' Fergus declared. 'I'll take him on the hill tomorrow. He'll need some guidance, but I think—or at least I hope—the rest of the flock will play ball. They'll curb his enthusiasm in a day or two.'

'He's terribly spoilt,' Flora said fondly, 'and he's sure to pine.'

'An older ewe will soon cure him of all that,' Fergus assured her. 'Want a cup of tea? Tom will be up from the loch in a few minutes.'

They inspected the new sheds while they waited.

'I'm terribly impressed,' said Flora. 'I didn't expect it to be all this good, but it certainly is a vast improvement all round. When it's finished we must have some sort of celebration,' she suggested. 'Like another barbecue.'

Ailsa, who was still conscious of Fergus's impulsive kiss standing like some sort of barrier between them, was quick to agree.

'Will we have it here or at the Lodge?' she asked.

'Cuilfail would be more appropriate,' Fergus decided. 'All the work has been going on here.'

He was very proud of it, Ailsa realised, because he had done a great deal of the work himself, toiling all hours to see it completed in the shortest possible time, and because that time had become precious to him he

decided that George should be penned in a small enclosure next to the caravan until he could finally take
him on to the hill.

George was less than enthusiastic about the decision,
however, trying to follow them to the caravan door where
they were about to eat.

'He's far too fat,' Tom reflected, adding cruelly, 'It's
time he'd gone to market.'

'You brute!' Flora cried. 'You can get *that* idea out
of your head straight away. If George goes to market I
go too!'

'You wouldn't fetch much of a price in the fat-stock
ring,' Tom grinned. 'You're mostly skin and bone!'

'But sturdy with it!' She pounced on him, ruffling his
hair. 'Apologise,' she demanded, 'or I'll take George
and disappear for ever!'

'I surrender, in that case!' He caught her to him. 'Life
without you wouldn't be worth the disappearance of
George, although he is the ultimate menace.'

Flora parted with the lamb, shedding a regretful tear.

'It's always the same,' she said on their way back to
the Lodge. 'They get right under your skin and play
havoc with your sense of proportion in a big way. I've
never known a hand-reared lamb to behave naturally
when it came to parting, and they have that awful rejected look in their eyes when you walk away.'

They helped in the kitchen, preparing their evening
meal. Martha Birch asked a few leading questions about
Fergus and why he had been unable to meet Flora's train
at Oban.

'Fergus is up to his eyes in work at the moment,' her
daughter explained. 'He's been working all hours at the
new sheds and on the hill. There's lots of paperwork to
do into the bargain,' she added, 'and maybe I could help
there with the extra orders and that sort of thing.'

'You're not a clerk,' her mother reminded her sternly.
'You could look for a teaching job in the meantime.'

'I'll think about it,' Flora agreed. 'Maybe I could get
something in the vicinity, but I'd like a few weeks to
myself first.'

'What does Fergus think about it?' Martha demanded.

Flora flushed scarlet.

'Fergus has nothing to do with my decisions,' she said. 'He'd never dream of giving me advice.'

'He wouldn't give you the wrong counsel if he did,' her mother returned. 'I'm sure of that.'

'Tom and I want to become engaged.'

The statement was so unexpected and so decisive that even Ailsa was surprised, while Martha Birch could only stare at her daughter in stark amazement.

'Have you gone out of your head?' she demanded.

'It isn't anything new,' Flora assured her. 'We've thought about it for a long time. Of course,' she added sadly, 'we know we can't marry immediately—not till the fish farm is paying, anyway, but we both want to live here in the end and be part of Truan.'

'You must be mad!' her mother managed at last. 'You must be out of your mind to reject someone like Fergus MacNair!'

'Mother,' Flora said patiently, 'Fergus was never mine to reject. I wish you could understand that. We're fond of each other—very fond, but it's because we were brought up together here, at Truan. He was the brother I never had and I'm no more to him than a younger sister. You must believe this, because it's no use living in a fantasy world hoping that one day I will be mistress of Truan. I never could be and I never wanted to be!'

At this stage Ailsa turned away, busying herself with setting the table in the small sitting-room across the back hall, although she could still hear the noisy exchanges in the kitchen where Martha Birch had eventually regained her breath. Flora was being remarkably cool and determined, she thought.

Going through to the dining-room for an extra serving spoon, she looked out of the windows which faced the loch, drawing back instinctively at what she saw. A fierce red glow leapt beyond the trees. Something was on fire!

Pulling open one of the long windows, she stepped out on to the terrace for a better view—only to freeze at the conviction that filled her heart. Down there beside the loch, and between it and the road, Cuilfail was burning.

For a split second she could neither move nor think, then she began to run back through the house in search of help.

'Flora!' She half dragged the younger girl towards the side door. 'Cuilfail is on fire! The sheds are burning and they must need help.'

'Tom and Fergus!' Flora gasped. 'They must be down there.' She began to run. 'We left them less than an hour ago. What could have happened? Ailsa, are you listening to me?'

'Yes, I'm listening,' Ailsa gasped in her turn, still running. 'Maybe we should have brought the car.'

'We can't go back now.' Flora was looking straight ahead towards the loch. 'Maybe it isn't Cuilfail after all.'

'What else could it be?' Ailsa refused to slacken her pace even though Flora was now behind her. 'Can you imagine what this will mean—everything gone, everything Fergus and Tom have hoped for? If the fire has really got a hold——'

She could not finish that thought because she knew what the result would mean—bankruptcy, perhaps, or a long, long way back to prosperity. It was then that Flora's words struck home with terrible certainty. 'Tom and Fergus! They must be down there.'

They reached the road where other people were gathering, most of them villagers who had run out just as they were, the women in their aprons, the men in shirt sleeves, and some of the forestry workers down from the hill, running with the long-handled spades and beaters which were kept for the control of forest fires a mile along the road.

Ailsa pushed ahead, oblivious of the fact that other people were standing back, and Flora ran beside her. They could see the flames now licking hungrily at the row of pines between Cuilfail and the road, while the crackle of burning wood was suddenly loud in their ears. The flames seemed to be leaping skywards, shouting for joy.

When they came to the gate a small group of men stood there silhouetted against the burning sheds. Hoses and buckets of water were everywhere, and something was lying on a stretcher beside the disinfectant trough. Ailsa's heart gave a great bound and lay still. Fergus? Tom?

She knelt beside the stretcher. It was Tom. She bent over him, steeling herself against the sight of his badly burned face as he opened his eyes.

'Sorry!' he said in a gruff, familiar voice. 'We did what we could.'

The district nurse was there, and Flora, kneeling beside her. Ailsa turned away, searching for Fergus with an anxious prayer in her heart. 'Please God! Please God, let him be all right!'

She heard the scream of the ambulance as it drew up on the road and the sound of running feet as men came towards her carrying another stretcher.

'There's someone in there,' one of them said, looking through the pall of smoke as the hoses began to do their work and the highest flames were subdued. It was then that Ailsa saw George standing on the bank at one side of a burned-out caravan with a bewildered look on his small, inquisitive face. He was neither bleating nor running around in panic; he was just stunned, while behind him was the broken-down fence of his temporary paddock. Fergus had penned him there for the night, she remembered, till he could take him on to the hill in the morning.

A figure staggered out of the pall of grey smoke.

'Fergus!'

She was first to reach him, although he was scarcely recognisable, but she had known he would be in there, fighting for what was left of Cuilfail. The district nurse led him away to where she had set up an emergency unit on the grass.

'We'll get Tom in the ambulance first,' she decided with professional calm, 'and then we'll see what's happened to you.'

'I'm all right.' Fergus was wiping his smoke-blackened face with the towel she had provided. 'Don't worry about me—see to Tom. He went right in there as soon as he saw the fire.'

Ailsa moved towards him, conscious that she was shaking in every limb, and suddenly it was Fergus who was doing the comforting.

'Don't worry about Tom,' he said. 'He'll pull through—I'm certain about that.'

'How can you be sure?' Her voice was unsteady. 'And how can you be so sure about yourself?'

'I'm not so easily destroyed,' he said, holding her for a moment longer in the sanctuary of his arms. 'Thanks for coming, anyway.'

The district nurse was at his elbow.

'Into the ambulance!' she commanded in her brusque but kindly way. 'The fire brigade is here from Oban. You can't do anything more.'

Fergus looked beyond her to the burned-out shell of the caravan where all their records had been stored.

'There goes all our good intentions,' he said harshly, 'and quite a lot of your capital, Ailsa. I'm sorry!'

'Get him into the ambulance,' the nurse instructed.

'Fergus, you've got to go,' Ailsa said. 'Your hands——'

She could not finish the sentence as he put his blackened hands behind his back.

'I have to stay here,' he said. 'I have to clean up this mess.'

'Tomorrow,' she said, amazed at how firmly the word came out. 'We'll look at everything tomorrow, Fergus, and assess the damage.'

He gazed at her in what could have been amazement.

'You never give up, do you?' he said. 'But I still don't think I should be rushed off to hospital when——'

'When you can't use your hands because of the pain?' she suggested, her voice breaking. 'And goodness knows what else there is——'

'Leave him to me,' the nurse said firmly. 'Mr MacNair, Tom Kelvin is in a poor way. You're not going to hold up the ambulance, now, are you?'

Flora was still kneeling beside the stretcher when they turned towards her.

'He can't speak any more,' she said, bewildered. 'He's very sick.'

One of the ambulance men lifted her to her feet.

'We're taking him to hospital,' he said.

'I'm going with him.' Flora met his eyes with a new determination in her own. 'I'm his fiancée,' she added. 'Surely that's enough.'

They made way for her to walk beside the stretcher while Ailsa and the nurse followed on either side of Fergus, supporting him as best they could.

'Get that damned lamb out of the way,' Fergus said as they passed a still bewildered George. 'He was the cause of all this. Seemingly he got out of the pen and the caravan door was open. Tom had left something cooking on the paraffin stove and there were all these papers. He must have climbed up on the bench and knocked over the stove. That's how it seems, anyway.'

'Poor George!' Flora wailed, and suddenly she was crying.

Ailsa waited till the ambulance had gone with Fergus and Flora seated inside with the nurse and Tom lying on the stretcher, then she turned swiftly and made her way back to the Lodge. The firemen had everything under control and only a grey haze of smoke and steam rose from the sheds now, but she could not bring herself to look more closely. The damage seemed to be complete.

When she drove back again half an hour later the fire brigade was winding up the hoses and making sure that the last remnants of the conflagration were extinguished.

'Are you in charge?' the fire chief asked.

'Yes—yes, I suppose I am,' she agreed. 'I have a share in the business.' She still could not bear to look too closely at what had once been the caravan. 'It's all so terrible I can't quite take it in. Can you tell me about the fish?'

'They're safe enough, all in the last shed over there. That was one of Mr MacNair's first concerns, I'm thinking. He rushed in to try to save as many of them as he could, I understand. You needn't worry about them now because there's no fear of the fire breaking out again, but we'll leave someone in charge just in case it does.'

'I want to go to Oban,' Ailsa said. 'I must follow the ambulance. I have my own car, and I—have to bring Flora back home.'

'Off you go, then,' he advised briskly. 'We'll clean up here.'

On her way back to the car she passed George, who had been penned safely away from the rubble.

'Oh, George,' she said wearily, 'what have you done?'

She could think of nothing but Tom, and Flora loving him as she loved Fergus. For her own part she knew that Fergus was safe, but Flora must be in an agony of uncertainty, her mind numb to the present while it searched out the future. Supposing Tom died?

It was unthinkable. The district nurse came to stand beside the car.

'You'll be fair worried, Miss Mallory,' she said. 'It was such a dire thing to happen, and all because of that stupid creature wanting to be in the caravan. It seems he knocked over the paraffin stove, and not a bit of his fleece burned either. Not even singed!'

'Will you see to him?' Ailsa asked. 'See that he doesn't get out again. It was an accident no one could have foreseen.'

'I'll do what I can. Would you like me to take him home with me?' the nurse asked. 'We've looked after motherless lambs before.'

But not one like this, Ailsa thought, although she said, 'If you would do that, Jessie, we'd be very much in your debt.'

She drove fast, eating up the miles on the road south to Oban, the little hired car behaving impeccably as her thoughts strayed to that first day when Fergus had come upon her stranded by the roadside. Not much more than two months ago, she remembered, yet a lifetime seemed to have passed since then. She tried to convince herself that nothing would be changed, that it wasn't all over now, that Fergus wouldn't pack up and go away if anything happened to Tom. Tom had been burned—badly burned—but miracles were accomplished with such cases every day, so now she was praying for a miracle for both herself and Flora!

Ahead of her on the winding road she could see the ambulance with its cross of St Andrew on the side, but it was a long way ahead on the far side of the water while she had yet to reach the head of the loch. It disappeared from view long before she got there, but luckily there was no oncoming traffic to hold her back between the passing bays and she was able to put her foot down on the accelerator once again.

At Oban she asked for directions.

'Oh, the hospital! Which one would you be wanting now?' The man looked at her curiously.

'I had no idea there was more than one——'

'Is it for yourself?' he asked.

'No. I'm following an ambulance.'

'I saw it go past,' he said. 'Now, you'll go straight along here and through the square. After that you'll see it posted. It isn't far. I hope there hasn't been a serious accident,' he added compassionately.

Ailsa had re-started the car.

'I—it was a fire,' she told him, pulling away from the kerb.

On the hill road leading to the hospital she could see beyond it to a blue ridge of mountains darkening against the evening sky. How beautiful it all is, she thought, and how still.

The ambulance was drawing away as she turned in at the entrance to the hospital and she parked her car where it wouldn't be in anyone's way, walking quickly towards the only door she could see. It opened and Flora came out.

'They've taken him away—Tom, I mean. He lost consciousness on the journey and I heard them say something about an oxygen tent. Do you think——'

'He's not going to die,' Ailsa said firmly. 'We must believe that.'

Flora tried to pull herself together.

'I'm not helping, am I, being so afraid?' she said.

'I know how you feel,' Ailsa admitted. 'What happened to Fergus?'

'They took him to have something put on his hands. They were badly burned. He saved most of the papers, you see, all the new orders and the ledgers. The rest were to be destroyed, anyway.' Flora hid her face in her hands. 'How long will it be before we know?' she asked of no one in particular.

'Not long.' Ailsa tried to console her. 'Shall we wait in the car?'

'I couldn't sit still. Maybe we could walk about,' Flora suggested. 'Not too far.'

They walked slowly round the end of a now deserted sun-lounge, looking towards the hills. Eventually someone came in search of them. It was Fergus.

Ailsa wanted to rush towards him, but she remained beside Flora who seemed to be rooted to the spot.

'You can see him now,' Fergus said, 'but only for a few minutes. They want him to get some sleep.'

'Oh, thank you! Thank you, Fergus!' Flora passed them on her way to the door.

'There's a nurse waiting for her inside,' Fergus said. 'She'll be all right.'

'And you?' Ailsa put her hand out but did not touch him, aware of his heavily bandaged hands. 'They've trussed you up like a chicken!' she joked shakily.

'I'm evidently all in one piece,' he said. 'It's Tom we have to worry about. Something fell on him—a roof beam, I think—but they're going to do something about that right away.'

'I'm glad Flora was able to go to him.'

'Her being his official fiancée all of a sudden apparently made a difference.' He offered a smile, although his eyes were still deeply troubled. 'She can only see him for five minutes before they operate, but she can come back tomorrow, probably in the afternoon.'

'She won't want to leave Oban,' Ailsa predicted.

'It's no distance back to the Lodge,' he said. 'I think she should go home.'

'And you, Fergus?' she asked again.

'They're not interested in me now, I gather,' he said. 'Jessie MacGregor can take off the bandages when the time comes, so you'll have two passengers on the way back, I'm afraid.'

They waited for Flora as the sun drew down towards the horizon, flaming the sky towards the west in coral and vermilion with a wisp of grey cloud floating in between.

'It's so beautiful here,' Ailsa said. 'Surely, surely nothing can go wrong!'

Flora came to join them, saying very little as they drove back down the hill.

'They say he'll be all right,' she managed at last. 'There's a terrible splinter of wood in his leg and his beard has all been burned away.'

'He told me it might be an improvement,' said Fergus. 'Tom always was an optimistic devil, even in an emergency. Do you want to stop somewhere for a bite to eat?'

Flora shook her head.

'But you do, if you're hungry,' she added. 'I'll just have some coffee.'

'Ailsa,' he asked, 'what about you?'

'I'm not hungry, and Mrs Birch will have something ready for us when we get home.'

She wanted to withdraw that last word, yet she knew in that moment what she was going to do.

When she came to the Lodge gates she drove straight up the drive to the main door.

'You're not going back to that empty cottage of yours at this time of night with no one to look after you,' she said firmly when Fergus would have protested.

He looked down at his bandaged hands.

'I'd make a poor job of catering for myself,' he admitted ruefully.

He had averted his head as they had passed the burned-out shell of the caravan and the blackened sheds, but Ailsa knew that Cuilfail was uppermost in his mind.

Martha Birch was relieved to see them and more than delighted by Fergus's presence in the car.

'You'll not go back to that cottage if I have anything to do with it,' she told him. 'My, my! Your hands!' she exclaimed. 'Are you badly burned? I heard you had rushed in to save your friend.'

'Tom has been kept at the hospital,' Flora said shakily. 'We won't know till tomorrow how he is—after the operation.'

'I heard he was badly hurt.' Martha led the way into the house. 'It was a terrible thing to happen.'

Ailsa was aware of Fergus hesitating for only a moment before he followed them through the main doorway.

'I'll make up a bed for you,' Mrs Birch told him, 'and then you can have something to eat.'

Ailsa followed Flora to the kitchen, but not before she heard Fergus say:

'I wondered what it would be like to come home for more than just a visit, Mrs Birch.'

'You'll be staying here till your hands get better,' the housekeeper assured him. 'I'll look after you, as I always have done.'

Her heart beating strongly, Ailsa put a comforting arm around Flora's shoulders.

'I'll take you back to Oban first thing in the morning,' she promised. 'At least we can ask about Tom and stay there till you're allowed to see him, even for a minute or two.'

'I'll never be able to thank you enough,' Flora began, until Ailsa silenced her with a kiss.

'Don't try,' she said. 'I know how you feel, Flora, but—but it's going to be all right.'

'I'm not even wearing Tom's ring,' Flora pointed out, 'yet I said I was his fiancée just to make sure I could go in the ambulance with him.'

'What difference does it make—an engagement ring?' Ailsa asked. 'You *are* his fiancée, the closest thing to being his wife. He has nobody else.'

'Nobody but Fergus and you,' Flora said thoughtfully. 'We couldn't have deserted him in an emergency.'

The supper table had been set in the small sitting-room and they quickly laid out another place.

'If my mother had known Fergus was coming back with us she would have opened up the family dining-room,' Flora mused, 'but I think Fergus would rather have it this way.' She glanced round the room with its circular table and well-worn chairs. 'It used to be the old morning-room where the family took their breakfast, a cosy place when the two boys were at home where everyone lingered as long as they could. When I was young I used to think it was always full of children running in and out of the garden, and Mrs MacNair was so kind to me, making me feel one of them. My mother remembers those days very vividly,' she added on a quieter note. 'I think that was why she wanted to push

Fergus and me together so much. It wouldn't have brought Fergus back to the Lodge, but at least I would have been a MacNair.' Flora sighed. 'She had great ambition for me, but I don't feel I have let her down so very much. I can teach somewhere in the vicinity, I hope, till—till Tom is well again.'

Her mother came in to say that Fergus was installed in his old room at the head of the back stairs.

'Was that wise?' asked Flora. 'Bringing back so many memories?'

'He said very little,' Martha Birch returned, 'but he seemed to feel at home.'

'Will he come down for a meal?' Ailsa asked.

'I offered to take it up to him on a tray.' The housekeeper's eyes were frankly calculating. 'But he preferred to come down. He says he isn't hurt, apart from the burns.'

When he appeared at the sitting-room door Fergus had made an effort to tidy himself up.

'I find I can use one hand reasonably well,' he told them. 'It's amazing what one can do even with the handicap of a mile of bandages!'

'There's soup,' Mrs Birch announced, 'so that won't be a problem, and we'll cut up your meat.'

He looked across the room to where Ailsa was standing. 'You're being too kind to me,' he acknowledged.

She wanted to ask him about being in his old room, but couldn't in front of Mrs Birch, who had made her own decision in the matter for a reason best known to herself.

They spoke about Tom and their return to Oban the following morning.

'I'd like to go down with you,' he said, 'if we could stop for half an hour at Cuilfail on the way.'

'That won't be any problem,' Ailsa assured him swiftly. 'It's only off the shore road.'

By the end of the meal he looked tired.

'It's up the wooden hill to bed now, I suppose,' he said. 'I feel that I might sleep, after all.'

'I put a wee tot of whisky in your coffee,' Martha Birch admitted.

'So I noticed,' he smiled. 'It was your unfailing recipe for everything, Mrs Birch!'

He passed Ailsa on his way to the door, looking down at her with an expression in his eyes which she could not fathom, wistful, perhaps, and sad.

'Thanks,' he said, 'for everything.'

Thank you! It was all he had to offer, Ailsa thought.

In the morning he was up before any of them, going out through the side door to prowl in the garden like some caged animal waiting to be released. He wasn't going to stay, Ailsa realised; he was too proud for that. Now that he had managed to dress himself unaided he was his old independent self again.

After breakfast they bundled into the car, with Flora choosing the back seat rather deliberately so that Fergus was forced to sit beside Ailsa on their way to Cuilfail. The fish farm looked completely desolate, with the burned-out caravan little more than a charred shell at one side of it and two of the sheds open to the sky. Two young boys who had worked for them on the fish traps came forward to meet them.

'The trout are all right, Mr MacNair,' one of them assured Fergus. 'We've been feeding them.'

Fergus drew a breath of relief, although his brow darkened again as he looked down at the sheds.

'There go all our good intentions,' he said, turning to Ailsa, 'and quite a lot of your capital.'

'We're fully insured,' she countered swiftly. 'We'll just have to start building again.'

There was frank admiration in his eyes as he looked down at her.

'I always thought you were the eternal optimist,' he said, 'and now I know!'

'Things will work out, Fergus,' she declared, 'if——'

She couldn't bring herself to mention Tom's name.

'There are so many "ifs",' he mused, 'but now that I've seen the damage I think we might be able to go on.'

That 'we' held a promise for her. At least there would be Cuilfail and their partnership.

When they reached the hospital at one o'clock the news of Tom was good.

'He's come through the operation like the trooper he is,' Fergus told Ailsa as they waited for Flora's ten minutes at Tom's bedside to end. 'He will be up and about in three or four weeks, they say, but if I know that man, he'll be back at Cuilfail long before that.'

He paused, obviously thinking about the burned-out caravan which had been Tom's house.

'Bring him to the Lodge,' Ailsa suggested. 'There's plenty of room.'

'He won't hesitate,' Fergus returned, 'if Flora can nurse him!'

A completely transformed Flora joined them several minutes later.

'He's marvellous!' she declared. 'Almost his old self again.' Her voice trembled suddenly. 'He may always walk with a bit of a limp,' she added quietly, 'but that won't matter at all. He—he said even his beard was beginning to grow again. Just like him, isn't it?'

'Very like him,' Fergus agreed, putting her into the front passenger seat where he had sat beside Ailsa on their journey south. 'You can phone him every day to enquire about the beard's progress!'

'I will,' Flora smiled. 'After all, we're engaged now—officially engaged. I told Mother last night.'

'And what did she say?' Fergus asked.

'Oh, not too much, as a matter of fact. I think she must have been lost for words for the first time in her life.' Flora blushed. 'She had—other plans for me, but she said it was always the way. Young people never listen to advice.'

When they returned to Truan Fergus decided that he had to start work right away.

'I'm perfectly fit,' he declared the following morning when he followed Ailsa into the garden at the rear of the house. 'I have to make a start at Cuilfail sooner or later, and now that Tom will be back it has to be sooner.'

'The contractors phoned a few minutes ago,' she told him. 'They're ready to start on the sheds. If we can transfer the young trout into the new building at the weekend they can set to work on the damaged ones. It

will be a complete transformation when it's finished!'
Her eyes glowed with enthusiasm. 'Something exciting
for Tom to come back to!'

'Thanks to you.' They had reached the shrubbery
where the dew was still on the grass, making it a fresh
and lovely morning. 'I couldn't take it at first,' Fergus
added as the giant rhododendrons hid them from the
house, 'allowing a stranger to invest in us, especially
when you owned Truan and were doing so much for the
estate into the bargain. That was pride for you—pride
of the very worst sort,' he concluded.

Ailsa halted on the grassy path.

'But now——?' she prompted.

'I'm seeing things differently,' he acknowledged slowly.
'I can accept that we are both working for Truan in our
separate ways.'

'Fergus,' she asked, 'does that make us friends? Does
it mean that we can bury the hatchet, at last?'

He smiled his slow, attractive smile.

'The hatchet was never very sharp,' he admitted, 'when
I really got to know you, although I suppose it dealt a
few blows to my pride, and everything was complicated
by the fact that I fell in love with you.'

She gazed at him, unbelieving for a moment.

'When?' was all she could think of to say.

'Does it really matter?' he asked, his eyes holding hers
with a depth of feeling in them she had never expected
to see but had always longed for. 'When and how? Some
time you had to know.'

She moved towards him with a cry that was almost
disbelief, and with a supreme effort he freed himself from
the restricting sling about his neck, taking her swiftly
into his arms to press his lips purposefully against her
mouth with an insistence she could not deny.

'I love you,' he said. 'I will always love you, Ailsa,
wherever you go.'

She clung to him, her arms firmly about his neck.

'I'm not going anywhere,' she declared, her voice not
quite steady. 'Oh, Fergus, I can't tell you how much I've
hoped for this—for you back here at Truan, where you
belong.'

'It's all so one-sided,' he began, until she silenced him with a kiss.

'Please,' she said, holding him close. 'I'm asking you to stay for always and—and to love me for always too!'

In spite of his heavily-bandaged arms he drew her closer still.

'I'm in love with both of you—you and Truan, in that order,' he said, kissing her once more. 'You were right for the Lodge and you always will be, and I know we are right for each other. We'll make a go of it, Ailsa, here and at Cuilfail, if we can.'

'Do you honestly doubt it?' She held him at arms' length, able to smile at last. 'With so much love about, how could we possibly fail?'

'Failure isn't a word I like,' Fergus admitted as they walked back along the familiar path to his ancient home.

'It won't be a word for the future, either,' Ailsa said, smiling happily at the prospect of the years ahead when they would be partners in the fullest sense of the word, together for always.

Have You Ever Wondered If You Could Write A Harlequin Novel?

Here's great news—Harlequin is offering a series of cassette tapes to help you do just that. Written by Harlequin editors, these tapes give practical advice on how to make your characters—and your story—come alive. There's a tape for each contemporary romance series Harlequin publishes.

Mail order only

All sales final

A compelling novel of deadly revenge and passion
from Harlequin's bestselling international
romance author Penny Jordan

POWER PLAY

Eleven years had passed but the
terror of that night was something
Pepper Minesse would never
forget. Fueled by revenge against
the four men who had brutally
shattered her past, she set in
motion a deadly plan to destroy
their futures.

Available in February!

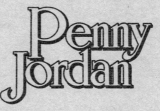

Penny Jordan

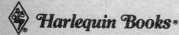

Harlequin Books ®

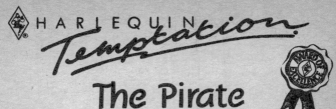

The Pirate
JAYNE ANN KRENTZ

At the heart of every powerful romance story lies a
legend. There are many romantic legends and
countless modern variations on them, but they all
have one thing in common: They are tales of brave,
resourceful women who must gentle and tame the
powerful, passionate men who are their true mates.

The enormous appeal of Jayne Ann Krentz lies in
her ability to create modern-day versions of these
classic romantic myths, and her LADIES AND
LEGENDS trilogy showcases this talent. Believing
that a storyteller who can bring legends to life
deserves special attention, Harlequin has chosen
the first book of the trilogy—THE PIRATE—to
receive our Award of Excellence. Look for it in
February.

AE-PIR-1